THE NEW KID SERIES

THE SWORD OF ARMAGEDDON

THE NEW KID: BOOK THREE

THE SWORD OF ARMAGEDDON

Temple Mathews

BORDERS.
exclusive

www.teenlibris.com

Developed for Borders, Inc., by BenBella Books, Inc.

Send feedback to feedback@benbellabooks.com

Printed in the United States of America
10 9 8 7 6 5 4 3 2 1

ISBN 978-1-935618-17-1

Copyediting by Oriana Leckert
Proofreading by Lisa Nold
Cover design by Laura Watkins
Cover illustration by Cliff Nielsen
Text design and composition by PerfecType, Nashville, TN
Printed by Bang Printing

ACKNOWLEDGMENTS

As I come to the end of the New Kid trilogy and recall what an amazing journey it's been, I must mention the wonderful and talented group of people who have supported me in this endeavor. I would very much like to thank my generous publisher, Glenn Yeffeth; my erudite, gifted editor, Leah Wilson; an ardent fan and talented note-giver, Susan Scarafia; my loyal webmaster and longtime fan, Hal Stellini; my biggest fan for over twenty years, Terri Mathews; my dear amour, Piedad Suarez; my talented and resourceful manager, Patrick Hughes; and my cheering section of Marsha, Beth, and Cameron Holand and Michelle Solis.

TABLE OF CONTENTS

Chapter One:
Love Hurts

Will was fleeing for his life, hunted by a horrifying monster. This monster was special; it was fate's cruel irony in the flesh, his absolute worst fear born into the world for the sole purpose of destroying him with as much pain as possible. He stumbled from room to room in the huge old mansion, his vision blurred, his sense of balance a distant memory. He felt like he'd fallen off a cliff, then been hit by a ten-ton truck. He desperately wanted to move faster, but every step he took was more agonizing than the last. Something was appallingly wrong with his body. He could feel the life leaching out of him, the Devil cackling in his ears. His steps grew heavier, his feet leaden, but he would not give up. It was imperative that the creature did not capture him, for if it did, it would surely mean an excruciatingly painful torture session—followed by an agonizingly slow death. Will shook his head, trying to clear away the visions swarming his brain. If only he were dreaming! But this was worse than any nightmare. The beast on his heels was no chimera, no grotesque product of his imagination. *This* beast was tragically real flesh and blood. He had seen it up close, all *too* close. It was a demon, the single most terrifying demon he'd ever encountered, and the very first demon he doubted he would be able to slay.

His head spinning, Will momentarily leaned against the hall-way wall for support. Was it his imagination, or could he actually *hear* his heart trying to pound its way out of his chest? Time. He needed more time. He paused to steady his breath. Somehow he had to evade his pursuer. As a demon hunter, or *everto venator*, like his father and grandfather before him, Will Hunter had endured much and suffered greatly. He was sorry about many things. And at this moment—as, unbeknownst to him, the clocks in the mansion ticked away the last precious seconds of his life—he was most sorry about one thing in particular: he was sorry that the creature chasing him, the beast that would probably end up killing him, was the girl of his dreams, the love of his life, Natalie Holand.

He thought back to . . . when? Had it really been only *minutes* ago when his world had come crashing down?

He'd rushed home from his half-sister Loreli's dank basement lair full of hope. Loreli had performed what she called "demon dialysis" on him, supposedly purging him of their father's evil blood. Believing that he was free of his demonic bloodline at long last, and that he and Natalie could finally be together forever, he had rushed to her, found her in her room. Like Romeo on bended knee, he'd proclaimed his undying love, a love destined to last an eternity. She was in enchanting repose on the bed, her eyes closed, a sly smile teasing her lips. As he spoke, she savored every word he said. It had been a moment of sheer bliss: heaven, ecstasy, paradise.

And then she had opened her eyes and fate had bitch-slapped Will Hunter. Natalie's eyes, her meltingly beautiful eyes, formerly an enchanting shade of blue, were now a stomach-turning liquid black. She was *infected*. Will's heart contracted like a fist. Suddenly he felt like a condemned man marching up the creaky wooden steps to the gallows. To be sure, it had shaken his world when he learned that the Dark Lord was his natural father. But *this*, now this! Discovering that the girl of his dreams had crossed over into the land of evil? This was beyond disturbing; this completely altered his universe.

He remembered staring down at her, the love of his life, now one of the very creatures he'd sworn to destroy. He was in shock. His blood felt like acid in his veins.

He nearly choked on his words as he spoke to her. "Nat . . . what have you *done*?"

Natalie blinked. Her eyes went from black to blue and back again.

No doubt about it, she'd gone over. And yet . . . there it was, the ugly truth: he was still drawn to her. This was *Natalie*. She was still beautiful. But now she was a vulgar kind of sexy. She shimmered with desire. Her body language told him she was ready to take him places neither of them had yet explored, places he could never let himself go with her, not when she was like this.

"Natalie, what on earth have you done?"

Her black eyes danced. She licked her lips.

"You *know* what I've done, Will. Isn't it awesome?"

She passed her tongue over her teeth, her canines now sharp, dangerous, deadly.

"Oh my god, Natalie . . ."

"Don't be sad," she said, her voice husky, velvety smooth, seductive.

Words lodged in his throat like rocks.

"I . . . I can't help it. It's not awesome, it's . . . it's . . . *horrible*."

Natalie reached up and gently twirled his hair. He pulled away. She bristled.

"Come on, Will, let's not play games. I crossed over for *us*. Loreli helped me see that this was what you really wanted."

Loreli, thought Will. Was it possible that she was responsible for this horror? Had she really and truly betrayed him in the most hurtful way possible? Had his sister really convinced the love of his life to become one of *them*?

"I *never* wanted this for you," he said.

Natalie made a deep purring sound, cocking her head to one side as she smiled. "Of course you did, but you were afraid. It's all right. I understand, baby, I really do."

She'd never called him "baby" before. He didn't like the way she said it now.

She sat up and licked her lips. She wanted to kiss him so badly she could taste it. She moved to do so. He turned away.

She hugged him and he could feel her heart beating wildly. It was insanity—even though she was a demon, he still felt a bond with her. Natalie's touch was electric. He shuddered.

For a brief moment Natalie's eyes changed back to their beautiful blue, and her face softened. As horrible as she was now as a demon, he could never, ever forget the Natalie she used to be. Maybe whatever they had together could never be killed, not even by something as horrific as this. Maybe they could somehow get through this scourge.

Will hoped so.

He gently pushed himself away from her and looked into her eyes. At the moment they were blue, but he could see so much else in them; they would, in the long run, become portals to a dark and lonely place of pain and suffering. Because demons were not capable of true love. They had lust covered in spades, but love? Love was something else. A creature that is all ego cannot fully love, because it cannot completely give.

Natalie was puzzled. She touched his cheek. Her fingernails were ruby red, sharp now, and pointed. She was menace and beauty combined. She could kiss him like he'd never been kissed before—or she could rip his throat out.

"Come on, baby," she said.

She was perspiring, the scent of lust rising from her skin.

"Please, Nat, not now, not like this . . ."

He breathed in her aroma. It was deeper and more pungent than before. It still smelled like strawberries, but now a more powerful scent was mixed in. Something sticky sweet and musky. Will was immobilized.

She put her other hand on his face. He shrank back from her dangerous touch. She grew angrier. He sensed that at any moment she could turn on him and slash his throat. He had to tread cautiously.

"What's wrong?" she asked. "I've become like *you*, Will. I'm a demon now. Like you!"

This wasn't permanent, he reminded himself. He could fix her. All he would have to do was subdue her and inject her with the same cure he'd given to Rudy.

"Natalie, listen to me carefully. I know you're not . . . yourself . . ."

"Oh, but I am! I am, Will. I feel sooooo good. In a *bad* kind of way."

She laughed harshly. Her eyes flashed, the irises shifting to saffron red. She looked so beautiful, and yet so evil.

"You were so afraid of hurting me before," she said. "You don't have to be afraid anymore. There's no reason we can't have each other now."

She stood and twirled around. She had always been in great shape, firm and toned, with the blessings of youth and health. But now she was even stronger and fitter and shapelier, like she'd had a sudden powerful dose of steroids. Will could not deny his attraction to her any more than he could control how much she repulsed him in this state.

She began unbuttoning her blouse as she gyrated. She took his hands in hers.

"It's time, Will . . . You and me . . ."

He had to do something. He cleared his throat.

"I . . . I don't feel well," he said. Maybe he could make a move if he could convince her that he was ill. It was, unfortunately, the cursed truth. His insides were churning, calamitous. His body was a war zone. What had Loreli *done* to him? Was he supposed to feel like this?

"I—I could use a glass of water . . . ," he stammered.

Natalie's deadly eyes flashed, and then she smiled at him.

"Sure, baby . . . we'll fix you right up." She moved into the bathroom and turned on the tap.

Will made a daring move—he dashed across her bedroom, out the door and into the hallway, down the stairs. *The lab.* He had to get to the lab. In seconds he heard her voice calling out.

"Baby, where did you go?!"

And then she came after him.

He lurched into the hallway, his eyes quickly scanning up and down it. His only chance was to get to the Demon Trapper and capture Natalie in it. Then maybe he could cure her; that was, if he could manage to stay upright long enough to do so. His blood was hot. His heart was beating erratically, skipping beats, like it couldn't make up its mind if it was going to keep pumping or not. He felt like he was dying. The door to his lab beckoned. He took a step toward it.

"Will!" He froze when he heard her voice, and then had the presence of mind to step back into a doorway. He knew he didn't have long: demons could smell out their prey like wolves.

"Where *are* you?"

He closed his eyes and thought of their first kiss. He still loved her. He had to save her. But first, he'd have to save himself.

Natalie prowled down the stairs, walking slowly, flexing her fingers, marveling at how sharp her nails were. She felt powerful, potent, and supreme. She was a new being. She was going to make damn sure she and Will were going to be happy together. She was growing angrier by the second. She hated that he'd left the room. Where was he? She squinted and scrutinized the downstairs but saw no lover awaiting her kiss. She closed her eyes and drew in a long breath through her nostrils. She could smell him. His pheromones. They made her dizzy with desire. She opened her eyes again and continued down the stairs.

"I know you're close . . ." she hissed.

Will was adjacent to the kitchen. He reached in and grabbed a plastic bowl lying on the counter. He waited one second, two, then flung it down the hallway, where it clattered loudly. Natalie instinctively crouched, whirled, and turned toward the noise. Her voice had a nasty rasp to it now.

"I don't like this, Will, I don't like this one bit! You better get your ass out here right now!"

She shrieked and ran the length of the hallway in two seconds.

"Where ARE you!?"

Will made his move. If he'd been feeling like himself, he'd have been able to time-bend and might have made it down the hallway to his lab. But he was a slug, a buffoon, his legs moving awkwardly, his balance out of whack. He staggered toward the lab as best he could, his vision blurring, his stomach lurching into his throat. He'd gotten as far as the lab door when Natalie's strong hands—which felt more like an eagle's talons—encircled his neck.

"There you are . . ."

She pulled him back into the hallway. Her voice was eerily composed. Her disturbing smile did little to calm him. She looked at him with merciless eyes. These were not the eyes of the girl he fell in love with the first time he saw her at the school bus stop back in Harrisburg. He remembered those eyes. They were a glorious azure, the color between blue and cyan, and they were honest and searching. He'd fallen right into those eyes when they met. But *these* eyes? These were the eyes of a bloodthirsty killer.

Will remembered that he had a Series 111 Cloaker—a device that could totally immobilize her—right in his pocket. He reached for it, but she was too fast for him—way too fast. Where was his strength?

"What have we here?" she said, ripping the Cloaker out of his hand. "One of your little boy toys?"

She was getting stronger every second as the demon blood inside her continued its onslaught.

"Were you going to use this on *me*?" she demanded.

Her eyes narrowing, Natalie threw the Cloaker aside. She clamped her right hand—it was rapidly morphing now, becoming a deadly claw—onto Will's neck. He was too weak to fight back. Realization was slowly dawning on him: this was more than just blood loss. The dialysis was supposed to make him stronger, to get rid of the rage that flooded him whenever he fought. But he didn't feel stronger. He caught his reflection in a hallway mirror. He was pale, pallid, his skin tinged yellow. There was only one explanation: Loreli had *poisoned* him. He was dying.

And Natalie, the girl whose body this demon now bewitched, was his only hope.

"Natalie listen to me. I need to find out right now if you truly love me."

"Of course I love you, baby."

"Then you need to let go of me."

"Sure, I'll let you go of you, Will. Right after we finish what we started."

With a throaty laugh, she started to yank Will's T-shirt up as she pushed him into a nearby sitting area, onto a padded window seat. She licked his neck.

He pulled away. "No!"

If he could just get her to hesitate long enough for him to get free and take the last few steps to the lab . . . Grab the Demon Trapper he'd used on Rudy . . .

Natalie's eyes narrowed into angry red slits. Will scrambled off the window seat and tried to take a step back toward the lab, but his brain began to spin. The floor seemed to shift beneath him. Lights pulsed and dimmed. Colors bled into one another as Loreli's poison attacked his central nervous system.

"Natalie . . ."

He stumbled, and she caught him before he could fall.

"Why are you fighting me?" she asked. "We can be together now, darling, just like we always wanted."

For an instant, Will allowed his mind to travel down the tempting neural pathway that she had just opened. It was a whole new world, a world in which Will Hunter was no longer the enemy of all demons, but their leader, their prince, and Natalie—a dark, beautiful Natalie—was by his side, his princess. In this tiny moment, demon Natalie saw something in Will's eyes—she knew he was considering the their life anew—and she seized the opening, pushing it wide.

"You and I . . . we can have anything we want," she said. "We can have each other completely. We can do whatever we want, whenever we want."

Will shook his head slowly. She was right, but she was so very, very wrong.

"No . . ."

"Come on, Will. You know this was meant to be!"

She tried to kiss him. He roughly pushed her away. He might as well have stabbed her in the heart. She was stung, burned, livid.

"I have yearned for you for so long! So *long*, Will. I saved your life! I went to Hell for you! Everything we've done . . . everything we've been through . . ." Her anger was peaking. Will could almost feel the temperature in the room rising. She did not so much speak her words now as growl them like a mad dog.

"And now . . . now you *turn me down*?!"

Her face warped, malicious. She roared and flung him across the room. His body slammed into the wall, knocking down a framed Ansel Adams picture of the moon. The glass in the frame shattered around him. Blood dripping from the back of his head, he tried to rise again, but she was across the room in a fraction of a second. She knelt down and held his head in her hands.

"Oh, god, baby, I'm so sorry . . ."

She had tears in her eyes. Will thought that this was a good thing. It meant that her human side could still feel. She spoke again.

"Sweetheart . . . precious. When I want to kiss you, you kiss me, understand?"

She lifted him to his feet and made a move to kiss him again. Will knew he could buy time by submitting to her desires, if only momentarily. But he could not help himself. He spurned her, again turning his head so her lips met only cheek.

Insulted, humiliated, she hissed like a feral cat. She dug her claws into his shoulders, jostled him, and then threw him across the room again. *Wham!* This time he crashed into the doorjamb of the lab. His neck snapped backward. As he fell to the floor, he wondered if his spinal cord had been severed.

Natalie approached him. He blinked up through watery eyes at what used to be the girl he loved.

For a few seconds she remembered how much she loved him, and she was conflicted. The demon part of her brain boiled with lustful thoughts, but her heart still had a voice, and that voice told her not to harm him, to remember how she used to daydream about their wedding day, how handsome she knew Will would look as they left the church, laughing, kissing, climbing into the limo.

A powerful, irresistible thought suddenly leapt into her mind. It was as though her demon brain had made a bargain with what was left of her uncontaminated human brain. She had always wanted a wedding. And demon Natalie, from the first few moments when she'd welcomed the flood of evil infection into her body, knew that she could now get *anything* she wanted. In her mind she flashed on a dress, flowers, rings. Quite suddenly she was on a mission. She picked Will up and carried him upstairs to her bedroom. She placed him on her bed. Her lips gently met his cheek.

"Do you promise to stay right here?"

"Yes." *No.*

She looked at him with a sly smile.

"I'll be right back," she said.

She turned and walked out. Will breathed deeply. She had left him alone. He had another chance.

Seconds ticked by as he tried to formulate the best plan. His body ached. His head felt like it had been kicked down the street like a soccer ball. But he was alive. If he could make it down to his lab, surely he could counteract the poison.

His thoughts of hope were quickly dashed as Natalie re-entered. She was carrying zip-ties, heavy-duty fourteen-inch cable ties like the ones cops used on perps.

"I know you promised," she said. "But these will make sure you're . . . sincere."

She splayed him out and zip-tied his wrists and ankles to the bed's iron posts, and when she was done, she took his head in her hands.

"One kiss."

He was too weak to struggle. Their lips met, the kiss a mixture of heaven and hell. Heaven was the taste of strawberries and sangria, the longing that welled up inside him, and hell was the acidic after-taste and the intense, hungry, angry look on Natalie's face. She rose.

"I'll be back."

"Where are you going?"

She shot a look over her shoulder and smiled wickedly. "Shopping."

Then she walked out.

Will struggled against the zip-ties. But they were capable of withstanding hundreds of pounds of pressure, and even at his best he'd have had difficulty breaking free. He only succeeded in hurting his wrists. He stopped struggling and fought against passing out. He had no idea how he could possibly free himself, or if he would even survive an attempt.

Chapter Two:
Thievery

Gillian Turner was one of many in Seattle who made a fortune in high tech during the boom years of the eighties and nineties. She first worked at Microsoft, then branched out on her own to create Spanway, a company that produced networking software applications that were integrated into wireless routers and cell phones all over the world. She had made millions while at Microsoft and millions more with Spanway, and through shrewd, fortuitous investments, her personal fortune eventually climbed into the billions. So it was not at all shocking—in fact, it was expected—that she would build a massive mansion on Mercer Island. But hers was different from other mansions. It sat not on the waterfront, where all the truly extravagant properties were, but inland, tucked deep within a wooded glen bordering Pioneer Park and surrounded by a tall security fence.

Gillian had always been a passionate environmentalist and a woman who cared deeply for those less fortunate than herself. She saw her wealth not as a means for bettering her own station in life, but as a vehicle for empowering the poor, sick, and downtrodden. She gave away millions each year and was a model philanthropist. So it was somewhat baffling to those who knew her that she was also one of Seattle's more voracious and prolific collectors of antiquities. Not unlike Charles Foster Kane in Orson Welles' *Citizen Kane*, she amassed an embarrassingly huge collection of ancient objects, both at legitimate auctions and on the black market. She did not, however, display these objects, but rather squirreled them away in her mansion.

Gillian had a security staff comprised of four ex-Navy Seals and two decorated Marines. It was rumored that since Gillian had never married, never had a partner, and spent so much time alone, she had become not merely eccentric, but had gone completely off her rocker. She was reclusive to the point that many speculated that she had actually passed away.

But Gillian was very much alive, and there was a method to her madness. She scoured the world for obscure collectables not because she adored them, but for the sole purpose of keeping them out of the hands of . . . others.

Every object Gillian collected had its own sordid history. She owned an ice axe, claimed by the seller to be the one used by Ramón Mercader to murder Leon Trotsky. She'd spent $2 million on it, even though authenticating the true history of the axe was next to impossible. The details didn't matter to Gillian; she was on a quest, a quest to suck up every single object she could that, in her estimation, harbored powerful evil.

Of course, it was evil that the Dark Lord was after, and he coveted some of the items in Gillian's collection. Though he might have sent dozens or even hundreds of his minions to fetch it, the Prince of Darkness deemed this assignment far too important to entrust to his common followers, or even his elite shedemons. Gillian Turner was an intelligent, resourceful woman. For many years she'd been able to keep the Dark Lord at bay with a cunning perimeter-defense system. But today would be different. Today the Dark Lord had help.

. . .

Lieutenant Bernard Howard was an ex-Navy Seal who had personally brought swift death to over twenty men in combat missions all
over the globe. Upon retiring from the Navy, he had been recruited
by Gillian Turner to head her security team. He was a savvy, battle-
hardened veteran who prided himself on his ability to smell a trap.
But even he detected no scent of what was to come this day.

Sergeant Peter Jeremy Wolcott had worked under Lt. Howard
for four years. Though at all times he appeared outwardly calm and
composed, inside he was in a perpetual state of conflict with himself. Why had he taken on this job? It was the money, of course, but
he desperately missed active duty. Guarding the Turner estate was
deathly boring. Peter Jeremy ached to fire his weapon, or even throw
some punches. But day after day he sat and stared at a surveillance
camera monitor, watching as the occasional vehicle or disinterested
jogger passed by.

So when the distant figure on the monitor began to approach
the front gate, Peter Jeremy's pulse quickened at the possibility of
confrontation. But when the figure came closer into focus, Peter Jeremy was confused and disappointed: it was a girl, woefully under-
dressed and drenched to the bone, even though it wasn't raining. She
appeared disoriented. Following protocol, Sergeant Wolcott alerted
Lt. Howard, and then he made a beeline for the front entrance.

At the steel gate he could see the girl more clearly. Her beauty
took his breath away. She was a strawberry blonde with striking
green eyes that were wild with panic. Something scary was going on
in this girl's head. Nonetheless, again following protocol, Peter Jeremy kept his distance and called out to her.

"Stop where you are!"

But Loreli didn't stop. She continued to approach the gate. Peter
Jeremy could not imagine shooting this helpless, unarmed girl, but

the opportunity to draw his Sig Sauer P226 pistol felt fine indeed. The Sig P226 was standard Navy Seal issue and its manufacturers claimed it had "To Hell and Back Reliability." Peter Jeremy loved the weapon, and he loved pointing it, which he did now.

"I said *stop!*"

He flicked off the safety. The girl's eyes, searching, drew Peter Jeremy into her, took hold of him, and did not let go. He was enthralled, mesmerized. Still, he steeled himself against her.

"Step away from the gate!" he said, aiming the Sig at her forehead.

Loreli did exactly the opposite. Her green eyes opening even wider—such a feat seemed impossible to Peter Jeremy—she stepped closer to it, her lips moving, a faint sound emanating from them. Peter Jeremy's finger tightened on the trigger. His hand, normally stone-steady, now began to tremble slightly. He yearned to hear what the girl was whispering. Still, there was protocol.

"Step back!" he said. And then, in a softer voice, "Please . . . ?"

Peter Jeremy could not help but stare at Loreli's body through her soaking wet clothing. He pulled his eyes back up to meet hers. This time he heard her whisper.

"Help me . . ."

She looked ill. And indeed she was, in no small part due to Gillian's defense system, which included a micro-mist moat surrounding the property. The dense fog diluted it this day, but the mist moat was still hazardous to those of the Dark Lord's ilk, since—though no one on Gillian's security team knew it—it contained molecules of Holy Water, gallons of which Gillian purchased directly from the Vatican at great expense. And the molecules had had their effect on Loreli. She was, after all, half-demon. Her system was growing weaker with each passing moment. Casting one last pleading look at Sergeant Peter Jeremy, Loreli's knees buckled and she collapsed.

"Damn!" said Peter Jeremy. He made the call he knew he had to make and gave his report. He listened to the response, then hung up the phone. He wanted to open the gate and scoop the beautiful wounded girl into his arms. But protocol . . . protocol. A few seconds passed. Then Lt. Howard was at Peter Jeremy's side, his own Sig Sauer pointing at the girl.

"She's not moving," said Peter Jeremy. "She looks pretty messed up. We should call the police."

"I did," said Howard. "They can't send a car right away. There was a pileup on Island Crest Way. Drunk driver, four cars, possible fatalities."

Peter Jeremy knelt down to get a better look at Loreli. "We can't just let her lay there on the gravel, can we?"

The girl wasn't moving. Lt. Howard holstered his gun and bit his lower lip. He, too, was torn, and he usually had a blink-of-the-eye instinct in situations like this. "It won't be good if she expires right there."

He paced back and forth a few times before making his decision. It was one that he would regret.

"I'm opening the gate," he said to Peter Jeremy. "Go ahead and pick her up."

Peter Jeremy was surprised by how solid the girl felt as he lifted her into his arms and carried her inside. *She looks slender, but she must be strong*, he thought as he moved down the main hallway and turned into a guest room. He laid her on the bed. He tore open a first-aid kit, removing an emergency Mylar blanket to cover her with.

As soon as the man turned his back to her, Loreli slid a tiny vial out of her waistband and popped the top. When he leaned in to cover her with the blanket, an ultra-sharp needle pierced Peter Jeremy's flesh and the chemicals rushed into his blood, immediately dragging him down into numbing darkness as he fell to the carpeted floor.

Loreli sat up, her eyes alert. She stepped off the table and moved slowly down the hallway. She quickened her pace. In seconds she came upon Lt. Howard, who turned and saw her. He recognized that he'd been fooled. This was no innocent girl they'd carried inside the gate. Loreli injected him with liquid from another vial and he, too, collapsed into unconsciousness.

An alarm sounded. Loreli looked down and saw Lt. Howard's hand on his belt. He'd triggered the alarm. No matter; she had breached the perimeter, and she was well on her way to accomplishing her mission. It took her less than thirty seconds to locate the mist-moat control station. Using a tube of acid gel, she disintegrated the lock and then shut the mist-moat down.

Up in her tower bedroom, Gillian Turner awakened from her nap. She reached under her bed and withdrew her protection, a Mossberg 500 pump shotgun. Jacking a shell into the firing chamber, she moved stealthily into the hallway, the weapon's laser beam searching. A laser-sighted shotgun was unusual, but Gillian's eyesight had deteriorated over the years, and she found the beam to be helpful. She would certainly shoot first and ask questions later, but she had a feeling that her trusty Mossberg, though a capably lethal weapon, would prove worthless if she were to come face to face with her darkest fear.

Once the mist-moat was shut down, the Dark Lord himself smashed through the gate, entering the Turner mansion. He searched swiftly, passing through Gillian's living quarters, which were impeccably designed and brimming with priceless artwork.

Lying in wait in the alcove near her bedroom, Gillian saw the Dark Lord's reflection in the surface of a silver vase and her heart froze in her chest. She'd always feared this moment.

Gillian's one and only love had been Daniel, a young anthropologist. They'd met at the University of Washington and moved in together, and were planning to get married and start a family once they were finished with school. Daniel's studies took him around the world as he began to gather evidence that proved the existence, the *real, physical existence*, of Heaven's fallen angel, the Prince of Darkness. The night before he was to present his thesis, Daniel inexplicably parked his Subaru in the middle of the Aurora Bridge, set fire to his thesis and all his evidence, and leapt to his death. There had never been a question in Gillian's mind who was responsible. And now the Dark Lord had come for her.

She was even more frightened than she'd imagined. Gillian's skin crawled as the Beast came closer. She saw his pebbled olive skin, breathed in his rank odor. Then finally, for a brief moment, she gazed into his maddening yellow eyes. She raised her Mossberg and got off two shots before the Dark Lord, his shoulder oozing puke-colored fluid from the shots, thrust his claw down the hall, grasped Gillian by the neck, and flung her out through a stained glass window.

Screaming all the way down, she slammed into her Zen garden, her face buried in the coarse sand, her head breaking against the heaviest of the carefully placed decorative stones.

On the second floor, Loreli stared down through a shattered window as the old woman's body twitched once and then went deadly still.

Inside the mansion, the Dark Lord prowled until he found the vault, his eyes glistening with delight as he gathered up the objects he'd come for. And then he and Loreli departed, disappearing into the forest moments before the Mercer Island Police arrived.

Chapter Three: The Seeding

With their stolen treasure in hand, Loreli and the Dark Lord returned to the Under City, a series of massive caverns six hundred feet below Pioneer Square in Seattle. It was populated, on any given day or night, by hundreds of demons. To access the Under City, one had only to go down through the famous "underground Seattle," the twenty-five square blocks that had burned down in the Great Seattle Fire of 1889 and had been subsequently built over, leaving a spooky subterranean "city." The good citizens of Seattle were proud of their quirky tourist attraction. They had no idea that far below their underground city lay a *real* metropolis, a colony of demons bent on the destruction of everything human.

It was here that the Dark Lord had been—with Loreli's help—recently raised from the near-dead. Being near-dead had been a thoroughly unpleasant experience for the Prince of Darkness, and he'd vowed to never let it happen again. He recalled how, in the bowels of Mount St. Emory, he had fought an epic battle with Will Hunter, his only son. He had been so certain that young Will would cross over to the darkness and rule by his side. Father and son reigning supreme! It was every father's dream. But no, not only had the foolish lad refused him, but he'd had the audacity to whack his head off!

Then had come the eruption of the Mount St. Emory volcano, during which the Dark Lord had been blown to smithereens, his body parts blasted asunder, his head fired out of the cone like a cannonball.

His zealous followers had painstakingly gathered up the thousands of bits of his flesh and bone and pieced them together in the vault in the Under City. But the idiots had been unable to find his head, even though he'd sent out clearly readable signposts of evil telling them where to look. No, it had been Will who'd finally had the wherewithal to locate his head. Luckily for the Dark Lord, his daughter, the boy's half-sister, was bent on winning his favor and facilitated reuniting his head with his body. But more had been needed for him to rise. Again young Loreli had prevailed, siphoning blood from Will and giving the Dark Lord a restorative transfusion, which had enabled him to roar fully back into the fray.

Now, there was revenge to be had. The Dark Lord would mercilessly punish Will, and then, finally, bend him to his will once and for all. Either that, or he'd just kill him. First, the Dark Lord would conjure into his possession the Sword of Armageddon. Then, his son dealt with, he would use it to bring an end to mankind's reign on Earth.

Of course, it would all take some doing. He needed to concentrate. There were details to remember, details from those fateful moments during the volcano's eruption.

Unlike humans, who foolishly preferred silence, demons did their best thinking with an abundance of noise, the more cacophonous the better. So the Dark Lord ordered his elite troops, the she-demons, led by Blue Streak, to spread the word that the Under City should become party central, with as much noise as possible.

In Spain they pride themselves on their long wild nights. In Argentina they wear their hangovers like a badge. But nobody, *nobody*, parties like a demon. This was to be a binge like no other because their Supreme Leader had risen from the dead and ordered it. The demons and the damned blasted grunge music and death metal, and they drank and danced and roared at one another until their throats were raw. They lit fireworks and held three simultaneous fight-to-the-death cage matches. They set a Mini Cooper aflame and drove it around until it exploded.

The Dark Lord's minions had been busy while he'd been away, building him a throne of bronzed human skulls. He sat upon it, closed his eyes, and concentrated on what had happened during the volcanic eruption while Loreli stood patiently at his side. She watched her father as his massive, ugly head dipped slightly, a sign that he was slipping into the trance he so richly yearned for. His eyelids trembled. She hoped the visions he sought would come to him, for if they didn't, all of his minions, herself included, would suffer.

Loreli wanted things to go smoothly. She knew she'd proven herself to her father, and she was biding her time, gathering the courage to speak to him about what she wanted. She knew the timing had to be just right. Because what she wanted was something very significant indeed.

The Dark Lord's brain was buzzing. Images swirled like grains of sand in a sirocco. He slowly took himself back to the eruption, honing in on it, and, though assaulted with a blinding white light in the memory, he forced his mind's eye wider open and drew a fateful image closer to him. The image was of two searing, white-hot crystal rods, two of the three legendary Power Rods, which, when joined with the third, formed the brutal, massively potent Triad of Power. The Dark Lord had intended to use the Triad of Power to open the portal to the Infinite Cave of Suffering Demons, unleashing them upon Earth to bring about the End of Days. But Will Hunter had thwarted his plan, flinging the Triad into the roiling lava, triggering both the implosion that had sealed both the portal to the damned and the ensuing eruption of Mount St. Emory.

All three Power Rods had been blown out of the cone of the volcano and flung in three different directions. Two of the rods, the ones not currently in the possession of Will Hunter, remained airborne, boomeranging through the atmosphere until they found each other and collided with tremendous force, creating a fulgent explosion that NASA scientists had mistaken for a meteor collision. The explosion was of sufficient impact that it caused the two rods to splinter and plummet straight down.

The Dark Lord's evil eyes sprang open. Loreli could tell that he'd accomplished his goal. He'd procured the vision he'd sought.

He rose and screamed, "Shut them up! Shut them all up!"

The word spread quickly. In seconds the Under City fell into an eerie, tomblike silence. Loreli could hear every rasping breath the Dark Lord took. He crooked a finger at her.

"Come closer."

She stepped toward the throne. He pulled out a dagger. Was he going to cut her? She tensed in anticipation. But to her astonishment, the Dark Lord turned the blade toward himself. He nicked one of his claw-like fingers and raised a drop of blood. His eyes swept the floor of the vault until they found a black beetle. Rising from the throne, he stood above the insect, which continued to scurry about as insects do, without apparent aim. With a puff of foul breath, the Dark Lord blew the blood from his finger, and it separated into smaller droplets. One found the beetle, and the insect paused as it absorbed the droplet.

"Observe closely, " said the Dark Lord to Loreli.

His eyes narrowed. The beetle moved back and forth in the dirt, dragging its tiny body with enough force to create a visible line. To and fro the insect crawled, until it had formed a perfect pentagram.

Loreli immediately understood. When the Dark Lord infused a creature with his blood, he could control it with his mind. She wondered if it were now up to her to take some of his blood into herself. But he did not draw more blood, instead he spit flame onto his small wound, cauterizing it. Then he snapped the blade off of the sword.

Loreli was shocked. Why would he break the blade off of one of the swords he'd so strongly coveted, which they'd gone to so much trouble to procure? The Dark Lord threw the blade into the dirt and held the handle in his hand, swinging it as though it had another invisible blade attached to it. He seemed pleased.

The Dark Lord stepped over to a circle of swords that were sticking up, their blades jabbed into the dirt. One by one, he pulled them out and snapped off their blades. Then he took the handles and tossed them into a melting pot. As he fanned the flames, he looked at Loreli with his compelling evil eyes.

"You are so very talented. I need you to make it rain."

She was perplexed. How could she make it rain? She wasn't a magician.

He moved to her and grabbed her by the shoulders, digging his claws into her flesh. "Use your *mind*, Loreli. Your training with chemicals. I need you to make it *rain* . . ."

He let go of her, then turned and tore through a stack of old books until he came upon one featuring a map of Puget Sound. With one bony finger he pointed to the map.

"Make it rain . . . *here*."

He was pointing to White Island.

Loreli stood on the bow of the ferry to White Island. She had figured out how to do the Dark Lord's bidding, and was on her way to do it. The wind was bitingly cold. She hugged herself to try and keep warm.

Earlier she'd jacked a 1999 Chevy Suburban that had belonged to Karl Mulligan, a retired chemical engineer who had worked as a consultant to the National Weather Control Board. Karl's specialty was cloud seeding, and he was one of the few experts in the field. That was why Loreli had paid a visit to his farm. The old man lived alone, so he was easy prey. She could so effortlessly have killed him, but she showed him mercy, leaving him alive but disoriented as she made off with his specialized equipment, which was now in a trailer hitched to the Suburban.

As the ferry docked, Loreli saw a hand-carved wooden sign that read: WELCOME TO BINGHAM, THE FRIENDLIEST LITTLE TOWN IN PUGET SOUND. She climbed into the Suburban and drove it off the ferry onto

terra firma, then sped through Bingham, up into the hills on a winding road, past Corwin's Tomato Farm and on up to Halstrom's Crest,
the highest point on the island. It was a large old farm, long over-
grown, having succumbed to neglect and nature. The farmhouse was
nearly demolished, and the adjacent tool and chicken sheds were in
shambles. The only thing still mostly intact was a sturdy old thick-
planked barn standing defiantly against the wind.

Loreli pulled into a meadow encircled with towering firs. At the
foot of the slanting meadow there was an old five-ton logging truck
sitting on its bare axles, the tires long rotted away. Loreli got out
and looked at the sky. She was pleased to see a gathering of growing
convective clouds that hopefully contained super-cooled droplets,
which would be necessary for her to accomplish her task. She saw
a rise adjacent to the barn and drove the truck over and backed the
trailer up onto it. From the trailer she wheeled out a cumbersome
device, a big bulky ground-based silver Iodide generator that Karl
had built himself.

She fired up the generator, then pulled a reeking bucket from the
back of the Suburban, using a bandana to cover her nose against the
stench of the Dark Lord's fetid blood. She added the blood to the silver
Iodide mixture. Gagging, she stood back and watched as the machine
chugged and belched plumes of acrid pink smoke into the sky, swiftly
impregnating the clouds with the evil mixture.

The clouds roiled and churned, growing darker. The air on the
ground was cold and becoming damper by the second. Loreli turned
her collar up against the wind as it began to rain. She climbed back into
the Suburban and sped off, leaving Karl Mulligan's machine behind.

She made it back to the tiny harbor in time to take the next ferry
back to the mainland. As the ferry pulled out, its iconic horn blasting three times, Loreli looked back at the island and smiled darkly.
Its inhabitants were about to experience a living nightmare.

Chapter Four:
Hot Red Rain

In downtown Seattle, Natalie moved swiftly down the street, lithe and mean. She felt liberated. No longer bound by moral constraints of any kind, she was on the hunt. She was thrilled as she looked at the world through her new demon eyes. She had a list of things to do, but with her newfound strength and cunning, it was hard not to get distracted, as when two pudgy middle-aged men, Josh and Guy, had whistled at her and laughed, lobbing lewd comments her way. She turned toward them with death in her eyes, but then smiled and struck a pose. They whistled some more. She motioned to a bar and went inside, though she was clearly underage.

The bar was a modern affair, very upscale, with lots of dark wood and candles. It served Mexican fare at absurdly inflated prices and had an extensive wine list. It took the paunchy duo about thirty seconds to arrive, doing their best to suck in their guts and appear younger than they were. Natalie found this sad and pathetic. She was sitting on the stool closest to the door when Josh sidled up, leaned close, and whispered what he must have considered an enticement into her ear. She forced a mechanical naughty girl smile and took him by the hand, and crooked a finger at Guy—*hey, come on, join the party*—then led them both into the small vestibule adjacent to the restrooms.

"You guys think you're pretty smokin' hot, huh?" Natalie purred.

Josh and Guy looked at each other and laughed. With their bloodshot eyes and flushed cheeks, it was clear that this wasn't the first bar they'd been in today. When Natalie noticed their wedding bands, she knew what she had to do. She was a demon, true, but that didn't mean marriage meant nothing to her. When she married Will, it would mean *everything*.

She grabbed Josh by the throat and slammed him against the concrete wall. His head hit with a revolting smack and he dropped to the floor, unconscious. Guy tried to bolt, but she aimed a kick at his groin. He doubled over as she hammered him with an uppercut, breaking his nose. He fell to the floor, moaning. She rifled through their pockets, smiling as she discovered that Josh carried a thick wad in a money clip and Guy had plenty of loot in his wallet.

"Well," said Natalie, clapping her hands. "Looks like this is my lucky day."

She stuffed the cash in her jeans pocket.

"Tell your wives I said hi."

She walked out, her blood running hot.

In Nordstrom, Natalie perused the wedding dresses, but all that white made her dizzy. So she departed and found a goth boutique down the street, where she put together a dark, threatening outfit: black tights, a lacy bustier, and a short leather jacket spiked with studs. Perfect. Now all she needed was a pair of kick-ass boots.

On the street again she felt a tingly anticipation, like a kid with a big rock in her hand who knew she was about to break something. It was a rush and it was coming on strong. She walked across the street and stood before Cache, Seattle's priciest shoe store. In the window a light shone upon a pair of thigh-high black leather boots with improbably tall spiked heels. She immediately swept in, yanked one of the boots from the window, and stared hard at the clerk, a sloppy, skinny kid, his face peppered with freckles. His watery grey eyes could hardly hold her gaze. She tossed him the sample boot, which he caught, the heel nearly impaling the soft flesh of his palm.

"Seven and a half," she said.

The clerk was bamboozled. This girl—her long hair shining, her eyes ablaze—was so strange and powerful that a ball of panic worked its way up into his throat. The best he could muster was a garbled grunt of consent as he moved on unsteady legs into the stockroom. He found the large box and pulled it down from the shelf, then ventured back out to face Natalie, whose flashing eyes continued to haunt him. He had been in her orbit less than two minutes, yet she was turning his world upside down. He knelt—supplication came naturally to him—took the boots out of their box, and slowly unzipped them. Natalie offered her feet, and the boots slid on easily, like they'd found their home. She stood and smiled at herself in the mirror, then caught the clerk's reflection. He was gaping at her. His throat was already constricted, so when she grabbed it, her hand strong as an eagle's talon, his brain, already buzzing from yearning, began to fade and his knees grew weak.

"Thank you for the boots," she said.

She released her viselike grip and he nodded, his face flushed, his freckles permanently darkened. He watched her walking away. It didn't even occur to him to protest that she hadn't paid. He would eventually pay for the boots, using his entire week's salary, on the idiotic hope that she would return and, in her gratitude for his generosity, reward him in ways he was already dreaming about.

Out on the street, her hair whipping in the wind, Natalie relished the feel of the boots as she strode down the street, her heels striking the concrete with deliciously succinct precision. Men lowered their umbrellas—better to be soaked than to miss a glimpse of this dark goddess—drank in her vision and instantly wanted her. Women gazed at her with vitriolic envy.

Natalie felt absolutely spectacular. She was the center of the universe.

She entered Maurer's Jewelry Store with a single-minded purpose. Her eyes swept the display cases. The burly guard registered in her vision, but she paid him no mind. Her eyes finally found a black diamond ring that suited her fancy. It was a simple yet elegant five-carat sable beauty. The unctuous salesman—concluding from her expensive boots that she was a customer of means—eagerly extracted the ring from the case and watched greedily as Natalie slid it onto her finger. It had flawless clarity. Light danced off of it. Natalie smiled radiantly, thinking of the moment she and Will would be bound together forever. She chose a plain gold band for him and thanked the salesman. With rings in hand, she began to leave.

"Excuse me . . . ," he said.

The manager, a stout middle-aged woman in a pantsuit, sensed foul play. She moved to intercept Natalie, making the terrible error of grabbing her by the shoulder. Natalie whirled, moving as though it were the most natural thing in the world, and leapt into a high kick. The toe of her boot slammed into the woman's nose. She shrieked. Her nose gushed blood. She dropped to her knees and pitched sideways onto the carpet. Natalie was already out the door.

In three seconds an alarm sounded. Out on the street Natalie was in no hurry. She walked two blocks, turning heads along the way. Then she heard the sirens. Two blue and white Seattle Police Department squad cars hurled past.

Natalie ran with abandon, laughing, flying through the city like the wind itself.

WHITE ISLAND

At the White Island Racquet Club, seventeen-year-old Jasper Sholes was lining up a serve when he felt the first few hot drops fall from the sky. He brushed his long flaxen hair out of his eyes, then fired the tennis ball across the net to his partner, Wendy Childress.

Waiting for the ball, she touched the expensive necklace that Jasper had given her for good luck and thought about their future together. They'd just started dating, but she could see it all clearly. They would hold out as long as they could before succumbing to their vigorous natural instincts. But she wouldn't get pregnant; no, they'd use birth control. She would be so giving and adventurous in bed that he would fall utterly, deeply in love with her. He would ask her to marry him. They would have a long engagement, long enough for him to go to college, and then they'd marry in the Lutheran church, honeymoon on Maui, and have their first child. They would buy a house, raise a family, and grow old together on White Island.

Wendy usually returned almost every one of Jasper's serves, but as she positioned herself under the ball, she felt a shudder crawl up her backbone. As the rain came down harder, she realized something was wrong. For one thing, the rain was hot. And for another, the rainwater pooling on the court was blood red. She felt faint, and her knees began to buckle. Jasper rushed over in time to catch her before she pitched sideways.

"Jasper . . . ?"

"It's only rain," he said. But even as he said it, he knew it wasn't true. They both knew it. Gathering Wendy in his arms, Jasper fled to take shelter under a willow tree. But the hot red rain found them. In moments they became dizzy and were sucked down, powerless, into a dead sleep.

Out on Farley Road sat a huge old two-story house. It was built along the lines of Victorian Stick architecture, the exterior walls ornamented with decorative half-timbering, brackets, rafters, and braces. It was white with a red shingle roof, and it belonged to sixty-one-year-old Janie Walker, who was lovingly tending the strawberries in her garden when the red rain began to fall.

Janie squinted up at the clouds. Did they look pink? They sure did. And was the rain that was falling in ever-larger droplets actually red? She held out her hand. It was indeed. It was also rather hot. But none of this frightened Janie. She'd seen red tides before, which were nothing more than an algae bloom—so why not red rain? Surely this was some kind of easily explained natural phenomenon. She was trying to piece together some kind of rational explanation, but suddenly she could no longer keep her eyes open. She succumbed to the dark slumber.

At six-foot-six and three hundred pounds of muscle, Boone Winter was a giant of a teenager. He was chopping wood in his father's backyard when he realized he was sweating more than usual. He ran his hand over his slick bald head, which he shaved every morning with his HeadBlade razor. He looked up into the sky. The rain splashing on his face felt hot. His huge dog, Killer, ran back and forth, barking.

"'Sup, Killer? Huh, boy?"

Killer kept barking but slowed down as he licked his coat. Boone cast another glance at the sky and then shrugged. Sure, he felt woozy, but he'd probably just had too many beers last night. He brought the axe down hard one more time, splitting a thick log in two. He felt dizzy and tired as he wiped the rain from his face. He sat down and was immediately overcome with drowsiness. He lay down on the ground next to Killer and slept.

All over White Island, similar scenarios were unfolding. Those who were inside when the hot red rain began to fall saw their neighbors crumble and, when they ran out to help, succumbed to slumber too. Although brief, the sleep was potent.

Awakening first, the island's teenagers all began to swarm up Porchain Road to gather at the First Lutheran Church. It was a storybook cathedral, painted a brilliant white with a cross-tipped spire that reached optimistically toward Heaven. As the teens arrived, they formed into a circle around the church and held hands, staring blankly ahead. Jasper Sholes was staring at a can of gasoline, which lifted up into the air, as if by magic, then went flying into the front doors, the liquid splashing and dispersing quickly.

Ronnie Salick, a stocky kid with curly brown hair and golf tee earrings, lit a cigarette. He took a few long drags, then flipped the burning stub at the pooling gas. The church caught fire in an instant, and the flames spread quickly. The gathered teens watched stoically, not at all bothered by the fact that their beloved church was burning. Their heads were filled with a commanding voice that was giving them implicit instructions to do His bidding.

The lone White Island fire truck arrived, laden with volunteer firemen who had roused themselves from their forced sleep. As soon as they got out of the truck, the teens surrounded them, holding them prisoner and forcing them to watch as church burned. The adults screamed in protest but were outnumbered and powerless.

Once the church had been completely engulfed in flames, the teens released the firemen, allowing them to do their job. They hooked up the hoses and sprayed the building, bringing the blaze under control in less than ten minutes. But the teenagers' mission had been accomplished. As the voice inside their heads had instructed them, they had transformed the church. The formerly snow-white building was now charred completely black, a fitting temple for their new deity.

Jasper looked at Wendy and then at Boone. Duty called.

They climbed into Boone's Jeep and left the smoking church while the rest of the group of boys marched the struggling adult firemen into the nearby woods.

Boone's Jeep sped down Possnack Avenue toward the bay, passing Sherriff Glenn Mertz's patrol vehicle, a Ford Explorer, parked by the side of the road. The driver's door was wide open and the police radio was spewing static.

Boone kept driving all the way down to the marina. As he pulled the Jeep to a stop, Jasper and the girls leapt out, moving quickly to a forty-foot Chris Craft cabin cruiser. The beautiful boat, which belonged to Wendy's parents, was christened *Reel Love*.

Boone moved over to the dock. The ferry terminal ticket booth was empty, the door open, an unfinished game of solitaire on the computer screen. Boone grabbed a sign, took it to the end of the dock, and hung it on a hook. The sign read: DOCK CLOSED.

Later that day there were signs of unusual occurrences all over Bingham. In Dixie's Diner, the counter stools were empty, cups of coffee steaming, plates of food half-eaten. The front door to the Thrift-T-Mart was wide open, but no one was at the register, even though the cash drawer was wide open. The neon lights on the front of Buster's Tavern blinked, and inside, a dozen steins of beer sat half-full on the bar. A couple of barstools had been tipped over. The jukebox played, but no one danced because no one was there.

Chapter Five:
A Dream Crushed

Having no idea that Will was bound to a bed back at the mansion, his life slipping away, Rudy and Emily had been criss-crossing the Seattle Center for hours looking for Natalie.

Emily and Natalie were twins, and each had always had a sixth sense for when the other was in danger. All week long Natalie had been acting strange. At first she'd only been jealous of that girl, Loreli, and how much attention Will had been paying her. But the jealousy had evolved into something much deeper and more hopeless. It had taken Natalie to a dark and lonely place in her mind. When Emily and Rudy had come home from school that day and found Natalie's bedroom door locked, Emily knew something was terribly wrong.

Rudy broke the door down, but Natalie wasn't there. In fact, she wasn't anywhere in the mansion, at least not that they could find. Emily thought hard. Figuring her sister would likely seek the comfort of memories, she decided that there was a good chance that she was down at the Seattle Center because when they were little girls it was their favorite place.

The first thing Emily and Rudy did was go up in the Needle because Emily remembered the romantic night Natalie and Will had shared up there. But Natalie wasn't up there now, nor was she in the gift shop below or anywhere near the monorail platform. They checked all the tacky game booths and the big old food pavilion. They circled the International Fountain and Key Arena and then the Peace Garden and the Fun Forest Amusement Park. They saw some kids they recognized from their last few days at Lyndon Baines Johnson High and asked if they'd seen Natalie. No one had. Rudy and Emily kept on walking.

Emily had been holding Rudy's hand off and on during their journey. When he casually put his arm around her at the fountain, she didn't resist. In fact, the more time they spent together, the more she seemed to touch him, brushing up against him, leaning on him while they searched the crowds for Natalie. Rudy kept finding people he insisted looked like movie stars. "Look, there's Brad Pitt and Angelina Jolie. Isn't that Jim Carrey?" Of course the people looked nothing like the stars, but it made Emily smile a little. Every time she touched him, Rudy felt tingles from his head to his toes. He suspected she was touching him so much only because she was so worried about her sister, and the last thing Rudy wanted to do was to take advantage of that, but he was so incredibly drawn to her.

He pulled her toward The Big Drop, a ride that climbed eighty feet into the air and then dropped with a sudden *whoosh*. Emily complained that they didn't have time for such frivolity, but when Rudy pointed out that they'd be able see more from up there, she acquiesced. They looked for Natalie as they rose but didn't see her. Then they dropped so suddenly their stomachs slammed into their throats. Afterwards they stopped by the funhouse mirrors to figure out their next move. Emily rested her head on Rudy's shoulder and his heart started banging against his rib cage.

Carpe diem, he told himself. His hands were shaking. He stopped and lifted her chin and looked into her eyes. He was going to do it; he was going to kiss her, and she knew it. But Emily caught a sudden warped reflection of Rudy that made him look strange and menacing, and she jerked away. The sudden reminder that Rudy had once been a demon—and could very well morph back into one at any second—shook her to the bone.

She turned and started walking away. Rudy jogged to catch up with her.

"Hey, I'm sorry, I didn't mean . . ."

She stopped and looked him in the eye.

"No, I'm sorry, Rudy. I just . . . had a moment back there. I kind of flashed back to when I was . . ."

She didn't have to finish the sentence. Rudy knew she was talking about when she'd been held captive by demons for all those weeks in the belly of the Mount St. Emory volcano. After she'd been tormented by the Harrisburg demonteens, it was a miracle that she even hung out with him at all. He'd been one of them, and they'd put a world of hurt on her. He wished he'd never crossed over to the dark side. But there was no erasing history. He was going to have to carry that with him for the rest of his days. It didn't exactly do wonders for his confidence.

"I don't blame you," he told Emily. "I guess I wouldn't want to kiss me, either." Rudy wondered if the world was ever going to cut him some slack for the mistake he'd made. Right now it sure didn't look like it.

Emily started walking toward the monorail, and Rudy followed. Then he saw an electronics vending machine selling phones, cameras, and video cameras. Living with Will did have its advantages, one of which was a nearly unlimited supply of cash and credit cards. Thanks to the *Demon Hunter* video game Will had designed and licensed years ago, he had a steady stream of cash flowing into his bank accounts. And he was generous with his money. Determined to cheer Emily up, Rudy whipped out an American Express card and bought a Sony HD DV camcorder.

• • •

Loreli returned to the Under City to find the Dark Lord welcoming her with open arms.

"You have done well, my daughter," he told her.

Loreli beamed with pride.

"Come," said the Dark Lord, and he strode from the vault into the main cavern and onto the large stone dais, with Loreli trailing him. Once she was next to him, he roared to get the attention of his army of minions.

"My daughter has performed admirably," he yelled. "Let us show her our appreciation!"

The Dark Lord slapped his mighty hands together. The sound was like a thunderclap. His followers did the same, applauding and banging sticks and drums and mugs and pots and pans and anything else they could get their hands on. It was a massive wave of noise that brought a flush to Loreli's face.

This was it. This was her moment! When the Dark Lord's malicious eyes found hers, she screwed up the courage.

"By saving your life, Father, and doing your bidding, I hereby claim my birthright. I deem myself a worthy heir and trust that you will reward my efforts."

His hideous face twitched with agitation.

"Of course your efforts will be rewarded. What is it you desire? Wealth? Fame? A mate? Name a man, any man, and he's yours."

She knew he could deliver on any promise. Her head swam with the possibilities. But she was on a mission, the same mission she'd been on ever since she was a little girl. It was time to reap the benefits from the years of hard work. He'd denied her the first time she asked, when she'd fought her way into the volcano near Harrisburg ahead of Will, but this time, surely, it would be different. Things had changed.

"I want what you were going to give Will Hunter. I want to rule by your side!"

A few agonizing seconds passed. Loreli blinked. It was as if time were turgid, swollen, slow, and cumbersome. She thought she saw dust motes frozen in midair. She watched her father's eyes narrow. His hand-claws clenched into fists. And then the Prince of Darkness began to laugh. It was a laugh that started deep in his gut and lifted up through his chest and exploded out his massive mouth.

He lifted his hands, exhorting the swarm. Now they, too, began to laugh, chirping and barking and squealing out their amusement. The laughs ricocheted around the cave, bouncing off the walls. Loreli stood frozen. Her ears burned. Was she being *mocked*? Did they *dare* to ridicule her?

The Dark Lord spoke in a low, deadly voice. "Have we not had this conversation before, daughter? You presume too much."

Loreli propelled herself forward. She stood in front of the most feared, dangerous entity on the planet. Yet she was defiant.

"Had it not been for me," she cried, "you would be dead!"

The Great Beast closed his eyes. Tick. Tick. Tick. Like a bomb, he was about to go off, and suddenly Loreli could feel her time on Earth growing short. The dirt beneath her feet shifted. The Dark Lord trembled with rage.

"Do you really, truly expect *me* . . ."

He was building up to it, his chest rising and falling rapidly, the scales upon it blooming, rising like the hackles on an angry dog, the quills of a porcupine.

". . . expect *me* . . . to *rule* next to . . . next to . . . a . . ."

He was working the word around in his mouth like a piece of bad meat. And then he spit it out, his voice full off venom.

". . . a *GIRL*?"

His eyes were filled with hate. He had told her before: A daughter, ruling by his side? Never! It would be his son, only his *son*!

Loreli tried to take a step backward, terrified in the realization that she'd just made—*had been making all these years*—a terrible mistake. When he threw her out before, she thought it was just because she had not yet proven her worth. She thought that once he had seen what she could do, her father would see that she, not Will, was the one worthy of sharing his throne. But she should have known better. She should have known that the Devil was and would always be the ultimate male chauvinist pig. That was why Will was chosen and not her. Not because he was smarter or more capable, but because he was a boy.

The Dark Lord grew even larger. His anger tasted bitter anger on his tongue. He was furious that she had tried to demand so much in front of his followers. It was blasphemy.

"You . . . have made a fool out of me!"

The anger and humiliation still coursed through her, but mostly she was afraid.

"I . . . I had no such intent, sir . . ."

With a roar, the Dark grabbed Loreli by her heel and lifted her into the air.

"You shall pay for your arrogance!"

She looked at the world upside down, the blood rushing into her pounding head. But she had saved him! Saved his life! Surely he would not—!

And then she was flying through the air—he had hurled her off the ledge!

Her head hit first, bending at a painful angle as she tumbled over rocks, her back scraping, her hands clawing for purchase, her nails breaking. Her forehead was badly gashed. Blood flowed into her eyes. Lights were exploding in her brain. The throng of faces, which only moments ago had looked upon her with respect and adoration, now regarded her with cold contempt. The minions snarled and spat. She felt someone kick her, then felt another blow to the head.

The pain was unbearable. She looked up at the Prince of Darkness, her *father*. There was nothing in his eyes but malice. He opened his maw and let loose another roar, his eyes widening, the veins on his face bulging. He held up a claw-hand and sent a force-beam upward. Loreli watched in horror as stalactites high on the ceiling above her began to break off, falling right at her. She rolled out of the way of the first two, but the third slammed into a boulder next to her and exploded, the fragments bursting like shrapnel into her left ankle. She cried out in pain. The crowd of demons cheered.

Her left leg wounded, Loreli still attempted to flee. Stalactites continued to bombard her from above. She was knocked off her feet. She tried to get up again but her left leg was numb. So she crawled.

The Dark Lord watched, impassive. His own daughter might as well have been a cockroach groveling on the floor of the cavern. She'd served her purpose—he had no need of her now. There was nothing she could do for him that his other followers could not. He motioned to Blue Streak, who instantly read his intentions. She signaled some comrades, and they swooped down upon Loreli like a pack of angry ravens, kicking her, slicing at her with their talons. They were thrilled to dish out punishment because she'd kicked their asses on more than one occasion. Then they lifted her, bleeding, battered, up into the air, suspending her in front of the Dark Lord.

"Take her away," he said. "Dispose of her."

"What is your suggestion, My Lord?" asked Blue Streak.

"Sink her in Puget Sound. Throw her off a cliff. In front of a bus. It matters not. Do whatever amuses you. Just make sure she takes her pain with her to eternity."

One of Loreli's eyes was nearly swollen shut, but she could still see her father, could make eye contact with her one good eye. And she used that eye to plead with him. How could he not feel sympathy, empathy, *something* for his own flesh and blood?

"How could you do this to me?" she cried.

The Dark Lord spat. "The answer is simple, my dear. It's my nature."

He waved away the shedemons and they exited, taking the Dark Lord's wounded daughter with them.

They rushed her upward through the labyrinth of tunnels and stairwells to the street. There, they set her on a bench in Pioneer Square. A light rain was falling from the ashen sky. Transients saw the wounded girl and the hard-looking, oddly attired teen girls. But they did nothing.

Blue Streak and the other shedemons debated in their high-pitched twittering how best to torture and kill her.

"Drowning her won't be any fun; we won't see her suffer."

"We could throw her off the Space Needle."

"Been there, done that."

They fired up a crack pipe and took hits. Their hearts were hammering and their brains were maelstroms. Loreli rolled off the bench and hit the ground hard. She didn't mind the pain; it was the only thing keeping her conscious. She knew if she didn't do something fast, she was in for a prolonged torture session.

Then she saw her escape coming, wheeling down First Avenue: a fourteen-ton Metro bus. She watched the light change from green to yellow, praying that the driver was in a hurry. He was, and he throttled the massive bus through the light, whooshing through just as it was turning red.

As the shedemons continued to squabble, Loreli heaved herself up onto her good leg, lurched into a crouch, and then, as a homeless woman screamed, she threw herself in front of the oncoming bus.

Chapter Six:
Capture

Rudy and Emily rode the monorail, its silver cars packed with tourists, in silence, zooming above Battery, Bell, and Blanchard Streets, gazing down at the cars and pedestrians, gliding the two miles down to the Westlake Center, where they got off and walked around. Rudy was still stinging from Emily's rebuff. He desperately wanted to change the mood, so he took the camcorder out and started filming some shots of Emily.

"What are you doing?" she said.

He kept shooting her, moving around, seeing her from different angles.

"Wow . . . ," he said.

"Oh, come on."

"No, really, wow."

Rudy lowered the camcorder for a second and looked very serious.

"You know, you could totally be a supermodel," he said.

She rolled her eyes. She thought the whole rewarding-people-for-how-they-looked thing was dumb. But secretly she still loved the compliment.

"There's no such thing as a supermodel," she said. "Unless they can leap over buildings in a single bound, they're just models. Human mannequins."

"Okay, so you're a super mannequin," said Rudy, as he kept shooting.

Emily was enjoying the attention, but she started to blush as she noticed people looking.

"Rudy, cut," she said. "I mean it. Cut!"

Rudy shut the camera off.

They kept scanning the shops and crowds for Natalie. Rudy thought maybe they'd have a better chance if they stopped walking around and stayed still for a few minutes, so they got a couple of caramel lattes at a Starbucks and sat, scrutinizing the waves of pedestrians. Then they crossed the street to the corner of Fifth and Pine and listened to a steel drum band for a few minutes.

Emily knew she'd hurt Rudy's feelings. She had to say something.

"Rudy . . . I'm sorry. I like you. I *really* like you. But I think it's going to take some time for me to . . ."

As she spoke, she touched his hand gently, but she stopped talking when he awkwardly jerked it away from her.

He spoke quickly, his words falling over each other. "No, I'm the one who should be sorry, you didn't do anything wrong, and I did just about everything. I mean, what an evil freak I was. If I were you, I wouldn't forgive me, either. So really, it's no problemo, seriously. You're an awesome girl, Emily."

"You really think so?"

"Of course. You deserve somebody who hasn't been . . . corrupted."

Emily thought that, one way or another, everyone was corrupted, no one was pure. People all made mistakes and messed up, that was what made them human. After all, she'd done things she wished she hadn't, especially before she'd been kidnapped back in Harrisburg.

She was going to tell Rudy that, but the words died in her throat when she looked up at him. He was suddenly utterly mesmerized, staring at something over her shoulder.

It was Natalie, crossing the street one block down on Sixth, but she cut such a different figure than Rudy was used to, it actually took him a moment to process who he was seeing. Natalie was terrifyingly beautiful.

He couldn't help but call out to her. "Natalie!"

Her ears pricked up. She spun as though threatened. She might have even hissed, though Rudy couldn't tell from where he was.

Now Emily saw her, too. "Nat!" she yelled.

The sisters locked eyes for two seconds. Then Natalie turned around and took off running.

"Let's go!" Emily called to Rudy.

They raced after her. They were both great runners because of all the training Will had insisted that they do, but there was just no way they could keep up with demon Natalie as she flashed down Sixth Avenue and took a right on Stewart Street. Even in those super-high heels, she moved amazingly fast.

She ducked into an alley, crouched down, and waited. She listened, and with her enhanced senses she could hear the soles of their shoes pounding on the pavement. Her nostrils widened as she breathed in and smiled. She could smell them. She heard Emily cry out plaintively, "Natalie?"

Like a hawk, she was on them. Rudy saw a shadow, turned, and found himself slammed facedown onto the sidewalk, his cheek smashed against a bottle cap, Natalie's boot planted on the back of his head.

"Nice," said Rudy. "Real nice!"

"I was just thinking to myself, why am I running from you two?" said Natalie. Then she laughed.

The sound of her sister's malevolent raspy laugh caused Emily's chest to constrict. She was too shocked to speak. It was like she was back in the amusement park, looking in the funhouse mirrors, only this time, it was as if a hideously distorted image of Natalie was glaring balefully back at her. Now that Emily had gotten a good look at her, she knew that Natalie had crossed over and become a demon. Her eyes were that sickening, fluid black ringed with burning red.

Natalie grabbed her sister and pinned her arm behind her back.

"What are you doing?" cried Emily.

"Right now? Enjoying subjugating you two, that's what," said Natalie.

"Well, you'd better let go of me, or I swear I'll . . ." said Emily

Natalie tightened her grip, twisting Emily's arm even harder. She cried out as the pain shot up her elbow into her shoulder blade.

"Or you'll *what*?" Natalie said. "What are you gonna do?"

Neither Rudy nor Emily had an answer, knowing full well that any threats would not only fall upon deaf ears, but only serve to inflame Natalie.

"That's right," said Natalie, "You're not going to do anything." She shoved Emily into the alley, where she fell next to Rudy. He knew enough to sit tight. He'd seen how powerful Natalie was, and he knew she was ferocious. Best to cooperate with her for the time being.

Natalie considered what to do with her twin sister and goofy Rudy. Her first thought was to kill them, but then she thought of an even better option.

"Don't move," said Natalie. "I've got a plan."

Emily started to sit up, but Natalie was on her in a flash and knocked her backward into the brick wall.

"Don't mess with me, Em," she snarled. "I could tear your head off if I wanted to. So don't make me want to, okay? I'm going to show mercy. I'm going to change you two."

Emily was dizzy. "Ch-change us?" she asked. "You mean infect us?"

Natalie didn't answer. She didn't have to talk. She didn't have to tell them anything. She knew what she was going to do. She was going to make them cross over to the dark side. Then they could all live together as one happily infected family. Sure, Emily would resist, but once she'd gone over, she'd see that her sister had done the best thing for her. And Rudy, he'd be fine; he'd already tasted the forbidden fruit.

Natalie looked into the street and then moved like a cat to a black Dodge Charger idling in traffic. She flung open the passenger-side door and climbed in. Three seconds later the driver, a petrified young black woman wearing curlers, leapt out of the car screaming, her left cheek crimson from where Natalie had sliced her with her nails.

Natalie jammed the car in reverse and backed it into the alley, where she popped the trunk. She grabbed Emily roughly and pushed her into the trunk. Rudy tried to struggle but was no match for her, and she shoved him in, too. It was a tight fit, and they had to contort themselves.

"We're all going home," Natalie said. "And once I convince you two to see the light—or, rather, the dark—we're going to be one badass family."

She saw the fear and confusion in Emily's face and leaned in low to sell it. "It's unbelievable, Em. It's like slipping into a whole new skin."

"But I don't want—"

Wham! Natalie slammed the trunk and got in the Dodge. The light changed. Cars behind her honked. She wasn't fazed. She took her time finding a death metal song on the radio, then jacked up the music and took off, driving like a bat out of Hell.

Loreli held on tightly to the undercarriage of the bus. She'd leapt in front of it and then dropped down. As the bumper had slammed into her head, she'd felt herself being pounded down into the hardness of the street, her skull bouncing, elbows pinging, her duster ripping open, her boots dragging. Using all her remaining strength, she'd reached up and grabbed the hot frame, her fingers burning. It felt like she'd grasped a white-hot fireplace poker, but she knew her only chance for survival was to hold on. The pain was hellish, shooting up from her hands and threatening to overtake her entire body. She took a deep breath and tried to embrace it. Fighting it would only drain what energy she had left, she knew.

The bus roared onward, rumbling up James Street, catching nothing but green lights. The driver kept his Red Wing boot pressing the accelerator to the floor, hurtling the big machine along.

Reaching Beacon Hill, the bus made a scheduled stop. Loreli released her grip and pushed herself out from underneath. She prayed that the syringe she needed was still intact in one of her duster pockets. Her legs were bruised, battered, and bleeding, her kneecaps raw. She limped across the sidewalk into José Rizal Park, which was perched on the hillside overlooking downtown Seattle.

A middle-aged man and his wife had tripods set up and were photographing the skyline panorama when Loreli limped into the park. After a quick whispered discussion, the woman approached her.

Loreli knew she was quite a sight, wearing one boot and all manner of leather and lace torn to shreds. She was like some version of Laura Croft who'd been tossed in a clothes dryer along with a bale of barbed wire. The woman's frightened heart was beating fast.

"My God . . . are you . . . all right?"

It was, of course, an utterly ridiculous question, for Loreli was clearly anything *but* all right, with her burned hair, her battered arms and body, blood flowing from her ears and scalp. But what else could the woman say?

Loreli nodded. Though it hurt to smile, she did. "Never been better," she said through gritted teeth.

Loreli dug through the pockets of her tattered duster. A few of her orbs and vials were cracked or broken but most of them were intact. She found the three that she needed. Kneeling on the grass, she mixed them together into one precious, lime-green potion, and filled a syringe with it. It was her only chance for salvation now. She stuffed it into the pocket of her leather shorts and turned her attention to the man, who was just concluding a cell phone call. She glared at him.

"It was just . . . nine-one-one," he said.

"Son of a bitch! I do *not* need this right now."

The woman was still hovering next to her, uncertain. Loreli pulled a thin deadly blade from the lining of her duster and put it to the woman's neck.

"I'd like to be polite, but there's no time. I need a ride. Let's go."

The photographers were terrified. Leaving their cameras behind, they took Loreli to their Toyota RAV4, then quietly followed her instructions. The man drove down across the Rizal Bridge on Twelfth Avenue South and headed for Queen Anne Hill, passing the international district.

Loreli brooded about her father and how her attempt at reconciliation had been such an unmitigated disaster. The devastation and rage she felt was unspeakable. She had wasted so much of her life yearning for what could never be. She had made a colossal mistake, and she knew it would haunt her forever—unless she did one thing. She clutched the vial. With it, she would save her brother, Will Hunter, and together they would vanquish the Dark Lord.

Terrified that she might already be too late, Loreli told the man to drive faster.

Will had struggled for what seemed like an eternity against the zip-ties, and all he'd managed to accomplish was to grow weaker. The ties had cut into his wrists as he knew they would; it would be impossible to break through them.

Think! It was time to try using brains over brawn. *If I ever get out of here*, he thought, *Loreli's going to pay for this if it's the last thing I ever do.* The poison she'd injected him with was stealing his life minute by minute, but even worse was what she'd done to Natalie. Turning the love of his life into a demon was the most spiteful thing she could have done. Better she should have just killed him—though it seemed as if she might have succeeded in that as well.

No! He told himself that he was going to get out of this. Somehow he was going to escape, and then Loreli would wish she'd never been born.

Natalie hadn't checked him for weapons, and he still had the Megashocker strapped to his right leg. He began to shake his leg, positioning his body so that the weapon would slide out of its holster. It took several minutes of excruciating pain, but he finally managed to get it out. The weapon's handle was nowhere within his reach, but he had another plan. Shifting his body on the bed, he was able to make the Megashocker roll toward his hip. *Good. Progress.* He used the pointy olecranon bone on his elbow to switch it on. The protruding blade immediately heated up. Using his hip again, he pushed the shocker to the edge of the bed. It was scorching the sheets already. Will worked his hips back and forth until the shocker slid off the mattress. He prayed for this to work, and then it wedged—*yes!*—against the metal frame of the bed. All he had to do was wait until the frame heated up enough for the plastic zip-ties to melt. It was a brilliant plan, with only one flaw: The bed frame was heating up all right, but the bed was starting to catch on fire.

Smoke billowed. Will held his breath. He kept yanking his wrists against the zip-ties—and they kept slicing into his skin. His eyes were burning, but he could see that the wrought-iron bed frame was scorching hot. Three possible scenarios went through his head. One: the ties would soften in time for him to yank one hand free and get out of this mess as planned. The chances of that were low. Two: he would die of smoke inhalation. There was a much better chance of that. Three: he'd be burned to death before either of the above happened. That one was the most likely.

He pulled on his right hand as hard as he could. The pain of the zip-tie cutting into his wrist was unbearable, and the smoke was beginning to fill his lungs. Images of his life swam through his head; the final highlight reel you see before succumbing to the inevitable and walking through Death's door.

As Natalie sped through the slick wet streets, the grinding, soul-scraping death metal music continued to blast out of the Charger's speakers. For Emily and Rudy, lying in the trunk, the noise was unbearable. Rudy had shifted his body and was banging on the trunk lid as hard as he could.

"Let us out of here!" he shouted.

There was scant light in the trunk, but his eyes had adjusted. He stopped kicking to catch his breath and turned to Emily. She still had a look of uncomprehending horror in her eyes.

"Why would she do this? Why would she cross over to the dark side and become infected?"

"I don't know," said Rudy.

"What are we going to do?"

"She said we're going home, right? Will should be back there by now. It's going to be okay. We're going to get out of here, and then . . . Will will think of something, I promise. He cured me. He can cure Natalie, too."

The Charger braked hard and their bodies were thrown around, the metal surfaces in the trunk dealing out pain. The music stopped. They heard the door slam.

They braced themselves, expecting Natalie to yank open the trunk and give them a good thrashing, or worse. If she was really cranky, maybe she'd twist their heads off. But she didn't open the trunk. Instead they heard her running toward the mansion.

The sight of smoke pouring from her cracked balcony door sent adrenaline coursing through Natalie's already amped-up system.

Will was trapped! He was going to die and it was her fault because she'd tied him to the bed! She growled at herself for her stupidity as she burst through the front doors and vaulted up the long sweeping stairway to the second floor.

In the guest bedroom, Will pulled with all his might on the zip-tie cinching his right wrist—and it snapped. He couldn't feel his hand. For a moment he thought he'd severed it. He coughed violently, then looked down and watched his fingers flex. He reached blindly for the Megashocker, his hand thrusting through the flames leaping up off the comforter. His hand wrapped around the shocker and he howled in pain. He'd grabbed the wrong end—the fiery blade of the shocker seared his flesh. He gasped and couldn't help but suck in more smoke. His lungs felt like they were going to explode. He held his breath, his scalp began to tingle, and then he passed out.

Chapter Seven:
Deadly Affection

The next thing Will knew, he was in the middle of a pounding rainstorm. Oddly, the rain was lukewarm. Was he in Hawaii? He opened his eyes.

He was in the huge tiled shower in Natalie's bedroom. She'd freed him from his inferno and placed him in here under the soothing water. Squinting, he could see out through the bathroom door to where Natalie was using a fire extinguisher to douse the burning bed. Even in his weakened, burned, dying state Will could not hold back a smile at the irony. When she'd acted all hot and bothered before, she'd wanted to set the bed on fire with him, but he was pretty sure *this* wasn't what she'd had in mind. A wave of pain rolled through his body. He clenched his eyes shut and bit down on a knuckle to keep from screaming.

Natalie came in and lifted him out of the shower as though he weighed no more than a stuffed toy. Holding him in her arms, she hurried down the stairs—each bouncing step an agony for Will— and took him into his lab.

"Don't worry, baby," she cooed. "It's going to be okay."

Her eyes were their usual beautiful azure. Will, slipping in and out of consciousness, wondered if he'd dreamed the whole thing.

Maybe she wasn't infected after all. Except even the way she moved was unfamiliar. Not like Natalie at all.

Natalie yanked open drawers until she found Will's miraculous healing balm, the salve she'd seen him applying when she'd spied on him in his secret basement lair months ago back in Harrisburg right after they met. She ripped off his shirt and began liberally slathering the potion all over his hands, arms, and torso. Despite her urgency, she took the time to enjoy touching his skin; it sent waves of pleasure through her.

"Look," she said. "It's working already."

The burns he'd suffered were already healing.

"Thank you," he managed.

"You're going to be good as new . . ."

She kissed his cheek, then picked him up and took him from the lab and into the guest bedroom, the same bedroom where he had brought Loreli to recuperate after she'd been wounded by the Dark Lord. Natalie laid him on the bed, stroked his forehead, and said, excitedly, "I'll be right back."

Will knew he needed to flee, but when he tried to move, pain shot through him like an electric current. The balm was working; his wounds were healing. But Loreli's poison was still coursing through his veins.

In less than a minute, Natalie re-emerged, wearing a black wedding veil and drinking from an open bottle of champagne.

"Do you, Will Hunter, take this . . . smokin' hot girl . . . to be your lawfully wedded wife?" she asked, unable to suppress the burst of giggles that followed.

As much as his instincts told him that good Natalie was gone, there was something in her girlish laughter that gave him hope, hope that he could somehow reach her. It was the only plan he had.

"Nat . . . Natalie . . . I know you're in there," he implored. "I know you care for me . . ."

"Of course I care for you," she said. But it was demon Natalie speaking, her eyes lighting up with the possibility of what was to come.

She came closer and began stroking Will's stomach with her nails. He knew that talking to her wasn't going to work. The demon was in control now. She leaned down and kissed him with burning passion.

This time the kiss held no allure for Will whatsoever. She tasted nothing like the old Natalie; there was only an acidic bitterness now. Will was repulsed.

Natalie reared back, her black eyes glinting. She had felt his revulsion, and suddenly she felt nothing but loathing for him. Hell hath no fury like a female demon spurned.

"I thought you *loved* me, Will!"

She began hissing and spitting. She slapped him hard across the face. It hurt, which was good—it meant he could still feel pain. He knew that if he didn't do something soon, his time on Earth would come to an end, but since he could hardly move and his brain was turning to mush, he could not think of one single move that might save his life. All he could think of was how angry he was at Loreli for betraying him.

Driven by the hurricane winds of her rage, Natalie started yanking open drawers in the bathroom, looking for something she could use as a weapon.

"I thought you'd *always* love me, no matter what! But that's *obviously* not the case!"

She was sweating and giving off toxic fumes. She angrily clawed through drawer after drawer after drawer, but found only hairbrushes and toothpaste, makeup and soap. She knew she could use her hands to wrench the life from Will, but she didn't think she could bear to kill him flesh to flesh. Touching him might make her hesitate. She needed something inanimate between them. A club of some kind.

She knelt down and opened the cabinet under the sink. She grabbed the drainpipe and yanked it out of the wall. She held it, dripping, in her right hand. The weight was good. It would smash Will's skull easily. She walked back into the bedroom. When he saw the pipe, he knew what she had in mind.

"Natalie, don't, please . . ."

She shook her head. She was done with him. It was time for him to die.

"You had your chance," she told him. "Remember that little thing they call unconditional love? The definition seems to have eluded you!"

To make her point, Natalie banged the pipe into the headboard, which, though made of solid old oak, nonetheless cracked.

"I've always loved you," said Will.

"NO!"

She smashed the pipe into the headboard again, right above Will's skull. He was too weak to even flinch. If death was coming, he was ready for it. He deserved it. He'd been a fool. He'd made the mistake of loving a girl and letting her love him back. He'd known all the way back in Harrisburg that this was a mistake. Actually, he thought, to die by the hand of his own living, breathing mistake had a sort of poetic justice to it.

"Natalie . . ."

When she looked down at him, he had love in his eyes because he was seeing not the demon that she'd become, but the girl he'd fallen in love with. His look crawled under her skin and made her crazy.

"No!" She shook her head wildly, her demon-self exerting control. "I've had enough of being shot down by you, Will!" She tossed the metal pipe in the air and caught it, deft as any battle-tested warrior. "You make me sick! It's obvious that you don't want me. So I don't have a choice!"

She was shaking. Killing him was going to be harder than she thought. Why did she have to love him so much? Why did she have to have a heart? *Damn it all!*

"The fact is, Will, I love you. But if I can't have you, then . . . well, nobody can."

She stepped slowly toward the bed with the pipe in her hand.

Loreli climbed out of the Rav4 and the man slammed his foot on the gas before she could even close the door behind her. She could hear the woman wailing with fear and relief as the SUV rocketed away down the street.

She took a step. Her left leg almost gave out on her. She was in bad shape, and sitting had only made it worse. Her body was stiff and sore. She bit into her lip and made her way toward the mansion.

Once inside, she stumbled toward the guest bedroom. She could hear shouting. Seconds later she pushed open the bedroom door and was flooded with relief when she saw that Will was still alive.

There was just one problem: Natalie was standing over him, about to swing a lethal-looking steel pipe into the side of his head.

"Natalie, wait!" shouted Loreli.

Natalie froze like a batter checking her swing. She looked over and saw Loreli, battered and bloody, standing in the doorway.

"Loreli . . . how very *stupid* of you to come back here," said Natalie. "But I'm glad you did. You, I'm going to enjoy killing you."

Natalie leapt across Will's body with feral speed. She circled Loreli, brandishing the pipe.

Wounded, bleeding, and dizzy, Loreli was no match for this demon, the very demon she had helped create. She saw Will lying on the bed and knew her poison was in the home stretch. She had to do something, and fast. Natalie continued to circle her like a jaguar.

"I'm going to enjoy watching you suffer," she said. "It might take a very long time for you to die."

Thump! Natalie slammed the pipe into Loreli's back. Pain shot through her shoulder and down to her toes. She collapsed.

"Have you ever wondered what it would feel like to have every single bone in your body broken?" asked Natalie. "Well, today's your lucky day."

Loreli rolled over and rose to her knees to face Natalie. "Listen to me. I lied to you. Manipulated you. Will never wanted you to change. He loved you just the way you were."

Natalie shrugged. "It doesn't matter. He bores me now. He's dead, you're dead, so get used to the idea."

Will was gasping for air, his chest heaving as his body convulsed. He was going into shock.

"Natalie, look at him."

Natalie turned. For a moment she appeared to feel some small measure of sympathy, but it didn't last long because her polluted blood was in control of her heart.

"He . . . *deserves* it." Natalie returned her attention to Loreli. "And *you* deserve what you're going to get, too."

Natalie swung the pipe around. Loreli blocked it, but when the pipe smashed into her arm, the pain was excruciating. Loreli knew she could not battle this creature and win.

"Fine, you can kill me. You're right. I do deserve it."

Natalie swung again and Loreli fell back to the carpet.

"But before you kill me, please listen. Try and remember what it feels like to love Will. Can you remember how strong that feeling was?"

A part of Natalie's brain sparked. She felt a pang in her heart. She softened for a second, remembering when they'd first met. How she'd fallen into his mismatched blue eyes . . .

Out in the trunk, Emily was beginning to cry. Being trapped in the dark was pulling her back down into a bad place, to the caves under Harrisburg and the months she'd been held captive there by the Dark

Lord. She wanted out. Claustrophobia was creeping over her body like fast-growing vines.

"Rudy . . . help me . . . please . . . ," she whispered, gripping his wrist.

Rudy kicked as hard as he could against the lid of the trunk again. It still didn't budge, but he'd be damned if he was going to let the girl he was crazy about suffer for one more minute. There *had* to be another way out. He changed his tack and began kicking the back seats, which, thrillingly, started to give. He was immediately pissed he hadn't thought to try that sooner. He gave another kick and broke through, and then he clambered up front and popped the trunk. He leapt out, ran around, and pulled Emily out.

She held him tightly. She felt so safe in his arms. And then she saw the smoke.

"Rudy! Look!"

They ran for the house.

In the guest bedroom, Loreli continued to plead with demon Natalie.

"Listen to me. You guys are in *love*! The kind of love that everyone dreams about."

It was working. Memories invaded Natalie's brain. A tear streaked down her cheek. As she remembered the fall dance, her eyes returned to blue. Loreli rose and stepped forward, believing that the tide was turning, that somehow, against the odds, love and goodness were winning out. With some luck, she could still redeem herself and save her brother. She slid the syringe from her pocket.

"Will is dying, Natalie. But I can save him. I can save his life. With this."

Natalie turned her head slowly, like a robot, gazing at the syringe. "Give it to me . . . ," she said.

In her wounded state, Loreli had lost her time-bending speed. Natalie surprised her and snatched the syringe—the only hope for

Will Hunter's survival—out of her hand. Her eyes were killing black. Loreli had miscalculated.

"What happens if we don't give it to him?

"He'll go into a coma," Loreli said. "Eventually, he'll die."

Natalie stared for several beats at the syringe, marveling at how pretty the green liquid was. Then she threw her head back and began to laugh, a sound that made the hairs on the back of Loreli's neck rise, a laugh of pure, wicked malevolence, the sadistic laugh of a killer. Loreli tried to grab the syringe, but Natalie was ready and caught her in the forehead with the pipe—*smack!*

Loreli dropped like a stone. Fireworks went off in her head. Her vision was mangled—she saw everything as though through a kaleidoscope. But she could still make out Will on the bed nearby. His mouth was moving as he silently gasped like a fish out of water. He was beginning the descent into unconsciousness.

Natalie placed the syringe on the nightstand and raised the pipe again. She was going to smash the syringe to bits.

Loreli croaked out a feeble protest. "Please . . . no . . ."

Natalie swung the pipe.

Chapter Eight: Spirit Drifting

The room erupted with brilliant, blue-hued shockwaves. Tendrils of energy snaked in and engulfed Natalie, wrapping around her like tentacles. And then she was yanked backward, sucked into the Demon Trapper that Rudy had just fired from the doorway.

"Holy crap, it worked!" Rudy said.

"Great shot!" said Emily.

The steel pipe bounced harmlessly off the carpet. The syringe was intact. Half blind, her body a maelstrom of pain, Loreli crawled over, grabbed the syringe, and plunged it into Will's neck before Rudy and Emily could stop her. She was overcome with dizziness. Everything was blurry, then black. She prayed: *Please let this antidote work. Bring Will back from the brink of death. Go ahead and take me, but spare him. He's the only one who can stop the Dark Lord.* Loreli continued to bargain for a few more seconds. And then she passed out.

Rudy set the Demon Trapper down. Emily stared at her twin sister in the trap, her eyes bugging out, her long red nails slashing at the Plexiglas.

"Emily, help me move him," Rudy said, grabbing Will by his shoulders. Emily rushed over and picked up Will's feet, and together they moved him into the lab. He looked bad.

"Will? Will can you hear me?" asked Rudy.

Will was soaring through clouds, his spirit seeking an exit. He wanted to leave, to be rid of the pressures that had been building up inside him for all the years since he'd seen his beloved adoptive father Edward carried away by his perversion of a biological father, the Prince of Darkness. Will was ready to let go. He flew higher into the sky, so high he could look down and see the city lights spread out below, tiny sparkling specks. Time sped up, then slowed to a crawl. He dreamed what seemed a thousand dreams.

Then he began to fall. He offered fate no resistance. What would be would be.

He found himself in his mother's hospital room in Swedish Hospital, where she was still in a coma. Familiar despair reached out, laying its spindly hands upon him.

How could he ever forgive himself for helping to put her in this heartbroken state? He remembered how he'd sent her away from Harrisburg for her own safety, how she'd found a supposedly secure house. By the time he'd been able to come for her, the Dark Lord's minions had found and imprisoned her. He'd attempted a rescue, but he hadn't been careful enough. Though he'd obliterated her captors, in the fracas his mother had suffered an injury that had pulled her down into the dark netherworlds of unconsciousness. And then the Dark Lord had entered her mind and stolen her will to live. It had been Will's quest to vanquish the Dark Lord and bring his mother back to life. And yet . . . here she lay, like Sleeping Beauty.

It was okay, though. They could be together now.

He cried inside. Floating to her bedside, he touched her cheek.

"Hello, Mother. I've come home."

Though she did not open her eyes or move her lips, April spoke to her son. *It is not your time yet, Willie. You still have much to do.*

"I want to join you, Mother. I want to be where you are."

We will be together, Willie. We will always be together. But right now, I beg you, do not let go.

"Why shouldn't I? I only cause people pain. I've been a fool. I've been manipulated. I believed lies. I couldn't see the truth. I've failed everyone in my life. You. Edward. Natalie. Everyone! Don't you see? I've let you all down. It'll be better for everyone this way."

No one ever achieves greatness without first failing. You must not give up, for if you do, then he will have won, and his hateful ways will spread darkness upon the land forever.

The mere thought of the Black Prince brought a trembling rage into Will's heart.

"Mother . . . I have so much anger. I hate the Dark Lord with every fiber of my being. I am angry at myself for not defeating him. I am angry at Loreli, at Natalie for doing what she did . . . some days it seems like I'm angry at the whole world!"

Don't be a slave to your anger, Will. When you let anger in, it crowds out everything else. It crowds out empathy, compassion, love. Experiencing anger is human. But it is how you deal with that anger that determines your destiny.

"But I'm *not* human. Not a whole human. Because of Him, I'm something else, something twisted and perverse."

Listen to me closely, Willie. You are but one thing, and one thing only. You are what you choose to be.

With his mother's words echoing in his mind, Will's spirit again lifted high into the sky. He was streaking out of the atmosphere toward the stars. He could travel to distant galaxies, slip away into the universe, transcending this life and ascending to another state of being entirely. He could *choose.* Over and over, the words rang like clarions in his head. He could choose to be whatever he wanted!

In a flash, he decided. He would choose to be . . . alive. A comet streaked across space and hurled toward the earth.

Will opened his eyes. He saw Rudy and Emily staring down at him.

"You're still with us!" said Rudy.

Emily looked shaken. "We didn't know if you were going to make it."

"How long have I been out?"

Rudy checked his watch. "Almost thirty-six hours."

Will looked over and saw Loreli lying on a table. She was still unconscious. Next to her was a packet of healing balm that had been torn open. It must have been applied to the worst of her injuries, if she was still alive. But she was still in terrible shape.

Will sat up. His head was spinning. He felt like he'd been run over by an armored truck. Every bone in his body ached. But the thought of getting revenge on his betrayer propelled him forward. He stood and took a shaky step toward Loreli, vengeance blazing in his eyes—but he stopped when he saw Natalie in the Demon Trapper. After what she'd planned on doing—bashing his head in with an iron pipe—he knew he should have felt relief that she was ensnared, but his heart was heavy. This never should have happened. And if it weren't for him, it wouldn't have. A terrifying thought leapt into his mind: *What if the real Natalie was gone for good?*

"Will, what the heck happened?" asked Rudy.

The question shook him out of his thoughts and back to Loreli.

"Help me tie her up," he barked, gesturing to Loreli's unconscious body. Then he grabbed some zip-ties lying on a workbench, and he and Rudy began lashing Loreli's legs to the lab table. Then Will peeled her duster off of her so they could bind her wrists, too.

"Why are we tying her up?" said Rudy.

"Just do it."

Emily placed a hand on Will's shoulder . . .

"Will, who *is* Loreli, really? She's obviously more than just some girl from school."

Will took a deep breath and looked at his friends. "She's my sister."

Emily and Rudy looked at each other, stunned.

Will knew he had a mountain of explaining to do to bring them up to speed. As they secured Loreli, he told them how she was related to him, about her alchemy, about how she'd manipulated him, how they'd infiltrated the Under City together, discovering the Dark Lord's headless body. He told them how they'd found the Dark Lord's head, and how she'd fooled him into believing that her "demon dialysis" would purge him of his father's evil blood. He still didn't know what her motives were, why she'd poisoned him and betrayed him, or how or why she'd convinced Natalie to become infected. The only thing he knew for certain was that when she woke up—and he would make sure that she did—no matter what she said, no matter what lies spewed out of her mouth, he would never, ever forgive her.

When he was done with the tale, Rudy let out a low whistle.

"Wow. She is one wicked witch, dude."

"That's an understatement."

Will checked the ties one more time, then turned his attention to Natalie in the Demon Trapper. She was hideous with anger, and had morphed into a revolting demon creature. Her eyes were bugging out, her skin scaly, her nails ragged claws. She pounded on the thick Plexiglas, just like Rudy had when he'd been trapped.

Emily's heart was nearly breaking because when Natalie was hurting, so was she.

Rudy tapped on the Plexiglas. Emily pulled his hand away.

"Stop fooling around! We've got to get her out of there and cure her, just like Will did to you. Right, Will?"

Will remembered how grueling and dangerous Rudy's cure had been. But he knew he had to do it again to Natalie. It was the only chance he had of bringing her back.

He moved to the cabinet, brought out a vial of the amber potion, and filled a syringe with it. Then he pressed a series of buttons on the trapper. With a *whoosh*, it released Natalie and, while she was still groggy, he pushed her onto the same table where he'd cured Rudy, and restrained her wrists and ankles with the same metal bands.

Her eyes were fearful as she looked at Will, Rudy, and Emily. "Em? Will? Where am I? What happened?"

Her voice was weak, but she struggled against the restraints.

"What's going on? Why am I tied down like some animal?"

Emily gently stroked her sister's forehead, pain in her eyes. "You were . . . we had to . . . catch you, in the Demon Trapper."

"Let me up, Em . . . please?"

Natalie sounded normal, but Emily had seen demons fake it before—Rudy, for one. Emily looked to Will. He didn't have to say a word. No way was he going to set Natalie free just yet.

He used surgical tubing to tie off her arm, and slapped for a vein. Then he picked up the syringe.

Seeing the needle, Natalie trembled, no doubt remembering what had happened when Will had injected Rudy.

"Will, what are you doing? Please don't . . . listen to me . . . it doesn't have to be like this!"

"Yes, it does," he said. "It definitely, definitely has to be exactly like this."

"Will, please, I'm begging you! I can behave, I can be good. I only did this for you!"

"I know. And now I'm going to change you back."

"I love you, baby, and I just know that my love is so strong . . . I could never hurt you. I will never hurt anyone if you don't want me to, I promise. I can stay like this and we can still be together. Please!"

Will gently pressed on the syringe plunger to get rid of the air bubbles near the tip. Natalie's whole body began shaking.

"No . . . NO! It's going to kill me! I just know it!" She began to wail.

Unable to stop herself, Emily, too, began to whimper. She closed her eyes and let the bitter tears fall. "Just hurry up and do it, Will!" she said.

Natalie was pale as a ghost. When she spoke, she sounded like a child. "Is it going to hurt?"

Will didn't answer. Instead, he slid the needle into her arm and pressed down. She bucked and screamed. The amber liquid was fire in her veins.

"I'll kill you!" she screamed. "I'll slit your throats and drink your blood!"

As the curative potion coursed into her bloodstream, she began a horrifying metamorphosis. Her skin turned bright red, then went terrifyingly pale, then took on a greenish tinge.

It hurt Will to see the girl he loved suffering so much. Rudy recalled his own ordeal and shuddered. As for Emily, she felt Natalie's waking nightmare as only a twin could. She doubled over, feeling like she'd just been kicked by a mule. She would have fallen if Rudy hadn't been there to help her to a chair.

"*Ahhhhh!!*" screamed Natalie. Her eyes bulged. Her tongue snaked out a good six inches as she hissed and spit and cursed. "You're going to regret this, I swear! I'm going to kill all of you! I'm going to—"

Will touched her shoulder, hoping to calm her. It didn't work. "Don't touch me!" she shrieked. "Don't—"

Her back arched as the pain clawed at her from inside out. She twisted into a grotesque position, her fingers curled, her face contorted. Will thought his heart was going to break.

"Oh my god," gasped Emily.

"It's gonna be okay . . . ," said Rudy.

Tears were streaming down Emily's cheeks. "You keep saying that," she whimpered. "But I can feel her! Something's really wrong!"

Natalie bared her teeth, growling. She wanted to bite the flesh from Will's bones. Her stomach began rolling and gurgling. She looked like she was going to explode. Her body shook violently. Her eyes shifted from demon black to bloodshot azure. She begged Emily with her eyes.

And then her eyes closed.

Alarm bells went off in Emily's brain. "She's dying!".

Emily was right. Natalie's body slackened. Her eyes rolled back in their sockets. She was a corpse-like parody of her normal, beautiful self. She let out a bloodcurdling scream that sent chills into Will's bones, and then her body went still. Will wasted no time hooking her up to an EKG. Her heartbeat was weak and erratic.

"What's going on?" cried Emily.

Will gently squeezed her hand. "Natalie . . . can you hear me?"

He looked at the monitor. She was flatlining.

"She's going into cardiac arrest . . . ," he said. Will had feared this might happen; the same thing had happened to Rudy. He raced to the wall, yanked open a metal cabinet, and pulled out the defibrillator kit. It was pre-charged. He ripped open Natalie's blouse and pressed the paddles against her chest, then delivered 700 volts. Natalie's body jerked spasmodically. She continued to flatline.

"This can't be happening!" screamed Emily.

Will increased the power to 1,000 volts and tried again.

"Come on, Nat!" he shouted.

Her body jerked a second time. Will did it again and sent a prayer to the heavens. He'd known there were risks involved in this process, but he'd never believed that Natalie could die. *Please, please don't take her!* he screamed inside his head.

Natalie wasn't moving.

"Oh no . . . Oh please . . . *NO!*" cried Emily.

Will delivered one more shock to Natalie's chest. The heart monitor continued to show her flatlining.

Finally, devastated, Will lowered the paddles. They all stared at each other in shock. Natalie was dead.

But then the monitor beeped. And again. Natalie's heart began beating. The trio began shouting with joy.

"She's back!" said Rudy. "She's gonna make it!"

"Is she, Will? Is she really?" asked Emily.

Will touched Natalie's cheek, then put an oxygen mask over her mouth and checked her pulse, which was strong and steady.

"Yes," he said. "She's back."

They watched in soft, careful silence for a full five minutes, staring at Natalie's chest rising and falling. Her heart was beating steadily and her blood pressure was normal again. She'd made it. She was stable.

Will leaned close to her and squeezed her temples.

"Emily, open one of her eyes."

This was the moment when they would find out if the cure had worked. Were her eyes demon black, or their normal blue?

Emily lifted one of Natalie's eyelids. One blue eye stared back at her. Sobbing in relief, she turned and buried her face in Rudy's shoulder.

Will hit a switch. The bands that had been holding her down released. He lifted her into his arms, carried her into the guest bedroom, and laid her on the bed. He turned the lights down low, then drew the curtains and laid down with her. He held her, listening to her breathe and feeling her heart beat good and strong. He didn't know when she would wake up, but he knew he'd be there when she did. He had never felt his love for her more keenly in his whole life. They were going to be okay. He could hardly wait for her to awaken and love him back. True love, not evil, had triumphed.

Twenty minutes later, he was lying next to her with his eyes closed, resting but alert. His own strength was returning quickly; Loreli's antidote had been effective, he had to give her that. He was still mulling over exactly what to do with his half-sister now when he heard a gasping sound. It was Natalie. She opened her eyes. He immediately touched her face.

"Natalie," he whispered, his voice full of warmth and love.

But her eyes were wide and wild.

"Will!"

"I'm right here," he said.

"WILL!" she screamed. The icy fear in her voice brought Emily and Rudy running in.

"What's wrong?" said Emily, moving toward the bed. Will held up a hand.

They kept their distance, watching as Will held Natalie and stroked her face. Her eyes darted around. She seemed to be looking all over the room, searching.

"Natalie, what is it?" asked Will, his fear mounting.

"Will, I can't . . . I can't see!"

"Oh my god!" said Emily.

Will clenched his jaw.

Natalie started hyperventilating. "WILL, I'M BLIND!"

Chapter Nine: Visiting Hours

Natalie was racing into a full-blown panic attack.

Will held her close. Emily ran over and took her sister's hand. "I'm here, Nat."

"Emily . . . ," she said. She was still gasping, but her sister's touch anchored her. "Emily, I'm scared . . ."

Will held her in his arms and kissed her forehead.

"Give it a minute," he told her. "Just hang on. The same thing happened to Rudy. Breathe normally, can you do that for me? Just breathe . . ."

Natalie forced herself to slow her breathing down.

"Even slower, please. Just . . . don't worry, it's going to be okay." He was doing his best to convince her. But what if he was wrong? His nerves were raw and he felt a rising fury. He wanted to run in and hack Loreli to pieces with his Power Rod. But instead he continued to hold Natalie. *Please don't let her be blind, I'll do anything, just don't let her be blind!*

Natalie began blinking. "Wait . . . I think I can see something . . . Oh god . . ."

She started to relax. Relief flooded through her body as her sight began to return, improving with each passing moment.

"I can see shapes . . . Things are starting to come into focus."

"Look at me," said Will.

Thank you, thank you, thank you.

Natalie looked straight at Will and continued blinking. In another few seconds, the floating patches of dark twinkled away and her vision cleared completely. She stared at Will.

"I . . . I can see you. I can see your eyes!"

A torrent of tears spilled over her cheeks. Emily and Rudy breathed sighs of relief, and Emily let go of Natalie's hand to hug her. "You're going to be okay," she said.

Natalie held on to Will like he was a life preserver. Emily got the message, and she pulled Rudy with her out of the room.

Natalie and Will were silent for a long time. Finally Natalie spoke softly. "Will?"

"Yeah?"

"Where I was . . . I don't ever want to go there again."

"Don't worry. We'll make sure you never do."

A few quiet moments passed. Natalie began to feel safe. But her body tensed when she heard Rudy yell.

"WILL!"

Will was up and into the lab in an instant.

Rudy and Emily were standing over Loreli. She was awake now, staring down at the zip-ties and frowning. She looked up sadly at Will as he entered.

"I'm not really surprised you tied me up," she said, closing her eyes against the pain.

"I should kill you right now," said Will.

"No one would blame you if you did."

When he examined her more closely, he saw how banged up and bruised she was. He was in no mood to be generous to his half-sister, but he was human—or half of him was, anyway. And he recalled his mother's words about how anger crowded out everything in its path. So he throttled back his anger a notch.

"How'd you get so messed up?" he asked her.

"I threw myself under a bus."

"Literally?"

She smiled. It wasn't a happy smile.

"And why would you do that?"

"It was either that or be tortured and killed by the shedemons," she said.

"I don't believe a single word you say."

"I don't . . . blame you." Her eyes clenched shut as another wave of pain hit. "I think . . . I'm . . . going to pass out again . . . ," she whispered. And she did.

Will paced back and forth, studying her, measuring the situation as Rudy and Emily looked on.

"What are you gonna do?" asked Rudy.

"After what she did to Natalie, I say throw her under another bus," said Emily.

Rudy winced at the thought. He countered: "She did save Will's life with that stuff she shot him up with."

"Yeah, but she was the one who tried to kill him in the first place!" retorted Emily.

"But she fixed it. She deserves a second chance," said Rudy. Having screwed up so thoroughly himself, Rudy was a big fan of second chances. And Emily had to agree that he had a point.

Will wasn't in the mood to forgive her, but he couldn't let her suffer, either. He angrily went to a cabinet and pulled out some more of his healing balm. He held the tube out to Emily.

"Here, rub it on anything that hasn't healed yet. I don't want to touch her."

Emily took the tube. "We're going to keep healing her? Even after what she did to you and Natalie?"

"What other choice do we have? We're not savages. I can't just let her lay there in pain. We're better than them."

Emily knew Will was right. Grudgingly, she began rubbing the healing balm onto Loreli's remaining scrapes and bruises.

"Ow!" cried Loreli, her eyes opening suddenly.

"Oh, did that hurt?" asked Emily innocently.

"Yeah."

"Good."

"I'll be back," said Will, turning and exiting the lab. He went into the kitchen for some ice cream and took a bowl in to Natalie, who was lying on her side, facing away from the window, where a single band of light had found its way in to bathe her face.

"I brought you some ice cream," said Will. "Strawberry. Your fave."

He scooped a big bite into a spoon and moved it toward her mouth.

"No, thank you," she said softly

Will put the spoon back in the bowl and set it down on the nightstand. Then he sat on the bed and lovingly touched her shoulder. Was it his imagination or did she flinch at his touch?

"Nat?"

"Yeah?"

"Can I get you something else?"

"No."

He could practically feel a chill coming off her. She wouldn't make eye contact with him and was acting like she definitely didn't want to touch or be touched. When she spoke, her voice was flat, loveless, dead.

"I'd like to be alone."

In all the time he'd known her, she'd never said anything like that to him.

"Are you all right?" said Will.

"I said I wanted to be alone," said Natalie sharply. "What part of that didn't you get?"

Her words jabbed Will in the heart. He backed slowly out the room, fighting hard against fear. Had becoming a demon fundamentally changed Natalie? Hardened her heart? He went back to the lab, his anger at Loreli rising again.

Emily was still rubbing the restorative potion on Loreli's wounds, which had already begun to improve.

Will met Loreli's gaze. She saw the anger coming off him like a vapor.

"Will, I know you don't want to listen to me, but you have to."

He glared at her.

"He means to bring an end to it all . . . the whole human race . . ."

"This is not new information," said Will.

"But—" Loreli gasped as Emily rubbed the salve on her leg, which was twisted at a painfully unnatural angle. Will leaned over and, after studying it for a moment, firmly manipulated Loreli's leg, pulling the dislocated bone back into place. She cried out in pain.

"Looks like she's got a deep bruise there, maybe even a fracture," he said to Emily. "You'll have to keep applying the balm, keep rubbing it in. It'll infuse the skin and make its way down to the bone eventually. It's going to hurt like a mother when it starts to heal the bone."

"Pity," said Emily. Loreli clenched her jaw in pain as Emily went back to rubbing the balm in.

Loreli's pleading eyes found Will. "Will . . . I'm going to pass out!"

"Frankly, I don't care."

"Listen . . . listen to me . . . You've heard of Gillian Turner?"

"Who hasn't? Filthy rich. Recluse. Some think she's a genius, others think she's crazy. What about her?"

Loreli was struggling to remain conscious.

"The Dark Lord and I . . . we broke into her compound and stole . . ." She was running out of gas. Her eyes closed.

Will leaned in close to her. "You stole what, Loreli? What did you and the Dark Lord steal?"

"Swords."

She passed out. Will tried his best to revive her to get more information, but her body was on sensory overload and her brain had shut down. There was no telling how long it would take for her to regain consciousness.

If she'd been telling the truth and something big was about to go down, Will knew he had to act immediately. Swords, Loreli had said. Was it possible that one of the swords she and the Dark Lord had stolen was the Sword of Armageddon that the Dark Lord had taunted him about? The one his family's demon hunter book had warned of?

Will moved to his bank of computers. Rudy had overheard everything and was right there with him.

"Swords? What kind of swords?" he asked.

"That's what we're going to find out."

Will did a search. Gillian Turner had been found by the Mercer Island Police and rushed by ambulance to Virginia Mason Hospital, where she was in critical condition. Talking to her was their best chance of finding out what the Dark Lord had stolen.

They had to hurry.

Will pulled his BMW 750Li into the Virginia Mason Hospital parking lot. Seeing the hospital reminded him of his mother. He hadn't checked on her since he'd awakened from his own near-death experience. He touched the screen of his phone and brought up an application that enabled him to check on her vital signs. They were good, but she'd made no progress toward coming out of her coma. It would be up to him to bring her out of it by defeating the Dark Lord once and for all.

Will looked over at Rudy, who was riding shotgun and was in awe of the BMW. It was a sleek beast, with 400 horsepower, dual nitro boosters, bulletproof glass, and front, side, and rear armor. When Will got out, Rudy climbed over into the driver's seat.

Will checked the surrounding area for demons. It looked clear, so he had time to quick-school Rudy. Rudy was rapt as Will described the Beemer's built-in weaponry.

"This," said Will, flipping open a compartment and pointing to a series of buttons, "is your offensive systems control panel. You've got your rear gas nozzles, which spray a gas of micro-tasers. Here you've got your side Vibroexploders in case they pull up on either side of you and you need to create some space. This one here is your main bad boy, a multi-shot laser mini-cannon mounted right under the hood ornament."

Will demonstrated the mini-cannon. The BMW hood badge slid aside, and up rose a small but lethal-looking barrel that tilted up and down, rotated 360 degrees, and was fired by a hidden button on the Beemer's gearshift knob.

"So what do you think, *compadre*? You get all that?"

Rudy was totally confused—but acted cool.

"Yeah, absolutely," he said.

Will wasn't convinced, but the clock was ticking. He had to find out whatever he could from Gillian Turner. He hoped she hadn't already succumbed to her injuries.

He squeezed Rudy's shoulder. "I don't want any of them coming in after me. If you see one, and you're certain he's dirty, make sure he doesn't see the sun come up tomorrow. Got it?"

"I'm all over it," said Rudy.

Will walked toward the hospital. Rudy wondered which button was which again.

Will got into the elevator next to a pretty young nurse. She reminded him a little of Natalie. He wondered what was going on in Natalie's mind. More importantly, what was going on in her *heart*? He let himself ponder these questions for a few seconds, but he knew he had to corral his feelings and concentrate on matters at hand. Which meant finding out anything and everything he could from the mysterious and reclusive Gillian Turner, whom Will had discovered was also one of the world's foremost collectors of antiquities. He rode the elevator to the fifteenth floor. He found the Critical Care Unit and Gillian Turner's room in less than thirty seconds.

A burly male nurse strode toward him. "You can't come in here!" he said.

Unfazed, Will smiled and quickly pricked the guy's neck with a drug that knocked him out instantly. Will caught him and dropped him into a visitor's chair. Then he went in and approached Gillian.

Her head was bandaged, her injuries so severe that her face was the color of an eggplant.

"Gillian? Mrs. Turner?"

She looked like she would never see the light of another day. Struggling mightily, she opened one swollen, bloodshot eye.

"My name is Will Hunter."

Gillian blinked, her one wise old eye studying him.

"I'm not going to hurt you," said Will.

She nodded. She fought to move her lips. When she finally won the battle, her voice was like rocks on sandpaper.

"I know."

"You had a theft at your house . . ."

Gillian again nodded and raised one shaking finger, pointing at a paper cup sitting next to a plastic pitcher.

"Ice . . . chips . . ."

Will took the small spoon on the tray and used it to scoop out some ice chips, then gently placed them between Gillian's lips. She sucked on them, and the liquid cooled her parched throat. Then she spoke, her one eye never leaving Will.

"It was the Devil," she said.

Will nodded, picturing the Dark Lord and Loreli vandalizing the old woman's mansion. Gillian motioned for Will to move closer, which he did. She peered deeply into his eyes.

"You have a connection to him. I can feel it. It doesn't make sense. You frighten me, and yet I feel safe around you."

"The Dark Lord is my father," said Will.

Gillian took a moment to grasp the implications, which made her sad.

"I'm so sorry," she said.

"Me, too. I don't want to disturb your recovery, but I think you can help me fight him. I know he took some things from you. Some swords. Can you tell me about them?" said Will.

Gillian thought for a moment, gathering her strength to proceed.

"Do you believe that an object, such as a knife or a sword, can harbor evil?" she asked him. "Do you believe in such things?"

"I've seen a lot. I believe just about anything, Mrs. Turner."

"Good. Then you will believe me when I tell you that I had amassed the largest and most important collection of evil weapons in the world. I thought I was making the world safe . . ."

Will looked into her eyes. He knew that she wasn't crazy, and had a feeling that what she was about to tell him was most definitely not going to be good news for mankind.

Chapter Ten: Evil Men

Rudy still had his eyes locked on the hospital entrance when he saw two teenage dudes come rolling up on skateboards. They had tattoos and wore the demon uniform de rigueur, complete with skulls and crossbones and other splashy images of death and destruction. They lit cigarettes and leered at a heavyset young nurse who was approaching the lobby.

"Somebody got some junk in the trunk," one of them said.

She ignored them, which only made them more intent on getting a rise out of her. They jumped on their skateboards and zoomed toward her, cutting her off and then rolling in circles around her while they stuck out their butts and grabbed their boy boobs.

The nurse worked in ER so she'd seen plenty worse than what these two could dish out. She kept quiet, hoping they'd get tired and leave her alone. But her stoic mask only spurred them on, until one of them went too far.

She'd studied Aikido since she was five-years-old, and when one of them reached out to goose her she caught him totally by surprise, grabbing him and then turning and leveraging his weight against him. She lifted him off his skateboard and flipped him skyward, right toward the BMW. He fell hard, his head smacking into the concrete.

His eyes flashed angrily. And black.

Rudy was just close enough to see, and suddenly he was on high alert, knowing he was going to have to take the two demonteens out. But which button controlled the hood laser?

He pushed the wrong one. The tail nozzles activated, spraying the street behind him.

"Oh, crap!"

By then he'd caught the attention of the demonteen skateboarders, and they immediately made for the hospital entrance. Rudy started pushing buttons like crazy, and the side Vibroexploders activated.

"Oh no!"

The shockwaves knocked the Camaro parked next to him, as well as a passing FedEx truck, right off their axles. No one was in the Camaro, and luckily the FedEx driver was only shaken up.

"Sorry! That was my fault!"

The FedEx guy crawled to the safety of some bushes, making a silent vow to go back to school and finish his engineering degree. His mother had always warned him that with all the freaks in the world, delivering packages was a dangerous job.

Rudy finally got control of the hood-mounted laser and blasted away erratically at the demonteens. He took out a row of stuffed giraffes and pandas on an outdoor gift cart as the vendor dove for cover. Then he got lucky and blasted both demonteens with one shot that pierced both of their skulls. They dropped like birds shot out of the sky. Their bodies sparked and dissolved into charcoal powder.

Up in Gillian Turner's room, Will heard the commotion. He moved to the window and looked down. Rudy had made one hell of a mess, but there didn't appear to be any casualties, so now wasn't the time to go down and clean it up. Gillian raised her one good eyebrow.

"Trouble?"

"Nothing I can't handle," said Will.

"You seem to think you're a very capable young man," said Gillian. "For all our sakes, I sincerely hope you are correct in that assumption." Then she coughed and closed her eye, fighting the pain.

"The swords. What can you tell me about them?" asked Will.

Gillian drew in a long breath.

"I spent billions. The sword collection, the one he took, was the only collection of its kind in the world. I personally have no attachment to weapons, you understand. I acquired them with one thing in mind: to prevent *him* from getting his hands on them."

"Who did the swords belong to originally?" asked Will.

"Men of staggering evil. A dagger belonging to Caligula, a scimitar from Genghis Khan, swords from Attila the Hun, Tamerlane, Joseph Stalin, the saber given to Hitler from the city of Nuremberg. A *dao* that belonged to Chairman Mao Zedong. Idi Amin Dada's saber, a sword owned by Pol Pot . . ."

Gillian closed her eye in pain at the thought of these men from history. Will had read about some of them. Pol Pot was the Cambodian leader whose rule of slave labor and murder contributed to the death of 1.5 million people. Idi Amin Dada was the president of Uganda whose ruthless dictatorship brought an end to half a million. Tamerlane was a particularly odious leader whose armies slaughtered millions. He once had a pyramid built out of the skulls of 70,000 of his victims.

Gillian opened her eye and continued. "The Dark Beast feeds off of malevolence. And those men . . . Well, the evil they propagated throughout history was unrivaled. I collected their weapons to keep the world safe from the evil they'd absorbed over the years. But now *he* has them, and all the badness they hold. He's going to use them somehow . . . I know he's up to something, something horrible."

Gillian looked at Will hopefully, wanting answers. Will considered telling her that the Dark Lord was intent on wielding the Sword of Armageddon, but he thought, *What good could it possibly do her to know that?*

He gently patted her hand. "It's going to be okay," he said.

Gillian continued to look deeply into his eyes. Her spirits sagged when she sensed that Will was withholding.

"He's growing more powerful every day," she said. "It's been happening for centuries. Pol Pot, Caligula, Hitler, they were all agents of his who tried to destroy what was good and pure on Earth. Fortunately, back then, there were heroes to stand up to them, and the monsters ultimately failed. But now? It's hard to believe there any heroes left. Will you be able to stand up to him? Are *you* a hero?"

"Yes," said Will, without hesitation. His answer momentarily placated Gillian, who closed her eye.

"I wish you Godspeed and good luck in your quest, young man," she said.

Will knew it was time to go. He stroked Gillian's arm affectionately.

"Get some rest. You're going to be fine," he said. And then he walked out.

Gillian kept her good eye closed until she heard the sound of his footsteps recede completely. Then she opened her eye as she heard a new set of footsteps. She suspected that her time to die had come. She wanted to believe that this young man could save the world, but she could not bring herself to do so. The boy would be no match for the Prince of Darkness, He who had seduced Eve into disobeying the Almighty, He who had wrought such evil in the world throughout history. Gillian did not believe that the young boy had any chance against the mighty Lucifer. And she did not want to be around when the End of Ends came.

When the shedemon entered her room, Gillian put up no struggle. She only watched as the shedemon unhooked her life support systems. Convinced that the world was on the verge of ending, Gillian willingly slipped away into her final sleep.

. . .

Exiting the hospital, Will saw the dark outlines of the remains of the demonteens on the concrete. He knew that Rudy had made a kill shot, but the collateral mayhem was unacceptable.

Will got in the BMW and peeled out. He drove fast, as he always did. Rudy was feeling pretty stupid, and Will giving him the stink eye didn't help.

"Hey I'm sorry, man. These controls, they're totally foreign to me. Anything on *Demon Hunter* I can handle totally for sure."

"No more weapons," said Will to Rudy. At least not anytime soon.

Natalie continued to recuperate in the guest room. She was physically sore and emotionally exhausted. She was thinking about all that happened in the past twenty-four hours and cataloging her feelings, putting them into order and making major decisions. There were some things she had to do.

She rose from the bed and went up to her own room. The sight of the burnt bed frame and what was left of the mattress and sheets turned her stomach. She looked in the full-length mirror at the mean, slutty-looking girl glaring back at her. She was going to put that dark demonic girl to rest forever.

She went into her bathroom and washed off the garish goth makeup. She trashed the clothes and put on jeans, a T-shirt, and a pair of blue Converse tennis shoes. She pulled her hair into a ponytail. Then she went downstairs. First things first: there were scores to be settled.

She stole a look into the lab and saw Loreli—the girl who was responsible for so much of her pain—lashed to a table like some animal, her hands swollen. Emily was applying healing balm to Loreli's arms and legs as Loreli winced. Natalie knew what she had to do. She slipped into the kitchen, her eyes alert, searching. On the counter was a knife block in the shape of a human head that Rudy had picked up at a garage sale. Natalie approached it and pulled out a twelve-inch butcher knife and examined the blade. She snagged a blood red apple from the hanging fruit basket and with one quick flick of her wrist used the knife to chop it in half. The blade was sharp. It would do the trick. Natalie took a bite out of the apple. She was ravenous. Then she walked slowly down the hall.

Loreli was looking up at Emily, thinking how pretty she was, just like her twin sister. Emily was just rubbing the last of the healing salve into Loreli's bruises.

"Seriously, thank you," said Loreli.

Emily was in no mood to accept her gratitude.

"If I were you, I'd just keep my mouth shut."

"I don't blame you for—"

Emily rubbed harder.

"Ow!"

"I warned you."

Loreli's eyes widened with terror.

Emily sighed. "Take it easy. I'm not going to hurt you. Or not, you know, seriously."

But it wasn't Emily Loreli was worried about. It was Natalie, standing in the doorway holding the butcher knife, her eyes intense and determined.

Loreli did the math and calculated she would only be alive for about another minute or so, provided Natalie was willing to grant her a swift and merciful death. Although, if she had some issues to work out, it could take much longer—and given what Loreli had done, Natalie probably had a few issues. As Natalie walked across the room, Loreli met her eyes and sent her a silent plea. *Be merciful.*

Emily turned and saw the murder in her sister's eyes. "Nat! What are you doing?"

"Please . . . ," whimpered Loreli, before even she knew she was going to speak. There was a tremor in her voice. "Don't do this, not yet."

But Natalie would not be dissuaded. She brought the knife down.

Loreli closed her eyes—then suddenly felt a tingling in her hands. She opened her eyes. Natalie had cut her hands free.

Emily stood transfixed, perplexed, trying to figure out what was going on. Did her sister intend to *free* Loreli?

"Um . . . Nat? What's going on? Talk to me!"

"It looked like her hands were going to be permanently damaged by those plastic ties," said Natalie. She put the knife down.

Free now to do so, Loreli sat up. "Thank you," she said simply, softly, humbly. She was more grateful to Natalie than she'd ever felt in her entire life.

Emily was still shaking her head in disbelief, flummoxed by her sister's act of compassion.

"Natalie, she poisoned Will and almost killed him. She tricked you into becoming infected," said Emily.

"She also injected him with an antidote and saved his life," said Natalie. "And yeah, she conned me. But *I'm* the one who let it happen. It was *my* decision. *My* mistake. There's nobody to blame but me."

She cut the tie holding Loreli's left foot, leaving only her right ankle still bound. That would ensure that, though she would be more comfortable, she still wasn't going anywhere.

"I just have one question," said Natalie to Loreli. "Why? Why did you want me to become infected? Did you think he'd come back to you?"

Loreli lowered her head in shame. "I didn't . . . it was never like that. He's my brother."

"Will told us," confirmed Emily, touching Natalie's arm.

"Then *why*?" demanded Natalie.

"You and Will . . . ," Loreli spoke with sorrow. "I'd never seen two people so perfectly, flawlessly in love. And . . ." Her voice rose an octave as her larynx contracted. She was crying.

"And?" said Emily.

"And no one's ever loved me like that . . . not for one single minute of my life." Her words were small and pathetic but genuine. The sad, true confession of a broken soul. Loreli let all the pain pour out of her, telling Emily and Natalie about her remarkable and twisted journey, and how she'd ended up here again, terribly wounded, seeking redemption.

Chapter Eleven: The Deal

When they got home, Rudy was still trying to convince Will that he could be trusted with a weapon. He was terrified that in the event of some kind of demon shitstorm, Will would leave him without one. He pictured himself in the middle of a huge fracas—something massive like in *Braveheart*, only with demons—with every creepy monster wielding a weapon and him standing there holding nothing but his wang.

"You know I got to level five on *Demon Hunter*," whined Rudy.

Will said nothing.

"When I met you, I was only on level three. I can *handle* weapons, Will! I just need to practice with them a little first. It only took me like two minutes to master the Gyrobuster on level four of *Demon Hunter*, so don't count me out, okay?"

"We'll see," said Will.

They went into the lab. Will stopped in shock, seeing that the twins had for all practical purposes liberated his dangerously evil half-sister.

"What the hell?" he said furiously.

He grabbed Loreli's wrist. She lowered her eyes in disgrace.

"I'm so sorry, brother . . ."

"Don't even try to go down that road," said Will. He glared at Nat and Em. "I restrained her for a reason."

"Her hands were about to fall off," said Natalie. Will looked at the butcher knife sitting on the table and shook his head. He was stunned. He would have bet money that the first chance she got, Natalie would have tried to kill Loreli. But instead she had shown compassion. She'd been able to see past her anger—the way he never could. If Natalie could do that, after all Loreli had done, maybe he should try to do the same.

He looked again at Loreli, and the anger rushed into him again. No, letting go of his anger was impossible. She didn't deserve his compassion.

"Whether or not she can feel her hands is the least of her troubles," he said. He moved to a cabinet and pulled out the Blaster Magnum, a nasty-looking handgun that fired white-hot pellets that exploded into shrapnel upon impact. Rudy's eyes got huge.

"Dude, what's *that* thing?"

"Blaster Magnum."

"Looks nasty."

"It could bring down a T.rex with one shot," said Will.

"Can I . . . ?"

"No," said Will. He pushed Rudy aside and pointed the Blaster Magnum at Loreli's head. She stared up at him.

"We've been here before," she said. She remembered when Will was on the verge of cutting her head off after a battle at the Calvary Cemetery with Blue Streak and a team of shedemons. And he would have, too, if she hadn't had such a snappy comeback: *I'm your sister.*

"This is different," said Will. He also remembered how close he'd come to smoking her before,. He wished he actually had.

"Will, don't . . . ," said Natalie.

"Which one of the swords you stole from Gillian Turner is the Sword of Armageddon?" he asked Loreli.

She didn't seem surprised by the question.

"None of them," she said.

Will pressed the Blaster Magnum into her temple.

"All of them," she said.

"These are not good answers," said Will, his finger tightening on the trigger. He turned to Rudy and the girls.

"You might want to step back a little; this could get messy."

The three of them looked aghast and stepped back. The room was eerily quiet.

"Any time you want to start making sense, it just might save your life," he said to Loreli.

"Here's the weird thing," she said, "I don't think any of them are, and yet somehow they all are. Or they're going to be."

Will clenched his jaw to control his irritation.

"Explain, please?"

"Before he beat me and threw me out like a dog, he broke the blades off of every single sword, and then he threw the handles into a melting pot. My guess is that he's going to make one handle from the combined metals."

"What about the *blade*?" asked Rudy. "What's he gonna use for a blade?"

"Excellent question," said Will.

"I was getting to that," said Loreli. "I think I know where it is."

"I'm waiting," said Will.

"I can show you."

"Or you can just tell me."

"No way. I tell you, you pull the trigger. And I want to help you kill him."

Will took the Blaster Magnum away from her head, pointed it at the wall, and pulled the trigger. With a massive *bang*, the weapon fired a screaming projectile that slammed into the wall and exploded, blowing a three-foot-wide hole. It didn't do anything to cool him off, but it made a statement. Will then cocked the Blaster Magnum and again placed the barrel back against Loreli's temple.

"I'm not going to play this game," he said.

"It's the only game there is. Will, listen to me—"

"Why, so you can tell me more lies?"

"No, this one's the truth. There's only one way I can make amends for what I've done, and that's to plunge the Sword of Armageddon right through our father's heart. So either you kill me now and pass up the opportunity of me showing you where the blade is, or we move our butts and get packing."

"If you think I'm going to forgive you for what you did to Natalie and me, you're crazy."

"I don't expect you to. What I'm doing is for me, not for you."

"Just as selfish as ever," said Will, disgusted.

Hesitantly, Natalie touched his arm, the one not holding the weapon. "It looks like we've only got once choice," she said.

Will looked at her.

"There's no *we* here!" he said. Why was everybody always so eager to jump onboard his ship and get themselves killed?

Natalie put her hands on her hips. "Don't argue, Will. You haven't won this fight once."

Will knew from the look in her eyes there was no way he was going to deter her, and he couldn't help but be a little relieved that, for the moment, Natalie seemed to be back to her old self. He moved to a cabinet and took something out. It looked like some kind of necklace. He carried it to Loreli, then motioned for her to cooperate. She lifted her hair as he clasped the necklace around her neck. It was beaded and had a heavy-looking pendant that hung just below where her Adam's apple would have been if she were a guy.

"It's lovely," said Loreli mockingly. "It'll shock me just like a dog, right?

"Yeah, it can do that," said Will. "But its real beauty is that it's a choker. Literally. You see this ring?" He held up a ring and then slid it onto his right ring finger. "Any time I am so inclined, I can use it to activate that puppy around your neck—and your head will be on the ground."

Will activated the ring and the choker tightened around Loreli's neck. She coughed. Will touched the ring again and the choker relaxed.

"Cool!" said Rudy.

Loreli nodded in understanding. One wrong move and she'd be dead.

"If that's what it takes," she said.

Will stood looking at Loreli, Natalie, Emily, and Rudy. His A-team, whether he liked it or not.

"So everybody's coming, then, I guess. I mean, Rudy, you're—?"

"Are you kidding me? I wouldn't miss this for the world! But you gotta fix me up with some firepower."

"We just finished talking about this. No weapons."

"Come on, Will! That is so uncool."

"No discussion."

Rudy's shoulders slumped.

Will stared hard at Loreli. "This place where we're going, the location of which you won't share with us, is it nearby? Jet plane? Overnight?"

"It's close enough. But I'd be prepared for overnight," said Loreli.

Will shot a look at the twins. "If you're going—and you know I think it's a bad idea—you're gonna want to pack, so let's get started," he said.

Loreli reached for her duster, but Will grabbed it.

"I need my coat," she said.

"No way," said Will. He carefully folded it into a backpack, then pointed a finger at her. "You, you don't move. You don't even *blink* unless I say so."

"Yes, sir," she said mockingly.

Will sighed. He needed this like he needed a hole in the head.

Natalie, Emily, and Rudy left the lab. Will packed up some heal-ing balm patches—he always seemed to need those—and two vials of the demon cure. Rudy hadn't needed any additional doses when he'd been cured, but Natalie had been acting so strangely earlier. Better to be prepared, just in case. Then he began putting together a cache of weapons.

"You want to give me *some* idea where we're going?" he asked Loreli.

"An island."

Will's shoulders tensed. "An *island*?"

"You know, a land mass surrounded by water?"

"Puget Sound?"

"Yep."

Will nodded. He changed his strategy. If they were crossing deep water, he would need to prepare himself, both with equipment and some mental adjustments. Come to think of it, some *huge* mental adjustments. Rivers he could deal with. Even the flood in the caves of Mount St. Emory he'd endured. But deep water, well, that was *not* his favorite thing. He stepped over to a closet and took out his com-bat vest and began loading it up.

As he packed Loreli spoke softly to him, explaining why she'd manipulated him and poisoned him, how the Dark Lord had again rejected her, and why she'd decided to come back to save him. She said she was sorry for the huge mistakes she'd made and wanted to make it up to him if she could. Will said nothing. He understood why she'd done what she had. But that didn't mean he would ever be able to trust her again.

The next morning they set out on their quest.

Will drove the jet black Hummer. It was built like a tank and had almost as much send-you-to-Hell firepower, with dual M-90 machine guns mounted on the front fenders over the headlights, and a Thunder Bazooka that could swing up from the roof and fire rounds big enough to blow a semi off the road.

Following Loreli's directions, they arrived in Beech Bay and pulled up to the ferry terminal, only to be met with a disheartening and clearly indisputable sign: FERRY CLOSED. Other cars that had approached were turning around and driving away.

Will parked the Hummer and shot Loreli a dirty look, then motioned to her.

"Out. The rest of you, stay put."

Loreli got out of the Hummer. Will followed.

"What did you do?" he asked her as the other three shot them worried looks from inside.

"Only what He told me to."

"Which was?"

"I seeded the clouds. Made it rain."

"That's it?"

"No.

"What else?"

Loreli looked uncomfortable.

"I kind of made it rain his blood."

Will closed his eyes to calm his rising temper.

"The ramifications of which are . . . ?"

"I'm guessing that anybody and anything on that island that the rain touched is under his complete control."

"For what purpose?" asked Will.

"No idea. I assume it has something to do with the sword, but he never explained it to me."

Will briefly considered telling the others about what Loreli had done but decided it would serve no purpose. Having everyone even more pissed off at her than they already were would only hamper their efforts.

He sighed. "Get in the truck. I'll be back in a minute."

She did. He passed a bait shop where a skinny blind girl was cutting the heads off of smelts. Her fingers slid over each fish before she placed the knife against the skin above the gills and then pushed it down into the flesh, empty eyes staring eerily out into the distance. He eyed her warily as he passed.

Shaking off a feeling of foreboding and putting a cordial smile on his face, Will approached the ticket booth. Inside was an official from the Washington State Transportation Authority. He was in his mid-fifties with a face flushed with rosacea. He looked like he was counting the hours until his retirement, which couldn't possibly come soon enough.

"Ferry to White Island's closed," he said.

"I can read," said Will. "When will it be running again?"

"Couldn't tell you."

"Can you tell me why it's not running?"

"Nope."

"Because you don't know, or because you don't want to tell me?"

"Both," said the guy. He closed his window.

Will paced back and forth on the dock, looking out at the water. Precious time was passing. He needed a solution, fast.

He saw hope in the form of an old fishing boat moored at the dock adjacent to the ferry terminal. An older man with an odd rolling gait was moving from the stern to the bow, no doubt doing one of the dozens of daily chores needed to keep his craft from falling apart and sinking, which it appeared on the verge of doing. The codger sported a gray beard and wore big floppy waders held up by suspenders over long underwear and a flannel shirt.

Will walked over and the closer he got to the old craft the more he wondered how in the heck it was still afloat. The hull—what was visible of it, anyway—was covered with a thick coating of barnacles. The few areas where the crustaceans had been scraped away were patched with some sort of marine tar.

"Permission to board, captain," said Will as he approached the scow.

The man looked up and blinked through his Coke-bottle glasses as though no one had spoken to him in a decade. He pulled his watch cap down and buried his head in his business.

Okay, thought Will, *we'll have to do this the hard way.* The closer he got to the water, the more nervous Will felt. But he forged ahead. He was sweating and his heart was banging as he climbed onto the boat, sending a terrified glance down at the dark green Puget Sound water.

"Yer tresspassin'. A man could get killed comin' aboard wit-out permissin'," said the old guy without looking up.

A thick wad of hundred-dollar bills landed on the worn boards of the deck. The guy was so shocked he started coughing violently, then took a swig from an oddly shaped bottle, knelt, and scooped the cash into his waders.

"Name's Cappy, and this here is the *Oleana*," he said, but he didn't offer his hand to shake.

"I need to get to White Island," said Will.

Cappy froze, took stock of the situation, then took the money out and tossed it back to Will.

"And I need to keep breathin'," said Cappy.

Will had dealt with stubborn vendors before. There was a simple solution: more dough. He produced three more stacks of hundreds. It was too much for Cappy to resist. He took the money.

"I'll have to take you 'round to the windward side. I ain't going anywhere near the harbor."

"Why not?"

"You want a ride or you want to sit around pickin' our butts and jawin'?"

Fifteen minutes later, after they'd loaded all the gear aboard, the *Oleana* pushed off from her mooring and chugged out into Puget Sound.

Chapter Twelve: The Crossing

The sky was the usual Seattle slate gray. Rudy climbed atop the wheelhouse and held on to a line. He loved boats and was happy to be on the water.

Will was a different story. He stared balefully ahead, then glanced at Loreli, his eyes full of silent accusations.

She spoke up. "You look like you want to kill me. Shall I just dive in, or do you want to hit me over the head and throw me overboard yourself?"

"Don't tempt me," said Will.

He decided to leave her alone with her thoughts, whatever they might be. On the shifting deck he stepped closer to Natalie but made no move to put his arm around her. She wasn't giving off the most welcoming vibes. In fact, every time Will ventured a look her way, she might as well have had a big sign on her forehead that said *leave me alone*. They hadn't been alone together since Loreli had woken up. Will had figured it was best to give her the space she clearly wanted, but he also didn't want this awkwardness hanging over them. He decided to make an effort to smooth things over.

"It's cold," he said.

Natalie said nothing, but her body shook just a little.

"Here," said Will, "take my scarf."

He was in the process of unwinding his scarf to give to her when she stepped away from him and walked back to the bow. He looked at Emily, who shrugged, then came over to him.

"She's been through a lot, Will."

"I know."

"She'll come around."

Will looked back at Natalie, who was gripping the rail, staring off into the fog, her expression bereft of emotion.

"Why am I not convinced of that?"

He knew he should be concentrating on his quest, but he couldn't get Natalie off his mind. Once upon a time the two of them—wrapped in each other's arms—could hardly believe the world could contain such happiness. They could barely wait for the sun to rise, to awaken, so that they could lay eyes upon each other. Now the mad darkness of sleep would be a welcome refuge. If only Will could sleep.

It didn't take long for Puget Sound to get ornery, the strong winds kicking up whitecaps. The *Oleana* rocked precariously in large swells.

"We got some wind comin' in from the north," said Cappy. He'd lit a cigar and seemed perfectly at home piloting the boat, his thick glasses so fogged he surely couldn't see. Will wondered if Cappy had been born on a boat, and if his weird lopsided gait was the result of all the years he'd spent on the water.

Natalie, Emily, and Loreli all seemed to weather the motion well. Rudy was, too, until he took out his camcorder and tried to record some of the action. Will had let Rudy bring the camcorder, figuring it would come in handy for the cover they'd concocted as amateur travel bloggers before they'd left. On the choppy water, looking through the viewfinder, Rudy's stomach quickly started doing flip-flops, and he put the camera away.

Will's stomach was fine. It was the rest of him that was suffering extreme turbulence. He tried not to look at the water, but it was next to impossible. He tried to fight it, but some things he just couldn't let go of. He found himself being dragged to a place where his innermost fear waited, like a shark in a watery hollow, poised to strike.

He was only four-years-old when it happened. His father Edward had taken him and his mother up to the Lake Chelan campground. Lake Chelan—from the Salish Indian word *Tsi-Laan*, meaning "deep water"—is a fifty-five-mile-long lake in northern Washington, the largest natural lake in the state and one of the deepest in the world. It's also exceedingly clear, and visibility is exceptional. So though the lake was cold on that summer day, Will felt safe on the air mattress as he floated on top of the water. He was under the watchful eye of "Noogie," a playmate twice his age whose mother had assured April and Edward that little Will would be just fine. But he was not fine, not when Noogie pushed him off the air mattress. He sank once, twice, three times, as though unseen hands from below were yanking him to his death.

April sprinted into the water and pulled Will out. She held him to her breast. He sobbed, his mind brimming with a plethora of terrifying images, each one worse than the last, wraith after wraith of death. Ever since, for Will, Hell was not a place of heat, fire, and brimstone, but the cold liquid depths of a lake—or worse, the ocean. He was more or less okay in shallow water, like the flood that he'd been caught in with Natalie in the caves of Mount St. Emory or even the shallow part of Lake George the sarcophagus had landed in after being blown out the mouth of the volcano, but deep water, deep *dark* water; that was something else.

Standing on the deck of the *Oleana*, he wiped the sweat off his upper lip and clenched his jaw tight. Cappy hooked off the wheel, took a few ungainly steps in Will's direction, and smiled—until he saw the terror in Will's eyes.

"Just be lookin' at the horizon and nothin' else," he said.

Will nodded and took Cappy's advice. It didn't help. Only when they chugged into a thickening fog did Will's terror back off to the point where he could steel his nerves. He gave Cappy a nod that said *I'm okay.*

"So why isn't the ferry running out to White Island?" asked Will.

Cappy looked over Will's shoulder at the others and spoke in a low tone. "Nobody tells me nothin'," he said.

Will looked disappointed.

"But I hear plenty," said Cappy. "'Tis contamination, that's fer sure."

"The ferries are contaminated? Or the island?"

"Maybe both." Cappy stared off over the bow as the *Oleana* lurched forward, crashing through the choppy waters. "Why you want to go to White Island anyway?"

"We're looking for something," said Will.

"You mind tellin' me what?" asked Cappy.

Will wasn't about to get into specifics with the old guy, so he changed the subject.

"Can this boat go any faster?"

Cappy nodded, set his jaw, then moved back to the wheel and pushed the *Oleana* to full throttle.

"No good can come of ya goin' out there," he said.

"Well, a whole hell of a lot of bad could come from us not," said Will.

Of course, Cappy had no idea what Will was talking about, hadn't the slightest inkling that Will and his four troopers were on a quest for the salvation of mankind. Cappy just shrugged, squinted into the fog, and then worked to pilot the *Oleana* back and forth through the rising swells. Will had the feeling the gnarly old guy knew these waters well.

A seagull cried out from above. Ten minutes later the waters grew less choppy, and when they began passing islets Will knew they were getting close. So he wasn't the least bit surprised when one of the gulls that had been escorting them from fifty feet on high suddenly came screeching down toward him and tried to take his head off. He ducked just in time as the crazed gull slammed into Cappy's wheelhouse, cracking both the window and its own neck. Cappy stood for a moment, dumbfounded, then came out and used a long, wooden-handled whaler's harpoon to snag the bird by its limp neck and fling it overboard.

"I ain't never seen that before," he said. He shook his head. "I'll tell you again, t'aint wise to be venturin' out to this island. There's some kinda curse out here. I wouldn't set foot on that rock for all the rice in China."

The fog cleared as the island finally came into view. They were approaching a cove with a broad rocky beach littered with gnarled driftwood and myriad ghastly visages. Cappy steered the boat closer, then killed the engine and tied off on a rock. They immediately began off-loading, each of them with a backpack on, most of the weight coming from Will's gear. Cappy kept looking at White Island and shaking his head. He yelled over the crashing waves to Will, his voice pitchy and trembling.

"If you have any thought about changing your mind, now would be the time to do it," he said. Cappy had a lifetime of worry already etched into his eyes. His plaintive stare gave Will pause. But Will knew there was no turning back.

"We'll be fine," he said.

Cappy didn't seem convinced. He reached into his pocket and pulled out a soiled old card with a number scribbled on it.

"Well, in case yer not, you give me a call if'n when you want me to come fetch you back."

"Thanks," said Will, taking the card.

Cappy cast off and put the *Oleana* into reverse, swung her around, and went full throttle back out into the Sound. When he thought he was far enough away from the kids, the old man crossed himself in the Catholic way. He didn't think anyone had seen him, but they all had. They watched him go.

Though no one spoke the words, they were all thinking the same thing: that they had just taken a one-way trip, destined never to return to the mainland.

Chapter Thirteen:
Flora and Fauna

Will led the group across the rocky beach through the clutches of crooked driftwood, grotesque shapes, poised, seemingly ready to strike. They walked through clumps of dune grass, then broke the tree line and moved into the forest. The air was damp. The landscape was fecund with oak ferns and salmonberry bushes, nettles and yarrow. They had to climb a gradual rise, making their way through a thicket as a wind came sweeping up behind them. The bushes on the ground danced to and fro.

"Ow!" said Emily, suddenly clutching her left hand with her right. "Something stung me!"

Will immediately recognized the stinging nettle plant. He knew that when you came in contact with these plants, tiny hairs on the stems and leaves would break off and leave traces of an intensely irritating chemical on your skin.

"It's the nettles," said Will. He was about to tell Emily how to recognize them when the wind shifted violently. A taller nettle plant seemed to reach down and lash at her face. She screamed as the plant stung her cheeks. Trying to get away, she lurched sideways into a thicket. Her hands sprung to her face as several plants appeared to converge on her.

"*OWWW!*" she screamed.

Natalie and Loreli both tried to help her, but within seconds they, too, were being stung by the nettles as the wind whipped the plants into a frenzy. *At least I hope it's the wind*, Will thought as he took out his Megashocker. With a half-dozen swipes, he cut through the nettles, which withered and died instantly, the air around them hissing as a white substance oozed from their slender stems.

"My skin! It's like it's on fire!" said Emily, who'd borne the brunt of the attack—if that was indeed what it was.

Plants don't attack you, thought Will as he and Rudy helped the girls to a clearing. He pulled a spray bottle of healing balm from his backpack and began spraying it on the girls' hands and necks and faces, which were rapidly breaking out in searing, painful hives.

"What *was* that, Will?" asked Natalie.

"Just the wind, and stinging nettles," he said. But he had a sinking feeling—especially when he made eye contact with Loreli, who looked guilty as a thief—that these were no ordinary nettles. The healing balm should have made short work of the nettles' stings, but the wounds were stubborn. The girls had to grit their teeth and bear the pain for longer than they should have.

"Here, squeeze my hands," said Will. The twins gladly obliged—anything to take their minds off the pain.

"Man, this sucks. So far I'm not liking this island. I'm thinking Maui would have been a better choice," said Emily, doing her best to lighten the mood. Rudy offered her his hand and she clenched her fingers around his instead of Will's.

"Whoa . . . that's some grip you got there," he said, smiling. She smiled back at him, suddenly very grateful that he was there. In a couple of minutes the swelling and redness abated and the pain subsided.

"Do you think we could possibly find a road or something?" asked Natalie.

"I'm on it, give me a second," said Will. He flipped open the ana-
log cover of his oversized watch to reveal a tiny screen and a micro-
phone, which he spoke into.

"White Island, 98450." The screen came to life and went to a
GPS image mapping White Island. Will spoke again. "Terrain view."
The image was too small to see well, so Will hit another switch. Now
the image was projected in midair as a hologram. Will studied it.

"Zoom in, please," he said.

The image enlarged.

"Track south . . . now west . . . .okay, hold . . ."

Will had their precise location pinpointed. He flipped his watch
shut and looked northward. The forest was dense in that direction,
with nettles and other potentially dangerous plant life, including
poison oak. Who knew how potent the demon version of *that* would
be? He pointed north.

"There's a road about four miles that way. But it's pretty thick
through there, so I'm going to try to locate a trail."

He turned Rudy around and began looking in his backpack.

"If you find a Snickers in there, even pack mules get hungry,"
said Rudy hopefully.

Will pulled out a tiny remote-controlled helicopter gizmo that
was basically a flying video camera. He turned it on and sent it airborne, then adjusted his watch and projected another hologram
while controlling the tiny chopper with a miniature joystick also on
the watch. The drone searched from just above the treetops, and it
didn't take Will long to locate a trail they could use.

"This way," he said, and started hiking, his Megashocker out in
front of him to cut down any threatening plants. Will looked up into
the trees. This forest was eerie, filled with ominous rustling as if the
trees were whispering secrets to each other. Will stepped carefully.
The others hiked directly behind him, with the girls in the middle
and Rudy bringing up the rear. They found the trail quickly and,
once on it, felt a little bit safer.

"This rain of yours," said Will to Loreli.

"It wasn't mine," she said.

"Okay, the Dark Lord's rain. Could it have affected the plant life?"

"I have no idea. But we both know that with *him* in the equation, anything's possible."

"Right. So here's the deal, everybody. We're going in with the assumption that this whole island is polluted with the Dark Lord's evil. Don't eat the fruit, don't drink the water," said Will.

He got no arguments from any of them. They didn't speak again until they came upon a ground squirrel on its hind legs in the middle of the trail facing them and chittering loudly.

"He's a cute little guy," said Rudy.

"So far," said Will.

"Oh come on, you don't think—" Rudy stopped as the squirrel was joined by several others, which started popping up all around them. Rudy whipped out his camcorder and started shooting. Suddenly two of the squirrels flew at each other and began fighting, their sharp little claws and teeth tearing into one another until the smaller of the two was dead. The others converged on the body of the fallen squirrel and began tearing it apart.

"Oh, my god, this is like a Discovery Channel horror movie," said Rudy, still filming.

"I used to like squirrels," said Emily.

"Better him than us," said Natalie. "Why are they acting like that?"

"They're clearly not normal," said Will. "In fact. I'm beginning to think that not much on this island is going to be."

They heard noises above them and looked up. A dozen Northern flying squirrels were swooping back and forth among the branches of the towering pine trees.

"Flying squirrels," said Rudy. "Cool."

"Yeah, it *would* be cool, except that they're nocturnal animals," said Loreli. "They're supposed to be sleeping right now."

"So why are they awake?" asked Rudy.

"I don't know, and I don't want to find out," said Will. "Let's keep moving."

They picked up the pace as they hiked along the trail, following it uphill. Up in the trees, the ranks of the flying squirrels grew until there were at least fifty of them that Will could see.

"Okay, this is getting totally freaky," said Rudy.

Aiming his camcorder up into the trees, he zoomed in, and on the LCD screen he saw that the rodents' eyes were glowing red—and they were staring right at him. His pulse quickened.

"Run!" he yelled.

"No! Don't run!" said Will.

But it was too late. Rudy was already hauling ass. One of the creatures dove down and smacked into Rudy's head, its claws raking at his forehead.

"Ahhhhh!"

"Get down and cover!" Will yelled at the girls, who immediately dropped to the ground and put their arms over their heads. Will pulled a knuckle pistol from his belt clip and fired a laser beam through the creature on Rudy's head, cutting it in half.

"Rudy, get down, *now*!"

Rudy dropped, his head bleeding. He fumbled the camcorder off and jammed it in his pocket. Will pulled something from Emily's backpack. It was a Broad-Beamed Shock Bombardier. While it was powering up with a terrifying whining sound, he took careful aim with the knuckle pistol and picked off as many of the dive-bombing rodents as he could. But the trees were full of them. They were diving like kamikazes, striking Rudy and the girls and biting.

"Will, do something!" screamed Natalie.

Will aimed the Shock Bombardier upward and fired off a long blast. The shock waves slammed into the trees and the forest shook. Pinecones rained down, and so did the varmints, dying as they hit the ground, their small bodies quivering, sparking, dissolving into sparkling dust.

Will looked around. The forest was quiet.

"All clear. You can get up."

"I am so not digging this freakin' place," said Emily.

"You and me both," said Rudy, helping her up.

They turned and looked at Will. He was stoic, but his mismatched eyes glinted with a hard edge.

"You insisted on coming. Once we get to town I can find a way to get you all back on the mainland."

Will then started hiking up the trail. As the land began to flatten out, Natalie caught up to him.

"I'm not going anywhere. I'm in this thing until the end. You know that."

Will stopped, turned, and regarded her. "What thing? *This* thing?"

He made a motion with his hand encompassing the two of them. There was no mistaking his meaning. If she wasn't arguing with him, she wouldn't even talk to him. Something was wrong, and he didn't know what. How could he, when she kept avoiding him?

Natalie wouldn't hold his penetrating gaze. "I'm talking about the job we have to do."

"Nothing more?"

She lowered her eyes. Her silence cut Will to the bone. All he could think was, *What happened?* Was her heart so fickle that it could change directions like smoke in the wind?

"Sorry for bitching, Will," said Rudy as he reached them. "I'm in, too."

"So am I," said Emily, right behind him.

"I shouldn't have to, but I'll say it anyway," added Loreli. "I'm in. You know I'm in. No matter what it takes." Her eyes were intense and hard.

Will looked at all of them and shook his head. "Let's keep moving," he said.

When he started hiking onward, they followed.

In a few minutes they found a paved road and began following its serpentine course through the forest. Using the GPS, Will calculated that they had several miles to schlep before they hit the one and only town on the island, Bingham. As they walked they kept a wary eye upon the surrounding woods, aware that at any moment they might come under attack from any one of the thousands of species of living things inhabiting the White Island forests.

They knew they had a long way to walk, but they got lucky when an old GMC truck came rumbling down the road and pulled over. A teen wearing a hoodie with the hood up rolled down his window.

"You need a lift into town?"

They all looked to Will. He stared at the kid and decided that even if he were infected, they need the ride badly enough to risk it. He smiled.

"Sure, that would be great."

They piled into the GMC. The kid gave them a twice-over and then went ahead and pulled his hoodie down. He was a ruddy-faced redhead. He put the big truck in gear and off they went, snaking along the winding road.

"My name's Milk," said the kid, "Milk Rottman. Go ahead and make the jokes, everyone does." Milk waited for a joke, but none was forthcoming. So he asked, "What are you guys doing all the way out here?"

"The ferry's out. We got a ride on a boat," said Will.

Milk nodded. "Yeah, I heard about the ferry. Weird. Some kind of virus, they said. But I feel fine, in case you were worried or something." Milk seemed to be turning something over in his mind. Then he said, "I have some apples in the back if anybody wants one. Go ahead, I picked them myself this morning."

Rudy turned and looked at a bushel of the most beautiful Red Delicious apples he'd ever seen. He picked one up.

"Thanks . . ."

When he saw Will's disapproving look, Rudy put the apple back.

". . . but we just ate. I'm stuffed like a Thanksgiving turkey," he said, patting his stomach, which then growled.

Will noticed that Milk had an open can of beer between his legs. Milk noticed him noticing.

"I got a half-rack under the seat. You want one?"

"No thanks," said Will.

Milk finished the beer, crushed the can, and tossed it out the window. It bounced off a road sign that said "$300 FINE FOR LITTERING."

This kid's just aching to get his butt thrown in jail, thought Will.

Rudy took out his camcorder and watched some of the crazy squirrel attack he'd filmed.

"You taking some video?" asked Milk.

"Yeah. Got some pretty interesting shots so far," he said.

Will noticed that Milk seemed disturbed by the presence of the camcorder, almost spooked. When Milk caught on that Will was sensing his discomfort, he pasted a big smile on his face and said simply, "Cool."

He steered around a corner and hit the gas hard. The old GMC's 403 hp engine blew them down the road. Milk smiled.

"First time in Bingham?"

"Yep," said Will.

"You're gonna love it. We were named the friendliest little town in Puget Sound four years ago," said Milk, throttling the truck through a long wide turn. The lush forests were flashing by in a green blur.

"Look out!" screamed Loreli as a figure came blasting out of the woods ahead of them. Milk slammed on the brakes. The GMC rocked and shuddered as its oversized tires tried to dig into the asphalt, and their screeching provided a surreal soundtrack to the image in front of them: a middle-aged man wearing only his Jockey shorts, running right at them waving his arms and yelling. His eyes were crazy.

"Help me!"

The GMC spun into a side drift and—*WHAM!*—smashed into the man and sent him flying fifty feet backward. His body did an awkward cartwheel in the air and then crumpled onto the road, his head hitting first, bending his neck at an angle so impossible that they could almost hear the bones snapping. The truck skidded into the ditch.

"Everyone okay?" asked Will. He was looking at Natalie.

"Yeah, I'm fine," she said.

Everybody else nodded. Will jumped out and ran to the man in the street. His underwear was filthy, and he was covered in dirt from his feet to his neck. He was moaning, his face flat against the asphalt. The others, except for Milk, joined Will and looked down at the man.

"Oh my god," said Natalie.

The man's head jerked a little. Blood flowed from his mouth. When he spoke, he gurgled.

"Help . . . me . . ."

Will bent down and felt for a pulse. It was there, but it was weak. The guy's skull had cracked open and he was gushing blood. Will knew there was no saving him. He had only seconds to live.

"What happened to you?" asked Will.

The man's eyes opened. He blinked up at Will. With his last breath, he whispered, "The . . . unholy . . ."

And then he died.

As Will got back to his feet, Milk backed the GMC out of the ditch and onto the road. Then he got out, went around, and opened the truck's large tailgate door. He motioned for help, and the three boys lifted the man's body and placed it in the back next to the apples. Milk stood there, appraising the situation, thinking so hard you could practically hear the gears in his head grinding away. He looked like he was shock, but then he collected himself and shook his head sadly.

"Poor Arliss . . ."

"You know him?" asked Will.

Milk was nodding now, in a weird way, like an idiot savant computing some inner math conundrum. Then he spoke rapidly, the words spilling out.

"Arliss Armenaki used to be the pharmacist. Owned the Price Rite Drugstore downtown. But when his wife left him, he kind of went south. He couldn't sleep, started getting paranoid, just withdrew, even from his friends. He got so he couldn't pay attention in the drug store, you'd have to repeat things to him over and over. Then he started ignoring his personal hygiene and rambling random things. He was crazy, just plain crazy." Milk paused awkwardly. "Guess we better get goin'."

They all got back in the truck, and this time Milk took it real slow. He looked grim and confused. But who wouldn't after having just killed a man?

Stung by seemingly sentient nettles, attacked by flying squirrels, and now running over a mostly naked man. So far, the island had been anything but hospitable. Will hoped that things would get better, but he was pretty sure that they would only get worse.

Chapter Fourteen: Uninvited

They drove for five miles until they reached Bingham, passing a large gaudy red-and-yellow sign anointing it, as Milk had claimed, THE FRIENDLIEST LITTLE TOWN IN PUGET SOUND. They passed some teens wearing hooded parkas, the best defense against the persistent Northwest drizzle. The teens were walking practically down the middle of the road, smoking and throwing rocks and dancing to the tunes of their iPods. When Milk drove by a convenience store, they saw a few more hoodied teens come out, stuffing their faces with junk food.

Milk kept driving. They passed the town library, which had two of the smallest marble lions Will had ever seen flanking the four steps leading to the double doors. No one was going in or coming out of the library. Will guessed it was a slow day for books. They drove some more and passed the local high school, with a sign proclaiming it HOME OF THE BINGHAM BEARS, which sat on a rise with a parking lot on one side and a grove of oak trees on the other. Some genius had spray painted the words HOT RAIN on the side of the gymnasium. There were cars in the parking lot and a few students milling about outside the school, smoking fearlessly, defiantly. Near the front entrance was a big plastic statue of the school mascot, a bear, but someone had sawed the head off. *Nice creepy touch*, thought Will.

As they pulled into the town proper, Will tapped on the truck's dashboard and said, "Here's good." Milk braked to a stop in front of the local greasy spoon, a place called Dixie's Diner. Will and the others got out.

"I'll take poor Arliss to the sheriff's office, and then the morgue, I guess," said Milk.

"Where's the sheriff's office?" asked Will.

Milk blinked. "Uh, end of Main Street, take a right, two blocks down. Can't miss it," he said. Then he smiled at them all, friendly face back in place. "It was a pleasure meeting you guys, I mean . . . under the circumstances . . ."

Milk drove away as Will and the others walked toward the diner, and Will noticed that when Milk got to the end of Main Street, he didn't go right, but left. Will watched as Milk drove up another winding road toward a hill that rose above the coastline. Where was he going? Clearly not in the direction of the sheriff's office. So he'd lied. Will figured it was just the first of many they'd be hearing that day.

Will looked down at the marina. A large sign identified one of the out buildings as the headquarters for the White Island Diving Club. Most of the berths in the marina were empty, even though it was a blustery day and Puget Sound was inhospitable. Rudy saw Will's eyes narrowing.

"What's up?" he asked.

"I'm not sure yet. But we'll find out. Eventually. Let's get something to eat."

They all went into the diner—the cute bell above the door ringing as they entered—and found a booth. It looked like the tables in the diner hadn't been bussed in days. A mountain of filthy dishes and burger baskets threatened to topple the dirty dish cart. There was a smattering of teens at various tables; some working on their laptops, some listening to their mp3 players or texting on their phones. There were no adults to be seen.

Seeing Will and the others come in and sit down at the only available booth, the other teens whispered among themselves and then departed, one by one. They didn't even bother trying to exit discreetly, and no one stopped to pay on their way out. Will didn't see any money on the tables, either. What was this? Free Food Day? There was definitely something majorly odd about the island's inhabitants. Milk definitely hadn't been normal either, though he hadn't done anything to confirm whether or not he was actually infected.

A tall blonde waitress, Misty Scott, was surreptitiously checking them out in an angled mirror that hung over the counter. When Will caught her eye, she turned around with a sweet smile pasted on her face. She was a big-boned girl who looked like she hadn't missed a meal lately. She approached them and passed around plastic-covered menus.

"Hi, welcome to Dixie's Diner. What can I get you guys?"

"Double cheeseburgers, fries, and cokes all around," said Will.

"Skip the coke for me," said Loreli, slanting Will a look. "I'll have a vanilla shake."

"Well, that was easy!" chirped Misty. She turned and was about to beeline to the cook's window when Will stopped her.

"Excuse me."

Misty turned and her smile was even brighter. "Yes?"

"Do you have any idea why the ferry's not running?"

"Gosh, no, except its some kind of health thing. I don't think it'll last long. I'll bet it will be up and running soon, and then you guys can go on back."

Missy took their order to the window and clipped it onto the order wheel. "Order up," she said.

A tall, stoop-shouldered kid with acne studied the order and then set to work building the burgers. Misty gave the counter a couple of cursory wipes, then slipped her cell phone out of her jeans and sent a quick text.

"Is it just me, or did she seem a little nervous?" asked Natalie.

"Definitely nervous," said Emily.

"One thing's for sure. Our arrival has not gone unnoticed," said Will. "It won't be long before somebody shows up and starts asking questions.

A few minutes later Misty served the burgers. Will took the lettuce and tomatoes off of his, just in case they were island-grown, and the others followed suit. Then they all dug in. For a few moments it was as if they were just some normal teens chowing down at the neighborhood diner after school without a care in the world. Except for the fact that this was hands down the messiest diner any of them had ever been in. Will was sitting across from Natalie and nudged her foot with his, trying to get her to look at him. She just drew her foot away, still not looking him in the eye. He could feel her continuing to distance herself from him, and it was eating away at his heart.

Emily was watching Rudy nibbling. Usually he was such a pig that he disgusted her, but today he'd changed his style and was eating slowly. He still savored every bite, though, moaning with pleasure and flicking little glances her way. She rolled her eyes at his not-so-subtle flirting, but when he wanted to play footsie under the table, she was game.

The old-fashioned diner had those quaint tabletop jukeboxes, little glass domes with song selections that you could flip through and feed quarters into. Rudy picked out an oldie, "Here Comes the Sun." But the sun was hidden today; the skies were a dull gray, the clouds full-to-bursting with precipitation, though at the moment it wasn't really raining so much as misting. Still, Rudy was eternally optimistic, humming along with Lennon and McCartney as he ate.

Will was seated so he could see part of the marina. He watched as a group of power boats, Chris Crafts and See-Doos; Sea Rays and Skaters, blasted into the harbor and docked.

Ten minutes later, two pickup trucks pulled up in front of the diner, their Thrush Glasspack exhausts rumbling. Will watched carefully as a half-dozen teenage boys unfolded from the trucks. They were big guys, townies wearing ball caps and down vests. One of the trucks had a big, mean-looking dog in its pickup bed, howling and barking and snarling, straining against his choke collar. Rudy was relieved to note that the dog was tethered to the floor of the truck bed by a strong chain. The dog, a huge bullmastiff, looked less like a pet than a weapon of destruction with his teeth bared, his jaws snapping like he couldn't wait to tear someone apart.

The largest of the hulking boys, Boone Winter, quieted his dog, Killer, and then led the others toward the diner. They entered, loudly banging open the door. Boone grabbed the cute little bell over the door to stop it from ringing. He looked like he might tear it off, but he let it be. Flanking Boone were two other big guys, Andy Grassman and Colin Ritter. The other three guys hung back and waited as Boone clomped over to the table and glared down at Will and the others.

"Friendliest little town in Puget Sound," said Will.

Boone clenched his teeth and balled his fists.

Rudy was thankful he was on the last bite of his cheeseburger, which he popped in his mouth and chewed quickly as he braced himself for the inevitable confrontation. With the muscle he had left over from his time as a demon, he was pretty sure he had a chance against every one of the guys except the biggest one, Boone. The guy had to be six foot six and over three hundred pounds. He didn't look like a teenager; he looked like a poster boy for the WWF.

"You're in our booth," Boone growled.

Rudy picked up his camcorder and turned it on. A couple of the townies exchanged worried glances. Will stopped eating and regarded the Incredible Hulk.

"This is your booth?" asked Will. He sniffed the air. "Come to think of it, I thought I smelled something bad."

Will knew he should have just let it go, but he simply didn't have it in him to back down. For the better part of his demon hunting days, he'd gotten things done by *refusing* to back down, instead pushing creeps who didn't want to be pushed. Boone Winter wasn't any different than the others.

Boone grabbed the table and tore it right out of the wall. The food baskets and Rudy's camcorder went flying. Rudy caught the camera in midair.

Misty shook her head angrily. "Dammit, Boone, you're gonna have to pay for that, whenever—"

"Shut up, Misty!" roared Boone.

There was a tense moment where everyone wondered which way this was going to go. Will knew, and he braced himself, smirking like a punk at Boone, pushing the big dumb ape, daring him. *Go ahead*, Will's eyes said. *Throw a punch.*

Boone did. Will ducked, and Boone's club-like fist smashed into the wall, punching a hole in the drywall. Before he could even yank it out, Will hit him with a right uppercut. The punch would have knocked a normal kid out, but Boone was far from normal. He just flinched.

"That your best shot?"

"Not even close," said Will.

For Will, during a fight or any other kind of physical confrontation, time seemed to slow down, even stand still, as punches were thrown, knives thrust, guns fired. The timeframe in which violence occurs is both terrifyingly rapid and agonizingly slow. Will, who was able to bend time, had time to think about things even as he was springing into action. His old friend, rage, surged up within him. He could feel it pumping through his veins. He knew he should fight it, but the red curtain that dropped over his vision was familiar and welcome. It made things so simple.

He aimed a hard kick to Andy's kneecap. When Andy reflexively reached for his knee, Will brought a fist up to meet his chin, lifting him off his feet and sending him crashing onto the table behind him, utensils and ketchup bottle flying.

Boone was watching Will with a mixture of awe and curiosity. He threw two punches, both of which landed in Will's mid-section. Well felt like he'd been kicked in the stomach by a racehorse, but he recovered quickly and dropped to the floor, body straight like he was going to do a pushup. Then he used his hands to flip himself over and back up, swinging his elbow and chopping Boone twice in his windpipe. The big guy grabbed at his throat and started wheezing.

Loreli jumped up and feinted left toward Colin Ritter. But he was an expert boxer, and he anticipated her move and then nailed her a good one, the punch catching the bone in her right cheek. Rudy thought he heard a cracking sound, and he picked up the heavy glass sugar dispenser from the floor and threw it as hard as he could. It smacked Colin square in the nose. Blood spurted. Colin's eyes bugged out. He stared hard at Rudy.

A chair came flying through the air. Natalie, Emily, and Rudy ducked as it smashed into the wall. Will glanced over, wondering who had thrown it, but there was no one there.

The other three boys rushed forward with fists flying, but they froze when they heard the front door burst open.

Jasper Sholes shouted out, "That's enough!"

Boone, Andy, Colin, and the other three boys reacted like automatons, like robots that'd just been switched off. Their fists unclenched, their arms dropped to their sides.

Loreli took the opportunity to kick Colin as hard as she could one more time, in the groin. He brayed like a calf being branded and crumpled to the floor. Will shot a look at Loreli. She held up her hands up as if to say, *hey, he had it coming.*

Jasper was the epitome of calm, striding confidently across the room—putting away his cell phone, which he'd obviously just been on. He had his hand extended, a politician garnering votes, smiling like a snake. His long blond hair was damp, probably from the drizzle.

"I'm Jasper Sholes," he said to Will, proffering his hand.

Will stared at him for a good five seconds before mustering a neutral smile of his own and grasping Jasper's hand.

"Hello."

A rapid truce was being negotiated, but Will knew it was all a façade. He took his time shaking Jasper's hand, as he often did with those he suspected to be demons. As far as Will could tell, Jasper had neither teeth, eyes, or tentacles housed within his palm. He was carefully eyeing the camcorder in Rudy's hands.

Will said, "I'm Will Hunter."

Jasper nodded. "Great to meet you. You'll have to forgive the Testosterone Troupe here," he said. "We've all been a little on edge ever since this quarantine thing came down."

"Why is White Island under quarantine?" asked Will pointedly.

Jasper looked genuinely puzzled. "You know," he said, "we've all been asking ourselves the same thing ever since the state guys came out with the order."

Will turned and looked at the other boys. "'State guys' . . . Is that the State Health Department?"

Every time he made eye contact with the other boys, they dropped their gaze to the floor, unwilling to risk sending Will even the slightest visual clue.

"Yes, the Health Department. Exactly," said Jasper.

Will nodded as though he understood, but the only thing he was beginning to understand was that Jasper Sholes had some kind of strong authoritarian hold over the other boys. He wasn't about to let anyone slip up and blurt out any information.

"So you have no idea why the island is under quarantine?" asked Will.

"Not a clue," said Jasper.

Will nodded to show how very much he totally believed what Jasper was saying. Of course they both knew he was lying, but there was a scenario to work through here, and Will was obediently playing his part.

"I have a couple of questions for you," said Jasper. "How did you get out here? The ferry's shut down, and the marina's been closed off since Sunday. And more importantly, *why* are you here?"

"Did you ever hear of Earthtrekkers?" asked Rudy. He pasted an affable smile on his face and started jabbering with a friendly lilt in his voice, explaining how they were Internet journalists, bloggers backpacking from California to Alaska, exploring the coast and writing about it online. He was laying it on appropriately thick, playing the part of a geeky blogger, making it sound they were having a spectacular time trekking from one picturesque paradise to another.

The night before they'd left, Rudy and Emily had hastily built a blog and crammed it with dozens of entries and photos they'd snagged off the web, tampering with the posting dates to make it look like the blog had been active for months, but taking care to put "Site Under Construction" tags throughout. Will figured Jasper and his drones would likely log on and check up on their story, so Rudy and Emily's handiwork would buy them some time.

"We're on a rippin' quest to find the most beautiful, peaceful place on the West Coast," said Rudy, wide-eyed. He pulled out his camcorder. "I get everything with this puppy. I've got it linked through my phone, and everything I shoot goes right to our server and onto our website with the push of a button."

Will could see the muscles working in Jasper's neck and jaw. Like it had Milk, the camcorder clearly made Jasper terribly uneasy, and Will wondered why.

But the moment of unease passed quickly—Jasper was a pro manipulator—and he nodded as though he were not only impressed, but also rather pleased. "Well," he said, still trying to out-smile everyone, "you won't find anyplace more beautiful or peaceful than White Island." He seemed so sincere, it was as if he almost believed himself.

"It didn't seem so peaceful for Arliss Armenaki," said Will. "Guy named Milk gave us a ride into town and ran right into him. In fact, he killed him."

Jasper briefly closed his eyes and nodded. "I heard about that. A terrible tragedy."

"Any idea why Arliss was running around in his Jockeys covered with dirt?"

"As I'm sure Milk explained to you, Arliss was a very disturbed man."

"Well, he's not disturbed anymore," said Will. "Actually, I was thinking maybe we could go and have a talk with the sheriff."

Jasper kept his cool, like he had nothing to hide. But Will knew he was hiding something. He knew they all were.

"Sure! I'll take you on over to the sheriff's office myself," said Jasper.

Will noticed a Jaeger-LeCoultre Master Compressor pro diving watch on Jasper's wrist. It was an expensive little piece of work, with a built-in mechanical depth gauge.

"You do some diving?" said Will.

Jasper's eyes flicked to his watch as though he'd forgotten he was wearing it. "Yeah. In Cabo, mostly."

"Not around here?"

"In these waters? You gotta be kidding me. Freezing, dark, nothing to see. Naw, I'm not one of those macho Northwest dudes with something to prove. When I dive, it's strictly tropical." He cleared his throat. "So if you're done eating, we can head over to see the sheriff now. Don't worry about paying. Lunch is on me."

As they left the diner, Jasper took Misty aside and spoke quietly to her. She nodded, then set about cleaning up the mess.

Chapter Fifteen:
The Black Church

Once outside, Jasper spoke in rapid, hushed tones to Boone and the other boys, who nodded glumly and then climbed into their trucks. Boone's massive bullmastiff was growling and straining at his chain.

Boone yelled at him, "Killer, shut up! Sit!"

The dog silenced, circled, and sat. Boone got in his truck and they drove down toward the marina. Jasper drove a big Ford Excursion, so there was plenty of room for Will and the others. Jasper sent a quick text, then signaled like he was taking a driving test, and pulled carefully onto Main Street.

They drove down the wide boulevard lined with cherry trees, passing other teens in cars, stereos blasting rap and heavy metal. Jasper waved to a couple of kids. They drove by a hardware store and a coffee shop where more teens were in evidence, most of them wearing hoodies and many of them openly smoking and drinking.

"Pretty laid-back town," said Will.

"Yeah, it's cool. I've lived here all my life," said Jasper. "My great-grandfather and grandfather were both fishermen, salmon and halibut mostly, but the quotas, the catch limits, pretty much put them out of business. So my father, along with just about everybody else on the island, started growing tomatoes. Lately they grow heirlooms."

Rudy and Emily and Natalie exchanged looks. Who on earth cares? But Will was paying close attention to every word. Jasper was very convincing. As they drove, he kept talking about anything and everything, except the one thing they were all wondering: What was *really* going on there on the island?

Jasper pulled up to the sheriff's office, a squat brick building with a small parking lot bordered by conifers. They all got out. Jasper was so accommodating, he politely opened the front door for them. Inside it was quiet except for the sound of fingers tapping on a computer keyboard.

A teen guy was smoking at a desk.

"Hey, Sean," said Jasper.

"Oh, I didn't hear you come in," said Sean, standing up.

Jasper shot him a quick dirty look. Sean put the cigarette out.

"Is the sheriff around?"

Beat. Beat. Sean thinking. *Forming the lie*, thought Will.

"Not now. He's out. On patrol. I can have him call you. What's up?"

Jasper indicated Will and the others.

"They wanted to talk to him about Arliss, and maybe find out about the quarantine."

Sean made a face.

"Um . . . well, there's still no news. But, uh, like I said, I'll have him call you."

"Okay then," said Jasper. He stood there waiting, looking expectantly at Will. Will took a few moments to scan the room, taking in details, looking past Sean through the window to the back parking lot.

"Thanks for your time," said Will finally. He turned and left the sheriff's office. Rudy and the girls followed. Outside they stared at the deserted ferry terminal.

"With the quarantine and everything, it looks like you didn't exactly pick the best time to visit our fair island," said Jasper. "Again,

I'm sorry about Boone and the boys being so freakin' rude. They're just blowing off steam. I can give you a ride back to the mainland in my boat."

"I thought the island was under quarantine. That means that once we're here we can't leave, right?" said Will.

Jasper stared at him.

"It looks like we'll have to extend our visit," said Will.

Jasper's eyes narrowed, but his smile came back quickly in full force.

"In that case, I know the best bed and breakfast in town. Come on!"

Will didn't argue, so Jasper drove them to Janie Walker's Victorian beauty. He pulled into the driveway, got out, and walked right in, motioning for them to follow.

"Belongs to my aunt, come on in and make yourselves at home."

They all entered, with Jasper playing the part of the affable host.

"The house was built in 1902, been in the family all these years. It's got three bedrooms on the second floor, and three more on the first, all totally pimped out. I mean, for an old person, you know?" He laughed and continued showing off the place. He seemed eager to have them settled someplace where he could keep an eye on them.

"Here's the living room, fireplace, kitchen, breakfast nook."

The interior design of the house was in the kitschy style of an older woman with too much time on her hands. She had macramé ducks on the walls and rocks that looked vaguely like frogs and salamanders and rabbits, which she'd painted in bright, cheery colors and scattered about on shelves and on the floor.

"Aunt Janie did all this artwork by herself," said Jasper.

"No kidding," said Will.

Seeing the homey handicrafts reminded Will of his mother and the colorful landscapes she used to paint before the Dark Lord kidnapped his stepfather, Edward. The sooner Will could thwart the Beast's plans and bring him down, the sooner he could free his mother from the Dark Lord's grasp. First he had to figure out why the Dark Lord had picked *this* island. And so far Jasper wasn't much help.

Jasper went into the kitchen and opened the fridge. He pulled out a large plate of cookies and a carton of milk and set both items on the counter.

"Just in case you get a snack attack," he said, eating a cookie. Then the smile again. He was looking at Natalie, Emily, and Loreli.

"Somebody must have left the gates of Heaven open because you three are some kind of angels," he said.

Emily blushed. Loreli and Natalie both tossed out the same comeback: "Don't be too sure of that—" They looked at each other in surprise.

"I'm sure you'll be totally comfortable here tonight," said Jasper, his smile never dimming. "You've got cable, but I don't think Aunt Janie's up to speed with her Wi-Fi."

"We'll make do," said Will. "Thanks." Again he found himself shaking hands with Jasper.

"You guys seem like really cool people. I hope you enjoy your stay in our little town," he said. "Well, I gotta go. Homework, chores, the usual." Jasper turned to leave.

"Excuse me. Where is she?" asked Will.

Jasper turned around. "Who?"

"Your aunt."

"Oh, she'll probably pop up soon. But don't sweat it if she doesn't. She's old, but she's independent, and quite the hiker. She's probably out there tromping around somewhere. I'll give her a call and let her know you're here. Catch you later."

Jasper exited through the front door, climbed into his truck, started it up, and with a wave, drove away, leaving them alone.

"Holy crap, all those phony smiles gotta be hurting his face, don't you think?" said Rudy.

"Probably," said Will.

Loreli began exploring the living room. "Hello? Anybody home?" she said loudly. "What did he say his aunt's name was?"

"Janie," said Rudy.

"She's not here, and I have a feeling she's not going to be," said Will. He put down his backpack and helped the others take theirs off. He lined them all up on the floor next to the living room couch. Natalie was looking out the side window at Janie's garden.

"Did you notice something weird about this island?" she said.

"You mean besides the *Little Shop of Horrors* plants, the zombie squirrels, and the dirty naked dead guy?" said Rudy.

"We haven't seen any adults," said Will.

"Except for the dirty naked dead guy," corrected Rudy.

"Yeah. Except for him," said Will.

"Oh my god, you're right," said Emily.

"What happened to them?" asked Natalie.

"I don't know," said Will. "But we'll find out."

Will looked at Loreli. "The blade for the Sword of Armageddon. Where is it?"

"If I knew that, we'd already have it," she said. "My guess, though, given how weird everybody here is acting, is that the teens on this island are busy looking for it."

"They creep me out," said Emily, and Natalie nodded in agreement.

"What are we going to do?" asked Rudy.

"What I always do," said Will. "Tomorrow we'll rattle some cages, turn over some rocks, shake things up. But first we've got to get through the night."

Rudy tensed up. "What do you mean *get through*? I don't like the sound of that."

"Will . . . ," said Emily. "Is something going to happen?"

"Something always happens," said Loreli.

This didn't help Rudy's mood. He started chewing a fingernail.

Will poked around on the first floor and found a thick door off the living room leading to a basement wine cellar. He went down and looked around. As far as he could tell, there was no way in or out besides the door—a good place to hide if they needed to. He came back upstairs and shut the cellar door behind him. The others looked to him for guidance.

"What's the plan for right now?" asked Rudy.

Will stared out the front window, watching as the last remnants of daylight succumbed to the oncoming night.

"Right now, we're going to have milk and cookies and then go to bed. I'll take first watch."

While the others ate, Will walked to the rear of the house and looked into the backyard. All was quiet. He used his phone to log into the security camera and vital sign monitors at the hospital; April was in the same state. Comatose. It all felt like the calm before a storm—quiet but ominous. He went back to the living room, pulled a chair up to the picture window, and stared out into the night.

The church parking lot was nearly full. Jasper arrived last and crowded his truck into the lot. He stepped out and walked toward the church, which was so black that it was almost invisible in the night, save for the light shining from within.

Wendy Childress appeared from behind a tree. She walked up to Jasper and slowly draped her arms around his shoulders.

"I missed you, Jasper," she said. "See, I'm wearing the necklace you gave me."

Jasper put his arms around her, too, but when she kissed him and went searching with her tongue, he pushed her away. She clung to him with one hand, fingering the necklace with the other, and, frustrated, he pushed harder.

"Ow! You broke my necklace!"

He had. She held it in her hand.

"We don't have time for this, Wendy. We have business to take care of."

"Fine, there's always later." Wendy pocketed the jewelry and grabbed Jasper around the waist. "You can buy me another one. Jasper, I feel so . . . alive! But also guilty, you know?"

"Don't feel guilty. We did what we had to do."

"But I keep thinking about them."

"We all do. Just put it out of your mind."

"How can I put *them* out of my mind?"

Jasper had no answer for this because he'd not been able to do it himself; in fact, he found himself thinking about them nearly all the time.

Distant thunder rumbled through the night.

"Why did this happen, Jasper?" Wendy asked. "Are we cursed?"

"No, we're not cursed," said Jasper. He drew Wendy to him again and held her tight. She was shivering.

"In some ways we're blessed, right? We're going to be okay," he said. "Everything's going to be all right. We just have to keep doing what we're doing, and then everything will go back to the way it was before."

His words calmed Wendy, but even though he'd said them with conviction, he himself had grave doubts. He wondered if indeed they *had* been cursed. Certainly a great evil had rained down upon them—literally. He looked up into the sky and remembered the day when the crimson rain had fallen.

It had, of course, shocked everyone on the island. No one had ever seen or felt anything like it. Every living creature on the island had fallen into a deep slumber that lasted for only six hundred and sixty-six seconds but felt like hours. Upon awakening, the adults had all suffered from pounding headaches. The island's plants and animals were infused with hostility. And the teenagers all heard the same voice in their heads, a deep thunderous, commanding voice, a voice that sounded like the Earth itself. They were terrified.

The Voice commanded them to perform a series of events that would change White Island forever. The Voice, that awful *Being* in their heads, reached deep into their cerebral cortexes, demanding to be not merely heard, but obeyed. One dissenter, Brian Sooner, a tall boy who had always been a strong-willed, independent thinker, refused the Voice, rebuked the call, but it grew louder and louder until it hurt his brain, until at last he had no choice by to obey it. He killed his father with a garden hoe. Then, overcome with remorse and humiliation, he hung himself from the rafters of his grandfather's barn.

After that, the teens understood that the Voice was not to be trifled with. Their terror turned to a grim determination to finish the task they'd been given, hoping that once they had, the voice would go away again and leave them alone.

Within hours they began to notice changes in their bodies. They became stronger and more agile. Their eyes took on a reddish-yellow glow. Some of them could move things without touching them. As the hours passed, their powers increased. And they obeyed the Voice, obeyed without question, like zombies. They gathered and conspired to capture every adult on the island. And then they did so, with startling swiftness and cunning.

Jasper had always felt different and special. He knew he was a natural leader. But this, this was something extraordinary. He was oozing power. Somewhere in the edges of his mind, he sensed that the force that infused him was wicked, but he didn't care. It felt so *good*. There was one thing that weighed especially heavily on his conscience. He had feigned illness to draw his mother and father into his room, where they were set upon by Boone and the others, bound, gagged, and taken away.

All over the town, similar scenarios played out, with teenagers turning on those who had not only given them life, but had sacrificed so much to keep them healthy and happy. The gathering was a painful process that simultaneously thrilled the new demonteens and broke their hearts. But it had to be done. It was the will of the Voice.

Boone had had a hell of a time with his own father, Dan, who, though elderly, was still in good physical shape. He was not a man to be threatened, especially when he was wielding a hunting rifle, as he had been when the demonteens came for him. Boone was afraid his father was going to either kill or be killed. Fortunately, Gwen Chin, the only Asian girl on the island, was clever. She approached Dan speaking Mandarin, momentarily confusing him. When she fainted, he dropped his rifle to catch her, which allowed the boys to jump on him. He cursed a blue streak as Gwen rose up, clearly having just duped him into capture. As he was led away, he swore vengeance.

The adults were all taken away. For the first several hours, as they were captured and subdued, their wails of agony echoed across the island. But eventually they were gagged and lined up and could only stand and watch in horror as the holes were dug.

Jasper gave Wendy another comforting hug.

"It's time we go inside," he told her. "We've got a lot to do."

She nodded and he took her by the hand. They entered, and Jasper walked directly to the front. The interior of the church had largely been spared by the blaze, and the pews held dozens of White Island demonteens who had come there to meet, just as they had every night since the hot red rain. Jasper addressed those assembled with undisputed authority.

"This meeting is called to order. Ongoing business. The feedings?"

A tall redheaded girl was holding a clipboard and scanning a list. "Completed on schedule," she said.

"Progress report?" asked Jasper, his gaze shifting to Andy.

"Thirty units, bringing our total to six hundred and sixty-five. It appears there's only one left. But so far we haven't been able to locate it."

"We will," said Jasper.

Andy massaged his sore kneecap and touched his chin where Will had hammered him. He had a deep, plum-colored bruise and looked angry and miserable. If he had his way, there would be hell to pay.

"All right," said Jasper. "Now on to the obvious new business. The visitors."

The demonteens murmured among themselves. Boone stood up into his full height.

"We gotta take them out," he said.

"He was kicking your ass, Boone," said Misty. "You'll have to use a gun." She was smirking. They'd dated briefly when they were sophomores, until he'd abruptly broken up with her in front of the whole lunchroom, so she'd actually enjoyed watching him get beaten.

"I was thinking an axe, but we'll take shotguns just in case," said Boone. "Or maybe I'll just dump drop my truck on his head. But I'll tell you one thing, I'm going to kick his ass good first, and *then* put him in a box."

"No. Direct confrontation is not a good idea," said Jasper.

"But they're a threat!" said Andy.

"What if they've come to expose us?" said Colin. "We've got control of the island now, but what happens if the State Troopers come around? The Voice will punish us for sure."

"The only solution is to put 'em down hard, man!" said Boone.

A few of the big dudes banged their fists on the pews and grunted in agreement. Others joined in. The noise began to swell. A bookcase rose from the floor, lifted toward the ceiling, and then banged down onto the black and white tiles. Jasper raised a hand and the church went silent.

"Listen to me. We have a quest. Who among us did not hear the Voice?"

Jasper looked out at the assemblage. No one raised a hand. They'd *all* heard the Voice.

"These . . . intruders . . . with their video cameras and who knows what else . . . We can't risk openly attacking them. If they got any of it on tape and sent it out there . . . ," he pointed. *Out there* was anywhere off the island. The teens all looked in the direction Jasper indicated.

"Unwanted attention could hamper our quest."

"But we can't have them nosing around in our own backyard! We've got to destroy them!" shouted Boone.

Jasper remained calm and held up a hand again to silence the protests.

"It's too risky," he said. "There are other ways. The island . . . it will protect us. We will be smart and call upon the powers that guide us. The visitors are at Janie Walker's. We'll take care of them tonight.

The demonteens nodded and exited the black church in an orderly fashion, getting into their cars and driving off in the direction of Janie Walker's bed and breakfast.

Chapter Sixteen:
Demonwolves

Rudy was sacked out on the couch. Loreli was curled up asleep in the recliner a few feet away, and the twins were sleeping upstairs. Will was acting as sentry, watching for movement in the dark outside the house. A few bats and birds and insects flitted around, and a couple of raccoons raided a trashcan. But other than that, the neighborhood was calm and quiet. Anyone else might have relaxed, but Will knew better than to let his guard down. Especially here. Out of the corner of his eye, he saw Rudy sit up on the couch, grab another cookie from the plate, and scarf it down.

"Rudy?"

"Yeah? What is it?" said Rudy, his voice suddenly full of alarm.

"Don't freak out. Just come over here a sec, okay?"

In seconds he was beside Will at the front window.

"What am I looking at?" he asked.

"Nothing so far. It's been pretty quiet. Take watch for a couple of minutes, will you?"

"Done," said Rudy.

Rudy squinted as he looked outside. Nothing but a light wind tossing a few dry leaves across the front yard. Will turned from the window and glanced at Loreli, asleep in the chair. He was still carrying so much anger toward her, he had half a mind to give her a good shock with the collar but decided to let her be. He grabbed a cookie and climbed the stairs to the second floor. The door was open to the room where Natalie and Emily slept. Will stood in the doorway and listened. Emily's breathing was strong and rhythmic; she was out. But Natalie's was uneven and shallow, and he sensed that she was awake. He took a couple of steps into the room.

"Natalie?" he whispered.

She rolled over and looked up at him. He marveled at her beauty. But then he felt a little piece fall out of his heart because her eyes were flat and emotionless. Her eyes used to light up with joy every time she saw him, but since her infection they just seemed dead. Was it just a side effect of her time as a demon? Or had something really changed in the way she felt about him? He hoped Emily was right, that she just needed time. But seeing her eyes like that made it hard to believe.

"You hanging in there?" he asked.

"Why wouldn't I be?"

She couldn't bear to look at him for too long, so she moved her gaze out the window, where a small bird landed on a thin branch and swiped its beak back and forth, preening. Will offered the cookie to Natalie.

"Cookie?" She shook her head.

"No thanks."

Who doesn't want a cookie? thought Will. She probably wanted it; she just didn't want to take it from *him*. He laid it on the bedside table, just in case.

"Nat . . . we haven't had much time to talk about . . . things."

"There's nothing to talk about," she said, which was a crock of crap. They both knew there was more to talk about now than there had ever been. Why was she acting this way? Why was she so distant?

"Let's start with you telling me one thing," said Will. "Do you still . . ." He wanted to say "love," the word he'd used to describe how he felt for her, but right now it seemed too loaded, brought fear racing into his heart. "Do you still have feelings for me?"

Will waited, the moment stretching into agony as every second she hesitated spoke volumes.

"Yes," she finally said.

Relief began to flood through him. But then she clarified.

"But . . . not like I did before."

He felt like wasps were stinging his heart. "Why don't you just say it?"

"Say what?"

"We both know what. Go ahead and say it. Say what your eyes have been telling me ever since I pulled you out of the Demon Tapper and cured you."

For a moment it looked like Natalie's hard veneer would split open and reveal the gentle, playful, loving girl whom Will had fallen impossibly in love with. Her lower lip trembled ever so slightly. Her eyes blinked away a potential falling tear. But then her face hardened.

"I don't think I love you anymore," she said.

The stars in the sky might as well have come crashing down. It would have been less painful.

"You don't . . . *think* . . . ?"

She amended what she'd said. Like a hammer hitting an anvil.

"I don't love you anymore."

There are sanctuaries in the heart, places to take refuge, to clasp comfort. But no such place existed for Will now. His world was collapsing, all the good feelings he had stored in his heart twisting into ugliness.

"I don't believe you," he whispered.

He had no idea where the words came from. Because he *did* believe her; his broken heart told him so.

"I'm sorry, Will. But when I went to the dark side, I guess something inside me just died."

The truth hung in the air between them, acrid and foul. Will's hands were shaking. He spoke softly.

"Maybe . . . maybe it will come back to life. Like your sight . . ."

A slender thread of hope, on which only a fool would hang his heart. And yet there it was.

"Maybe," she said.

But they both knew the chances of such a resurrection were slim.

"Look, Will, I'm really tired . . . I need to sleep," she said.

She rolled over, turning her back to him. Slowly, Will walked out of the room. He told himself he wasn't walking out of her life, that it wasn't over. But he knew better.

When he went downstairs and looked outside again, he saw that the night had put on her darkest veil. In fact, he thought that this was the darkest night he had ever seen in his entire life.

He conjured a mental picture of the Dark Lord. This was all his fault. He pictured killing the Dark Lord—*yes, my father, my father!*— over and over, a loop of gory retribution going round and round. It made his blood boil. So when Loreli stirred on the couch and Will looked over at her, his eyes filled with loathing. This was her fault, too.

He had many scores to settle, and no forgiveness to render. He almost wished that some of these island punks would hurry up and come after him, because when they did he could strike them down unhesitatingly, without mercy. He was a pressure cooker ready to blow.

Will gritted his teeth. He knew he needed to catch some shut-eye. Compared to the average human teenager, he needed very little sleep, but he did need *some*, or else he'd crash and burn like anybody else. Something told him that this island was the worst possible place for that to happen.

"Everything okay?" asked Rudy.

Will was hard to read, but Rudy had been hanging out with him for awhile now, and he could tell his friend was in a bad way. But Will was not about to go all Oprah on Rudy now; all he needed was a few minutes of sleep. He thought about waking Loreli up to stand sentry, but he still didn't trust her.

"I'm gonna crash on the couch a few minutes. Keep your attention focused, okay?" said Will. "If you see *anything*, you wake me."

"You got it, man," said Rudy.

Rudy blinked and squinted out into the night. He put himself on full alert, even though he was dead tired and felt like his eyelids were made of iron. He wouldn't let Will down. He glanced over and saw that Will's eyes were already closed. Rudy looked back outside and his mind began to drift.

Up in her room, Emily opened her eyes. She'd heard everything Will and Natalie had said to one another. She felt a pressure on her chest, felt as though she'd somehow slipped into a parallel universe where down was up and black was white. *I don't love you anymore.* Her sister's words still echoed in the room, resonant with ruin. Emily gazed at her twin. She was still as stone, no tears of regret rolling down her cheeks. Had she truly meant what she'd said? It should have been easy to tell because all Emily should have had to do was to look into her own heart.

She'd *always* felt what Natalie felt. In a small place in her heart, she, too, had been in love with Will Hunter. Twin sisters, twin hearts, beating together and now breaking together. Emily could always feel Nat's grief and pain, her pleasure and joy. But now all she felt was turmoil, as though a great war had erupted within her sister's psyche. She knew this because her own heart beat anxiously, like a bird fluttering in a glass ball. Emily had to find out what was really going on. They couldn't survive like this. She resolved to talk to Natalie first thing in the morning. Then she shut her eyes and pictured herself on a sailboat, felt the warm sun shining down on her body. In less than a minute she was asleep again.

The White Island demonteens convened deep in the woods surrounding the old Victorian home. A dense fog carpeted the forest floor, so that the demonteens appeared to be standing on clouds.

They stood well apart, at intervals of twenty yards. It was a chilling sight, this group of teenagers standing calmly in the woods at night. From five hundred feet up in the sky, it would have been clear that they had formed a pattern, what Jasper had called the Gate of Death. It was, of course, the Dark Lord's most beloved geometric shape: a pentagram.

The forest was deathly quiet. Few nighttime creatures were stirring. The aberration was coming. Boone was adjacent to Jasper, and he had Killer on a leash next to him. He knelt down to pet the dog, rubbing his thick head and whispering to him.

"Good boy, Killer, such a good dog."

Jasper looked over at Boone and nodded. Boone nodded back. Then he let go of the leash. The big dog cut loose with a howl and began running toward Janie Walker's place. Boone watched him go. He'd had the dog since they were both pups, and he had a feeling that he'd never see him again.

"I'm gonna miss you, boy . . . ," he said quietly.

Killer picked up his pace. In a few moments, a dozen timber wolves appeared out of the pale grey mist. Their teeth bared, they joined Killer, moving as swift as shadows, their heads low to the ground.

Over in the recliner, Loreli began snoring. The sound woke Rudy up, and he turned to look at her. He was continually amazed at how beautiful she was. But Emily was beautiful, too, and his song was for her all the way. Thinking about how and when he would kiss her, he turned and looked back out the window and his skin started to crawl. *This must be a nightmare*, he thought. In the distance was Killer, the monstrosity of a dog he'd seen at the diner, and behind him were a dozen wolves. It looked like the dog was leading them because when he paused on a small rise about twenty yards from the house, the wolves all paused, too. No way could this be anything but a bad dream.

"Wake up, man . . . ," Rudy said to himself. He shook his head and breathed deeply. "Come on, dude, wake up!"

Will had fallen into a hard sleep, the kind that grabs you and yanks you down into the black void and doesn't want to let go. But something was happening up there on the surface, and Will knew, somewhere deep in his brain, that he needed to claw his way back up to consciousness. He could feel sleep fighting him, and then felt what he thought were the claws of the Dark Lord himself on his shoulders. He jolted upright.

"What?" he said.

It was Rudy, shaking him awake.

"We've got company!"

Will turned and looked at the front window just as Killer came crashing through, showering glass everywhere. The beast landed, his right ear cut and bleeding, hanging down. He shook, and blood splattered everywhere. He raised his head and howled, then looked over at Will and took two bounding leaps. He was arcing through the air when Will rolled off the couch and unstrapped his Megashocker. Thankfully he'd set it to charge when he'd flopped on the couch, so when he brought it upward with a powerful stroke, it was sizzling hot and breached Killer's shoulder, tearing through his muscles and scapula.

Killer's eyes blazed a hot red. He was wounded but not down, not by a long shot. Will yanked on the Megashocker, pulling it back through the dog's scapula bone.

Killer flipped sideways and began to morph, his paws growing larger, his teeth elongating, every muscle in his body doubling in size.

Rudy's eyes were huge. "Um . . . I don't think this is a regular dog, Will!"

"You think?" said Loreli sarcastically. She'd woken up when the window broke and, seeing Killer, had taken cover behind the couch.

Three wolves bounded in through the jagged, broken picture window and landed with tremendous force, their expanding claws tearing into the old polished hardwood floor. Like Killer, their eyes burned fiery red and their growls rattled the pictures on the walls.

Rudy was ready to wet his pants. "Will, what the heck *are* they?"

"Demonwolves," said Will. "Take cover!"

Rudy dove to the floor, rolled to the fireplace, and grabbed an iron poker. He turned and swung it with all his might. He got lucky and connected with the jaw of a charging wolf.

Loreli reached out for Will, shouting above the roaring animals. "Will, my duster!"

Time crawled. Will stared at his treacherous half-sister. He didn't—couldn't—trust her, but her life was at stake here too. And he didn't think he could take this threat alone—not without Rudy getting hurt, or something getting past him and up the stairs to Natalie and Emily. So he grabbed a backpack and tossed it to her.

She opened it with one deft move and whipped her duster out and on. It was still dirty and bloodstained from her escape from the Dark Lord, but at least now she was armed. She pulled out a small ceramic orb and threw it hard at the front door. It exploded into an expanding ball of green gas that caused the demonwolves to blink their glowing ruby eyes and snap at some unseen prey. Rudy heard a scream from upstairs.

"Emily!"

He ran for the stairs, leaping over a disoriented demonwolf.

Will continued to battle with Killer using the Megashocker, but the dog was immense. When Will thrust the weapon up through the roof of the creature's mouth, it shook with rage and pulled the shocker right out of Will's grasp. Without a second to lose, Will pulled the Blaster Magnum out of its holster on his hip. As Killer chomped at him, he dropped and rolled sideways and came to a stop, firing—*blam-blam!* The shots were thunderous and shook the house, but both missed, and Killer leapt through the air, all four hundred pounds of him ready to pin Will to the floor and rip his throat out.

The room filled with a whistling sound.

Zzzzzzzap! A deadly tendril of electricity lashed out, wrapping around Killer's head, jerking it sideways. Will quick-rolled out of the way as Killer's massive body slammed into the floor next to him. The dog's face was lacerated, but still it scrambled to its feet, and Will dove over the back of the couch. Killer leapt again, and again the room filled with the whistling sound. Killer was caught in midair by three of the white-hot electric strands, and they wrapped around his neck, tightened, and sliced his head off. It landed with a *thunk* next to Will, its jaws still snapping madly. Will grabbed one of Janie Walker's painted rocks and jammed it in Killer's mouth. Then he stood up and saw that Loreli had pulled one of his weapons out of a backpack.

"Thanks."

"Don't mention it," she said. "What do you call this thing?"

"Deathwhip," said Will.

"Nice."

Loreli cracked the whip again, this time connecting with one of the disoriented demonwolves and cutting its tail off. The beast shrieked, then charged. Will took it out with a couple of shots from his Blaster Magnum, blowing its demonwolf brains all over the ceiling. As with all demon creatures, the demonwolf, when it died, disintegrated into a swirling mass of heated particles that burned out in two seconds. As two more demonwolves knocked down the front door, Will reloaded the Blaster Magnum and fired off six shots. The reports from the gun sounded like the big guns on a battleship and seemed to do almost as much damage, blowing the wolves away and blasting four immense holes in the front wall of the house. Will and Loreli heard screams from upstairs. Loreli quickly cracked the whip, fending off another duo of demonwolves. She yelled to Will: "Go!"

He did, running across the living room, snagging a backpack, and then taking the stairs three at a time. *Natalie!* In the upstairs hallway, a demonwolf came crashing down through the ceiling onto Will's back, knocking him to the floor. Will pulled a Flareblade from his side holster and thrust it upward, gutting the creature, who howled so loudly as it died that a nearby vase burst into tiny fragments.

Will raced into Natalie and Emily's bedroom, where the twins were crouched low by the bed next to the wall. Rudy stood in front of them, swinging the fireplace poker at an attacking demonwolf that must have come in through the window. The wolf was smart. He ducked low and came up at Rudy so fast that he knocked the poker out of Rudy's hand. Then he bit Rudy on the arm.

"Ahhhh!"

Will was across the room in a flash, pulling the demonwolf off of Rudy and slitting its throat with a Flareblade. As the wolf's body slumped to the floor, sparking and smoking, Will whipped out a healing patch and tossed it to Rudy, who slapped it directly on his wound as he got down next to Natalie and Emily. Above them, the ceiling was being torn apart as more demonwolves scratched their way through.

Will holstered the Flareblade, then took out the Shock Bombardier, set it on level 9, flicked it on to charge, and waited three seconds as the room filled with a high-pitched whine. Then—*KA-BOOM!* A massive shockwave radiated upward. It felt like an earthquake. The whole house shook. Demonwolves were knocked off the roof and fell to the ground below, howling in rage. Will looked out the window and saw even more demonwolves, pack after pack, racing toward the house. They were under siege. In the distance Will thought he saw the shadow of several humans. The island teens? He couldn't tell. But it was time to take advantage of that cellar. He reached out for the twins.

"Come on!"

Natalie and Emily jumped up, and after a moment's hesitation, Will tossed Rudy the Blaster Magnum.

"Be *careful* with that!" he shouted.

KA-BLAM! Just catching it, Rudy had inadvertently fired off a shot that whizzed by Will's head and took out one of Janie Walker's insufferably cute driftwood wall sculptures.

"Sorry!" yelped Rudy.

They ran down the stairs to find Loreli throwing another of her explosive orbs at a horde of charging demonwolves. The orb exploded with a tremendous *bang!* The ensuing gas cloud created a whirling vortex of minute razor-sharp particles that sliced and diced, tormenting the wolves, who yelped and snapped at the air around them.

Will ran to the cellar door and yanked it open. Natalie, Emily, and Rudy went through, and Will tossed their backpacks after them. He yelled to Loreli:

"Let's go! Down here!"

She'd sustained some minor flesh wounds and was all too willing to join Will in the cellar. As he slammed the door behind them, a demonwolf crashed into it. The door shook but held.

Will knew it wouldn't be long before the horde clawed and chomped their way through the door, so, after tossing Loreli a healing patch, he unzipped one of the backpacks and removed a small device that looked like a futuristic air horn. It was an Ultrasonic Sound Blaster that sent out sound waves via powerful piezoelectric emitters.

The wolves continued ramming and clawing at the door. Will switched on the sound blaster. It took a few seconds to power up, and then emitted a high frequency sound wave that humans couldn't hear—but animals could. The demonwolves paused in their fervor, their ears perking up, then flattening. They began circling, then attacking each other in their agony, their sharp claws and teeth gnashing and tearing and quickly drawing blood from the weakest of the pack as they converged on her, releasing all their pain into her, ripping her to shreds. After a few moments they could take no more and retreated from the sound, scrambling out of the old Victorian.

Will looked over at Loreli and watched as she tended to her wounds. So far, she was doing a good job of acting like she was part of the team. The question was, could he trust her? It *seemed* like she was sincere, but she'd certainly seemed sincere before. He thought about all the ways she'd betrayed him—taking his blood, using it to resurrect the Dark Lord. Driving him and Natalie apart. Tricking Natalie into turning into a demon. Trying to kill him. She *acted* like she regretted having done those things, but did she really? Maybe she *had* changed sides, maybe she *was* on their team now. But even if he did choose to trust her, at least for the moment, that didn't mean he had to forgive her.

Out in the fog-shrouded woods, Jasper and the others watched as the demonwolves rushed past them covered in blood. Jasper smiled, mistakenly concluding that the blood on the wolves' coats was that of the human intruders. He turned to Boone and nodded.

Boone ran through the woods until he reached Janie Walker's place. He opened the door and stepped inside. The room was silent and empty. No sign of the visitors. But all that remained of Killer was his collar. Boone picked it up. Rage and sorrow flooded his brain. He looked around and, seeing all the blood, deduced that the wolf attack had been successful, that the demonic beasts had killed and eaten the human intruders. Boone took solace in that.

He ran back and reported to Jasper. Jasper turned to the other demonteens and gave a thumbs up as he began walking back toward Plorret's Field, where they'd parked their trucks and cars. There, they opened beers and cranked up heavy metal music. They drank and smoked and made out. The inevitable drunken fistfights broke out. Without fear of recrimination—other than by the Voice—they were running wild.

Jasper pulled Wendy into his arms and bit her on the neck. She squealed in mock horror.

"You seem happy," she said.

"It's all good," said Jasper. "They're taken care of. The threat is over. We're going to get it done."

But Jasper and the other island teens had badly miscalculated. It was going to cost them.

Chapter Seventeen: Hammering Man

The Dark Lord stood over the pot, staring down at the burbling golden liquid metal. It was ready to be cast, and for this he needed a great artist. The mightiest sword the world would ever see deserved no less. So he donned a hooded robe and stepped over to a shaft. Raising his arms, he rode an updraft to street level. When he came sweeping out of the alley on First Avenue, the few souls whose eyes were assaulted by his ugly visage figured that he was just another crazy homeless wretch in search of tonight's boozy refuge.

The Prince of Darkness was in a fine mood, so he refrained from causing any sudden heart attacks or making anyone break out in boils, as he had done with Job, the pious freak. He was on a mission. He had battled his heavenly adversary for control of Earth since the dawn of time, enraged about being thrown out of Heaven, and he felt that a final victory was nigh. The world was tipping in his favor. All one had to do was look around.

He strode up Skid Row until he hit the intersection of First and University, where he stopped and looked up at the forty-eight-foot metal sculpture, "Hammering Man." During the day, Hammering Man's left arm held a hammer and came down slowly once every fifteen seconds, symbolically striking a blow for the working class. But now, late at night, Hammering man's hammer was still.

As the Dark Lord looked at the statue, he was pleased to see the man he'd come to find, a local sculptor, Jared Wasserman, an introspective intellectual with thick glasses and a head of wild hair. Jared had been hired by the city to make repairs to Hammering Man. A true sociophobic, he preferred to work at night and had lights set up around the statue.

"I'd like a word, please," said the Dark Lord.

Jared was busy tinkering, only slightly annoyed at what he thought was another Skid Row loser asking him for money. Jared did what he always did in these situations, repeating his inner mantra: *Ignore them; don't make eye contact.* He stayed on his ladder, working a bolt loose with a crescent wrench, but then he felt a sudden pain shoot up his backbone. Thinking he might be having a heart attack, he clutched his chest, which caused him to teeter on the ladder. Arms pinwheeling, he lost his balance and fell hard to the sidewalk, croaking out in pain as he sustained a severe bruise to his right hip. He spewed out a string of curses and heard a man—or what sounded vaguely like a man—laugh a rumbling laugh.

"Excellent. Such poetry!"

"Who the hell are you?" asked Jared, looking up at the tall figure in the robe.

The Dark Lord's eyes glowed from within the hood. He smiled. Jared felt a sensation, like worms curling around his spinal cord.

"Your new employer," said the tall figure.

Seeing the glowing eyes, and realizing he was in the presence of unspeakable evil, Jared began to tremble. He was too wounded to run. He wondered if the next words he spoke would be his last.

"Please . . . I'm in pain."

"As are we all," said the Dark Lord. "I will pay you well." He dropped a large diamond onto the sidewalk. Jared eyed it but did not pick it up.

"I don't want your money. I don't want any trouble," said Jared.

"Ah. I see you will require alternative motivation to perform the necessary work."

The Dark Lord worked up a formidable snoot full of phlegm, then spat it onto the feet of Hammering Man. The phlegm infused the metal, caused it to shimmer and, much to the astonishment of anyone who bothered to look, the giant metal man lifted his feet and began stomping down the sidewalk, wildly swinging his hammer. The first to be hit was Guy Major, an obese con artist and pickpocket who had worked Skid Row for years. Hammering Man's mallet caught him behind his right ear and split his skull in two. Guy fell, hitting the sidewalk like a bag of pork fat.

Jared trembled at the power of the creature he was facing as the many small sins he'd committed in his lifetime raced through his mind. He was being punished; he must be.

The Dark Lord bellowed with laughter as Hammering Man stomped away, cutting a bloody swath down First Avenue. Then the Dark Lord lifted Jared up and slung him over his shoulder.

"I'll do whatever you want, just, my wife and daughter . . . Please don't hurt them!" he said.

"Your wife is a cheating slut and your daughter's a drugged-out imbecile," said the Dark Lord. "Why would I harm them? They're already mine."

Again the Dark Lord laughed. He was in a fine mood. Each step he took was moving him closer to bringing the Sword of Armageddon into his possession. What followed from that would be the Black Prince's version of Nirvana: the end of mankind's rule on Earth. His son was in for the biggest shock of his young life.

An hour later, after the necessary tools had been stolen by a gang of demonteens, Jared Wasserman was in the Under City, drinking whiskey and working on a mold for the handle of an exceptionally large sword.

• • •

After the demonwolf attack ceased, Will waited for a good fifteen minutes, listening. Then he cautiously opened the cellar door and looked around at the interior of the house. He saw the blood on the walls, broken windows, torn and tattered drapes, slashed and over-turned furniture, and holes in the wall where he'd fired the Blaster Magnum. Someone was going to have their hands full cleaning up this mess.

"Will?"

He turned and saw the four of them looking up at him. It was Emily who had spoken.

"What do we do now?"

"Stay down there. I'll be right back."

"I'll go with you," said Loreli.

"Stay," said Will, holding up a hand.

Loreli made a face but stayed put.

Will moved quickly through the house, assessing the damage. The place was really torn apart, but they'd managed to survive and keep possession of their weapons backpacks as well. Will grabbed as many blankets and pillows as he could carry, then retreated into the wine cellar.

"Everybody get some sleep," he said, passing out the pillows and blankets.

They all lay down. The floor was cold and hard, but after the ordeal they'd just survived, they were so exhausted that the concrete felt like a pillow-top mattress. They fell asleep quickly and slept for hours.

In the morning, Will was shocked when he woke up alone. Where were the others? Taken by the demonwolves? By the White Island teens? Overcome with panic, he jumped up and grabbed the weapons backpack closest to him, then ran for the stairs. That's when he smelled something cooking.

When he got upstairs, he found Rudy, Loreli, Natalie, and Emily in the kitchen scarfing down a huge breakfast of eggs, toast, toaster waffles with plenty of butter and syrup, and peanut butter and strawberry jam sandwiches. Rudy had the Blaster Magnum on the table in front of him, right next to the Mrs. Butterworth syrup bottle. Will set the backpack on the table.

"We didn't want to wake you. Figured you needed your sleep, captain," said Rudy.

Will took a seat. Natalie put a plate of eggs and waffles in front of him. He stared at the food.

"You'd better eat." she said. "I have a feeling we're going to have an interesting day ahead of us." Her voice was totally neutral.

He tried smiling at her, hoping for a reaction. "Thanks."

She just held his gaze for a moment and then turned away. Last night, before he'd fallen asleep, he'd hoped she'd get cold and maybe come and spoon with him—for warmth if nothing else—but no such luck. Now here she was being her new distant self again, even after they'd nearly lost their lives to a huge pack of bloodthirsty demon-wolves just a few hours ago.

Sending her a last troubled look, Will started on his breakfast, eating quickly as he gathered his thoughts. He knew he had to come up with a plan of action. He noticed that Natalie and Emily had donned identical clothes and both had their hair back in ponytails, though he'd never seen them dress the same before. It would difficult for someone who didn't know them to tell them apart. What was going on? He supposed he'd find out soon enough.

They finished breakfast in silence, with the exception of Rudy's moaning when he took a particularly good bite, which seemed to be every other one. When the last fork was laid down, everyone looked at Will. They were waiting for him to break down the coming day for them. He wiped his lips with a napkin and tried not to think about Natalie. He knew he had to stop trying to second-guess her and focus on the task at hand—finding the blade of the Sword of Armageddon before the White Island demonteens did.

Rudy spoke up. "The attack last night . . . those monster wolves. They were led by that big dude's dog, Killer. I saw them outside. It definitely looked like he was, you know, leading the attack," said Rudy.

"Which probably means his owner was behind the whole thing," said Will. "Which means they want us dead."

When he thought about what almost happened to Natalie—to all of them—his anger returned, a red curtain of rage that started to fall over his vision. He closed his eyes and breathed, letting the feeling pass right through him.

"So why not just kill us?" asked Rudy.

Will opened his eyes.

"I guess they wanted it to look like some kind of bizarre animal attack," said Will. "Did you notice how nervous they got about Rudy's camcorder? I think they're kind of freaked out about the whole 'real-time video uplink to the Internet' idea."

"You're welcome," said Rudy.

"Yeah, you probably bought us a little time. But sooner or later, they're going to figure out what we're after, and then it won't matter. They'll do whatever they have to get rid of us," said Will.

An ominous look was passed around.

"The good news is everybody's in one piece," Will continued. "Now I have to find that blade."

"I was thinking," said Natalie. "It's stupid for us to go tromping around all clumped together. If they don't want us here, and that certainly seems to be the case, then being in a big group just makes us an easier target."

"Plus, it looks pretty suspicious," added Loreli.

Will had been thinking the same thing. He had a solution. He pointed at the Blaster Magnum on the kitchen table in front of Rudy.

"Rudy, you think you know how to fire that thing with any accuracy now?"

Rudy flicked off the safety on the Blaster Magnum and pointed it across the room. He was about to fire when Will gently interceded, pushing the barrel of the Magnum down with his index finger.

"I'll take your word for it. I want you to stay here in the cellar with them," Will indicated Natalie and Emily, "while I take Loreli, and we go poke around."

"Second part of the plan is good," said Emily.

"But the first part sucks," said Natalie. "We have a plan, too. Emily and I are going to go see if we can find an adult. If we can, then I bet we'll find out what's going on in the 'friendliest little town in Puget Sound.'"

Will was already shaking his head no. No way was he going to let the twins go traipsing off by themselves. It wouldn't be safe. He couldn't risk it.

"And no Rudy," said Natalie. "Just the two of us." When Will opened his mouth to protest, she added, "We'll be fine."

"Sometimes being a twin has its advantages," said Emily, her voice purposefully identical to her sisters. Standing next to each other, looking so incredibly similar, they had a weird, almost vertigo-like effect on Will, like his brain was telling him he was seeing double so he must be dizzy.

"Also, we want some weapons," said Natalie.

"Will, we respect you, we admire you, and we owe our lives to you," said Emily. "But you can be a little thick sometimes. We keep telling you we're in this thing together come hell or high water, and you keep treating us like fair damsels in distress or whatever."

"So just get over yourself and pull your macho head out of your rump and cough up some firepower," said Natalie.

Rudy was watching with his jaw dropped, his eyes blinking.

Loreli was smiling. "You know they can't be any worse with the guns than Rudy is," she said.

"Hey!" said Rudy.

Natalie pushed the weapons backpack that Will had put on the table over to him. Will was about to protest, but he knew it would be futile. Once Natalie made up her mind about something, there was no changing it. He'd known that since they'd first met and she'd insisted upon teaming up with him to find Emily. If he didn't help her, chances were she and Emily would sneak out anyway after he left. He didn't have a lot of faith in Rudy's ability to keep them there against their will. So he unzipped the backpack, reached inside, and pulled out a set of handheld weapons no bigger than a deck of cards.

"These are Vibroslammers. They fit over your fingers, like this," said Will, demonstrating. "You activate them with this blue switch, and when you want to fire, you press the red button."

He pointed the Vibroslammers at one of Janie Walker's larger painted rocks—this one masquerading as a beaver—and pressed the red button. An invisible wave of vibrations blasted out of the device and knocked the rock across the room, where it slammed into the fireplace hearth, cracking a brick.

"Excellent," said Natalie, reaching for the Vibroslammer. Will withheld it.

"Be careful," he said.

"Duh," said Natalie. She grabbed the Vibroslammer from Will, picked the other one up, and handed it to Emily, who slid it onto her fingers carefully, getting the feel of it. Satisfied, she took it off and put it in her pocket.

Though Rudy tried to talk the twins into letting him go with them, Emily put the kybosh on that. She wanted some alone time with her sister to talk about what had happened with Will. So Rudy would be going with Will and Loreli, headed to the place where they figured they might run into the most teenagers: Bingham High School.

Will went out into Janie Walker's garage and, since he hadn't been able to find the keys, hot-wired her Jeep Wagoneer. Then he and Rudy and Loreli climbed in and drove into town.

Chapter Eighteen: School's Out

Will, Rudy, and Loreli pulled into the Bingham High School parking lot. It looked like someone had dropped a bomb. Cars and trucks were parked all helter-skelter. Nobody had bothered to pay attention to the white-lined spaces.

"Parking anarchy. I like it," said Rudy.

They parked the Wagoneer in a marked space and got out. Will flipped the hood up on his jacket. Loreli and Rudy did the same. They looked like the other teenagers on the island. Will and Rudy were wearing backpacks. With Loreli in between them, they walked toward the entrance of the main school building. They passed the headless mascot and discovered that the unfortunate creature was named Barney the Bear. They kept walking, drawing cursory looks from kids, but since they had their hoods up they didn't ring any alarm bells. They went to the front entrance and glanced up. Carved in stone above the doors were the words RESPECT, HONOR, INTEGRITY. They went in.

The first weird thing they noticed was the big screen monitor with a sign over it that read BINGHAM HIGH TV: OUR STATION, OUR PRIDE. Instead of the usual boring informational slideshow about athletic events and extracurricular activities, the station was showing *Night of the Living Dead*. The zombies were winning.

Will kept walking. Rudy and Loreli followed, their eyes searching. They passed the trophy case, which had been broken into. Most of the awards and trophies had been trashed or defaced. The plaque that identified Bingham High as a WASHINGTON STATE DISTINGUISHED SCHOOL had a jock strap draped ignobly over it. Rudy shuddered. So far, despite its awesome taste in films, this school was making him feel like he had ants crawling in his clothes.

They rounded a corner into the main hallway, which was littered with debris: pizza boxes, broken bongs, beer and soda cans, underwear, Barney the Bear's head, a bicycle with no rear wheel. They passed the lunchroom and looked inside. It was a disaster area too. The dishes that weren't broken were in a huge pile in the corner, apparently tossed there from a great distance. The floor was a minefield of spilled and discarded food items: chicken bones and half-eaten hot dogs and squares of red, green, and yellow Jell-O.

"Looks like the janitor has the day off," said Rudy.

There were a few students in the food line, helping themselves to pizza and brownies. There wasn't a vegetable in sight. Against the far wall stood a half-dozen vending machines. The locks had been broken, and a kid was helping himself to some Sun Chips and a Coke. There weren't many of either left.

Will motioned for Rudy and Loreli to keep moving with him, and they continued their journey through the bizarre school. Down a hallway they came upon a couple of girls, a blonde and brunette, who were behind a counter at a window with a little plaque on it that said ADMINISTRATION. The blonde, Mari Wilson, was giving the brunette, Jackie Gatewood, a henna tattoo—a goat's skull—and they had a big can of Red Bull, which smelled like they'd spiked it with a pint of vodka. They looked up at Will and Rudy and Loreli. Mari jumped.

"Geez! You guys scared me! Oh god, look, I messed up! Shit, now I'm gonna have to start over."

"Tragic," said Will.

As the girls stared at Will, Rudy, and Loreli, it slowly occurred to them that they'd never seen any of them before. They must be the interlopers that everyone had been buzzing about. Mari was taken with Will's good looks and his weirdly handsome eyes, but because he also looked kind of scary, she flinched when he took a step closer and spoke.

"Where's the principal?" he asked.

The girls looked at each other like they were trying to decide which one of them was the better liar.

"He's . . . around," said Mari.

"Yeah, he's doing his rounds," said Jackie.

"Oh, okay," said Will, playing dumb. "We'll just go find him."

Jackie didn't like this idea. "But . . . you can't," she said.

Obviously these two brainiacs were supposed to have been the lookouts and had blown their assignment big time. Mari did what she thought was some quick thinking.

"You . . . don't have a hall pass," she said.

"I won't tell if you won't," said Will, turning on the charm.

The girls' eyes widened. They looked at each other and went for their Blackberries.

Will was over the counter in less than a second. He grabbed both phones and smashed them together so hard their screens cracked. Then he dropped them on the table. Rudy picked one up and put it to his ear.

"I don't think you have service," he said.

Jackie's eyes bulged out. The veins in her forehead throbbed. "You son of a bitch!"

Concentrating, she caused the wall clock to come flying off and hit Will in the back of the head.

Loreli's eyes went wide.

"Telekinesis . . . ," she said, in awe.

Mari stared hard at a metal stapler, and it levitated. Rudy ducked as the thing zinged over his head and banged into the wall behind him. Jackie glared at a drawer and it flew open. Loreli pulled a tiny glass ball out of her duster and smashed it on the desk. The pink gas cloud made both girls cough and then slump over, unconscious. Will looked at Loreli disapprovingly.

"I was going to ask them some questions."

"Gee, Will, I'm sorry. I wanted to put them down before they got to the scissors."

Loreli pointed to the open drawer and the half-dozen lethal-looking pairs of scissors lying within.

"Let's go," said Will.

They moved down the hallway.

"Telekinesis? How?" asked Will, looking at Loreli.

"Just because I made it rain Satan's blood doesn't mean I have all the answers," she said. "It's probably just another one of his paranormal mutations, a power he chose to bless them with."

"But why *that* power?"

"I don't know. Let's hope it was an isolated case. If they all have it, we're going to be in for a shitstorm," said Loreli.

"I'm betting on the shitstorm," said Rudy.

They heard some rock and roll as they were passing a door marked TEACHERS' LOUNGE. Will signaled for Rudy and Loreli to hang back, then gently opened the door and peeked inside. A couple were going at it hot and heavy on the couch. Will decided against interrupting them and closed the door as quietly as he'd opened it. They kept going.

They'd walked another twenty feet when—BANG!—Rudy almost jumped out of his skin. The noise came from a locker right next to him. Someone was inside. He looked at Will.

"Why don't you knock on the door and see if anyone's home?" said Will.

Rudy knocked on the locker.

"Hello?"

Silence. Then a small voice said, "Can you let me out please? Twenty-nine, twelve, seventeen."

Rudy dialed the combination and was about to open the locker when Will put his hand out and stopped him, reaching into a backpack and pulling out a metallic glove which he slipped onto his hand. Then he nodded to Rudy.

Rudy opened the locker. A skinny, goofy-looking kid tumbled out onto the floor.

"Thanks. I've been in there since yesterday," said the kid.

He had tufts of brown hair that had once been spiked but now just jutted out at odd angles.

"My name's Garf. Short for Garfield. But everyone calls me Frag. You know, Garf spelled backward? I've never seen you guys before. Are you the new kids?"

"Bingo," said Rudy, though he wasn't sure being the new kid was going to get them quite the same kind of attention here that it had back in Seattle. Frag reached up a small hand attached to the skinniest wrist Rudy'd ever seen on a boy. Rudy took his hand and helped him to his feet.

"I'm Rudy. This is Will and this is . . ."

Frag was gawking at Loreli like he'd never seen a girl up close before. He made a move to hug her and she took a step back.

"Whoa. Back it up, partner," she said. Frag dropped his arms, looking disappointed.

". . . Loreli," Rudy finished.

"We're looking for the principal," said Will.

Frag blinked.

"Um . . . I don't know where he is."

"Okay, how about the vice principal?"

Frag shook his head quickly.

"Teacher?" Nothing. "Custodian?"

Frag just kept shaking his head. He wasn't prepared for this. Subterfuge was counterintuitive to his nature. He was sweating like crazy and starting to shake. His eyes found a big metal trashcan, and it began to wobble.

Oh, great, they've all got the power, thought Will. Loreli had picked up on it too and was already moving between Frag and the trashcan. The wobbling stopped.

"Why so nervous, Frag?" said Will.

"I . . . I . . . I'm n-n-not nervous."

"Of course you are," said Will. "You're nervous because this whole island's gone apeshit and you know why. And you also know that I'm going to find out everything I want to know. Because you're going to tell me."

Will reached over with his left hand and flicked the switch on the metal glove he was wearing on his right. It began to hum.

Frag eyed the device. "Wh-wha-what is that?"

"Paralyzer Glove," said Will. "How about you tell us a story?"

Will reached out and touched Frag's shoulder. A current passed from the glove to Frag's body. He shook wildly for two seconds until Will let go of him.

Frag was on the verge of a total meltdown. He slumped against the lockers, slid to the floor, and started blubbering, cowering, covering his face with his hands.

"Why are you picking on me?" he whimpered. But he was a sly little fox. Through his fingers and through Loreli's legs, the metal trashcan was in his line of sight again, and he was concentrating with all his might as he pretended to cry.

They heard it in time, but barely. The trashcan had levitated behind them and came zooming across the hall like a rocket. Will ducked. The trashcan clipped Loreli and Rudy, spinning them sideways. Then it careened off Will, knocking him down. Trash was flying and dust was swirling. By the time they all got to their feet again, Frag was halfway down the hall and rounding a corner. Loreli started after him.

"Let him go," said Will.

Loreli looked annoyed, but nodded.

Will knew the feeling. White Island was getting on his nerves in a big way. He wanted to kick some ass just to let off some steam.

In room 108, Darcy Lakes was sitting at the desk up front. She swiveled in her chair when the door opened and Will, Rudy, and Loreli came in. There were several kids in this classroom, mostly girls with a smattering of boys, and Will wondered if they were all infected, if they were all demonteens.

"What class is this?" he asked.

Everyone looked at Darcy.

"Um. English 201," she said. "Who are you?"

"The new kids," said Will. "Where's the teacher?" He picked up the little wooden triangle on the desk that had Miss Winter painted on it in cursive letters. "Miss Winter?"

"She went to the bathroom."

"Right. And she asked you to take over until she came back."

"That's right," said Darcy.

"Okay," said Will, "we'll wait for her."

He picked up a stack of essays from Miss Winter's desk.

Darcy looked furious. "Wait a second, you can't just come in here and—"

Will put a finger to his lips. "Shhhh . . ."

He fanned through the stack. Every one was marked A++. He speed-read through the first few, then looked quizzically at Darcy.

"Letters to your parents? This is an assignment?" he said.

"Yes," said Darcy.

Will nodded, then started reading one out loud.

"Dear Mom and Dad, I never in a million years thought I would be writing a letter like this one. I know it must be hard for you to understand what happened, and I don't blame you if you hate me. I promise you it will all be over as soon as we find what we're looking for, and then we can be together again. Hopefully before my birthday because I really want a PlayStation and the new *Demon Hunter*."

Will couldn't help but smile at the mention of his game. But not for long. As he'd been reading the letter, the students had been squirming unhappily in their seats. Rudy and Loreli could practically see the angry energy working up inside them. Will scanned their faces.

"Who wrote this?"

Of course no one spoke up. But one kid looked even more agitated than his comrades. Randy Pierce. Coke-bottle glasses, his left arm in a cast. Will approached him, carrying the letter.

"Was it you? Are you the birthday boy?"

Will looked down and saw that the handwriting in the letter matched the writing in Randy's spiral notebook.

"'As soon as we find what we're looking for'? What are you looking for?"

"None of your damn—"

Randy yelped in pain as Will grabbed the back of his neck with the Paralyser Glove.

"I'd like you to tell me," Will said, without releasing his grip.

Randy tried to take a swing at Will, but he was overcome with pain and could only crumple sideways.

"What are you looking for, Randy? The blade?"

A girl had stood up in the back clenching her fists. "Leave him alone or—"

"Or what?" asked Will, as he applied more voltage to Randy's neck.

"Or you're going to die," said the girl, quite calmly.

He ignored her. "What are you looking for?" Will asked Randy, putting more pressure on his neck. "Have you found it? Where is it?" Randy still refused to speak. He was starting to pass out from the pain.

"Down!" screamed Loreli as one of the metal desks flipped into the air—three girls were staring at it, their eyes wild with rage—and then right at Will. He released Randy and ducked into a crouch as the desk smashed into the blackboard behind him, shattering it. Will knew he could have just had his head taken off.

He rose up out of his crouch. "Is that any way to welcome the new kids?" he said.

The girls were focusing their eyes and evil energy on more desks, which were rising into the air and hovering, vibrating like jets on the deck of an aircraft carrier about to take off. And then take off they did, rocketing across the room toward Will.

But this time he was ready, as was Rudy. Rudy fired the Blaster Magnum—successfully, for once—blowing two desks to smithereens. Another whizzed at Will, who cut it in half with his Megashocker. Rudy kept firing—*BLAM! BLAM!*—and another desk bit the dust. One flew across the room at Loreli, who dove out of the way. Will's attention was drawn to her, and he didn't see the next desk coming until it was almost too late. He bent time and lurched backward, but the desk's metal leg caught him on the chin. The shock reverberated up his jaw into his brain. He felt like he'd just been tagged by a heavyweight.

He was momentarily vulnerable. Another desk flew right at him. Rudy used the last load of the Blaster Magnum to blow it up. But the girls had plenty of evil energy built up and had levitated another half-dozen desks, which they were about to fire across the room. They'd no doubt cream Will, who was still dazed. Loreli took out a Medium Flash Orb, lobbed it, then dropped and shielded her eyes. Rudy did the same, pulling Will down with him. The Flash Orb exploded, creating a blinding white blast of light. The demonteens screamed as they went temporarily blind. Loreli already had Will by the collar, pulling him out the door. Rudy was right behind them.

Will was in pain and visibly pissed. He sucked in a long slow breath and tried to calm down. He pulled a spray can from the weapons backpack and coated the door. The orange foam expanded, then hardened, forming an impenetrable seal. The demonteens inside started screaming and banging on the door. Will hoped it would hold long enough for him to figure out what to do next.

"You're bleeding," said Loreli.

Will touched his chin. He pulled a healing patch from his jacket pocket and applied it to the wound. He was still woozy from being clipped by the desk. He heard a rumbling sound, which he thought was coming from inside his head, so he closed his eyes and leaned against a locker to try to make it stop.

But Loreli and Rudy heard the rumbling too, and they looked down the hallway. Way at the end they saw little Frag marching toward them with enough bravado for a guy twice his size. He had a nasty smile on his face. Rudy thought he looked kinda like the Joker in Batman. But where was the rumbling coming from?

In two seconds they found out. Rounding the corner behind Frag was a heavy steel rolling trash bin, one of those industrial ones that had to weigh a half a ton. Frag wanted payback.

"You mess with the bull, you get the horns!" shouted Frag.

The bin went airborne—flying down the hallway right at Will. Loreli dove and pulled him out of the way a millisecond before the bin smashed into the wall with the force of a bomb, obliterating the lockers and the wall behind them.

Loreli pulled two balls from her coat and threw them at Frag. The balls were connected by a thin wire—this was Loreli's own design, a weapon fashioned after the Spanish Bolas used by Gauchos for hunting—which wrapped around Frag's ankles. Loreli yanked the cord and he fell over sideways, his head banging into the floor.

"OW!" he yelped.

Loreli yanked on the lead wire and Frag found himself being dragged toward his enemies.

"Noooooo!"

He tried to reach down and free himself, but by the time he got his hands around the Bolas, he'd come to a stop at Loreli and Rudy's feet. Rudy, who had reloaded, was pointing the Blaster Magnum straight at him.

"Are you feeling lucky, punk?" he said. He turned to Will and Loreli and smiled. "I couldn't help myself."

Will slipped the Paralyser Glove on and pulled Frag to his feet.

"Hey listen, I just—YEOW!" He went limp as Will zapped him.

Will slung him over his shoulder. They heard more furious pounding at the sealed door, which was starting to splinter. Will pulled a small ball from his backpack, flipped a switch on it, and then sent it down the hallway. It rolled as though it had a life of its own and began emitting human voices.

"Diversion Ball," said Will. "That should keep them busy for a little while. Come on."

As they marched down the hallway, Will turned to his half-sister.

"Thanks for saving my butt." He had to admit that Loreli was proving to be a valuable partner.

"Twice," she said.

"Yeah," he said. "But don't get it into your head that I forgive you."

She shook her head. "I'm not expecting anything, except to help find the blade."

They found an empty room—the book supply room—where they could interrogate Frag. Will locked the door behind them and dropped him on a counter. His eyes blinked nervously.

Rudy almost pitied the little guy. The key word being "almost." After all, the creep had just tried to crush them.

Will took out a test tube that held what looked to be an inch-long cockroach.

"You know what this is?" said Will.

Frag nodded and squeaked out his reply. "A . . . a . . . c-c-cockroach?"

"Actually, it's a probing robot. One hundred percent mechanical, and very powerful. I made it *look* exactly like a cockroach. Kind of heightens the effect, don't you think?"

"A p-p-probing robot?" said Frag. "Who *are* you people?"

"We're the ones who are going to save the world," said Loreli. "So we hope you'll cooperate."

Frag was staring wide-eyed at the probing robot. "You *made* that thing?"

"Yes. It can eat right through steel."

"Will, that thing is *nasty*," said Rudy, recoiling.

"I know."

Will pulled the probing robot out. It began moving its little feet, mandibles, and antennae.

"We've only seen one adult on this island and now he's dead. There are no teachers, no principal. The whole town's anarchy. So why are you here? Why is anyone at school?" asked Will.

Frag stared at the cockroach. "Jasper wanted us to have structure, so those of us who aren't searching are supposed to hang out here."

"Searching for what?" asked Will.

Frag quickly knew he'd said too much. Determined not to say more he lowered his eyes.

"Looks like we're gonna have to use the probing robot," said Loreli.

Frag couldn't help himself. He looked up and stared in horror at the cockroach. "A probing robot . . . ," he whispered, his eyes never leaving the thing. "Wh-wh-where does it go?"

"Wherever I want it to. Now, pick an orifice. Nose? Mouth? Or . . . ?"

Will didn't even have to finish because Frag was already squirming. He knew that either he was going talk or that thing was going to crawl inside him and chew him up from the inside out. Frag tightened his sphincter and clenched his fists. He wondered how long he could hold out.

Chapter Nineteen:
Mystery Town

After Will, Rudy, and Loreli had taken off in the Jeep Wagoneer, Natalie and Emily had grabbed their purses from the backpacks and taken Janie Walker's clunky 1998 Volvo station wagon, the perfect nondescript car, for a little White Island recon. The ignition key had been hanging on a cutesy little wooden duck key holder by the front door. So they were free to roam in search of an adult who might tell them what in the hell was going on.

The car needed gas, so they pulled into the Rapid Mini-Mart gas station. A sign told customers to PLEASE PAY FIRST. So Natalie got out, armed herself with her Vibroslammer, then flipped the hood of her parka up and went inside, leaving Emily to guard the car. There was no one behind the counter. Down one of the aisles was a tall kid with a thin goatee. He'd chosen a bag of chips, two candy bars, three packs of snack cakes, and a six-pack of energy drinks. He went to the counter and set the stuff down. Natalie grabbed one of the so-called women's magazines, pretending to be engrossed in an article on how to "Rock Your Guy's World in Bed!" She watched as the tall boy bagged his groceries, then moved behind the counter to a computer that regulated the gas pumps. Natalie sidled closer and saw him key in thirty-five dollars worth of gas on pump number four, then he grabbed his stuff and went outside. So *that* was how it was done. Natalie fought the urge to shout out, "Hey, you didn't pay for anything!"

Natalie slipped behind the counter and, locating pump number two, punched in twenty dollars worth of gas. Either there was some weird honor system at work in Bingham, or the town was in total anarchy. She guessed the latter. She noticed a free White Island visitor's map that showed the local "points of interest" and pocketed it. She was about to leave without paying for the gas, but she just couldn't do it. She left a twenty-dollar bill by the cash register and went out, pumped the gas she'd paid for, and then started the car back up.

They drove in silence for a bit. Natalie already knew what Emily was going to say. Emily looked over at her.

"I heard what you told Will last night . . . before the attack."

Natalie bit her lip, but otherwise gave no indication that she was interested in pursuing the topic. *I don't love you anymore. I don't love you anymore.* The words were so burned into her brain, she could never forget them.

"I thought I was dreaming at first because I could never in a million years imagine you telling him that," said Emily.

Still Natalie stayed mute, hoping the conversation would wither and die.

"Is it true? What you said?"

A beat.

"Of course it's true, otherwise I wouldn't have said it." Natalie was working hard at being cold-hearted.

"People say a lot of things they don't mean. I kind of thought you were trying to hurt him on purpose. But I couldn't figure out why," said Emily.

"I told you, I meant it. Things change. Feelings change. Especially when you've been through what I've been through." She flashed a hot look at her sister.

Emily felt betrayed. All this time, ever since Natalie had fallen in love with Will, Emily had sailed along with her, riding the currents of adoration, feeling the same feelings in her heart. In her own way, *she* was in love with Will Hunter, too. It was practically impossible *not* to be when her twin sister loved him so passionately, loved him with every beat of her heart, and Emily often felt both her pleasure and pain. And now this. Emily was deeply confused. She spoke softly.

"My mind hears your words, but my heart is telling me a different story, Natalie. I can feel your heartache, remember?"

Natalie was aggravated. She felt like her skin was tightening.

"Well, maybe you've got it *wrong*. Maybe when I went to the dark side something happened between *us*, too!"

Emily felt as though someone were clutching at her throat. She swallowed hard and wiped away a tear.

"Maybe," she said in a small voice. "But I hope not."

Natalie could see her sister's pain—hell, she could *feel* it—and she wanted to comfort her. But not at the expense of bringing her feelings for Will to the surface to be dissected.

"Look, we've got bigger things to worry about, right? Let's . . . let's just get through this whole thing right now. We'll figure it out later. Everything will be fine."

"Yeah. Okay," said Emily. But she didn't sound any more convinced than Natalie had.

They saw a PriceLand grocery store and pulled into the parking lot. They parked the Volvo, got out, and went inside. Instead of the usual quiet elevator music, the store speakers were blasting Linkin Park. The store was practically empty, except for three girls who were filling two shopping carts with cans of soup. They had another cart filled with beer and wine and plastic baby bottles.

Natalie and Emily hung back, watching, silently deciding to avoid any kind of contact. They hid in the bakery aisle until the three girls left PriceLand without so much as a glance at the cash registers, which weren't manned by checkers anyway. After the girls had loaded their booty into an old Dodge Durango and took off, Natalie and Emily walked through the remaining PriceLand aisles.

"Looks like everything in here's got the five-finger discount," said Emily.

"Let's check and see if anybody's in the back."

They found the manager's office and the break room and the stock rooms, but there was not an adult in sight. So they left Price-Land and drove into town.

Natalie pulled over and parked at a meter. Every meter on the street was expired, but none of the cars had parking tickets. Natalie was about to shove a quarter in the meter, but Emily stopped her.

"If you do that, we'll stick out like a sore thumb," she said.

Natalie nodded. They looked up and down the street. Rain was coming down in its usual misting fashion. A few teens in ball caps and hoodies came and went, but not one adult. The twins looked over at Daphne's Boutique and decided to check it out. Maybe the owner was inside waiting to tell them everything. Probably not, but it was worth a shot.

Daphne had good taste. The clothes on the racks looked hip, comfortable, and flattering. There was a girl—or was it a woman?—flipping through a sale rack toward the back. Natalie and Emily exchanged a hopeful look and approached her. She looked like an adult from behind.

"Um, excuse me . . . ," said Natalie.

The figure turned. She was maybe seventeen or eighteen, just tall. She had red circles under her eyes and looked dangerous as she sneered at them.

"What do you want?" she said.

"Um . . . ," Natalie grabbed a top from a nearby rack and held it up.

"Do you have this in blue?"

The girl looked annoyed. "What are you, an idiot? I don't *work* here." Her eyes narrowed. "Wait a second! You guys are the—"

BLA-WHUMP! Emily had pulled out her Vibroslammer and fired it. The blast knocked the girl backward with such force that she slammed right into a dressing room and was out cold. Her legs stuck out like a big doll's.

The twins looked around. There was no one else in the store. They folded the girl's legs up and closed the dressing room door. Emily couldn't help herself and began looking at the clothing, holding a top up to herself as Natalie moved behind the counter looking for clues.

Emily put the top back and tried on a hat. "Daphne has impeccable taste."

"I wonder where she is?" said Natalie.

Emily saw a sweater and fell in love. "Oh my god, look at this! I'm *so* taking it."

"You're not taking anything," Natalie said.

"Are you kidding me? We're on Freak Island trying to find the blade to some sword that the Devil is going to use to bring an end to mankind, and you're telling me I can't jack one lousy sweater? Natalie, this could be the end of the world."

"All the more reason not to steal. Let's go."

"You know, for someone who was possessed by the Devil only a few days ago, you're annoyingly angelic."

"Thanks," said Natalie sarcastically.

As they were leaving, Emily saw a scarf she liked. She grabbed it and started to wrap it around her neck.

Natalie gave her a look. "Put it back."

Emily groaned and tossed the scarf in the air. As the door closed behind them, it floated to the floor.

Outside they kept walking, passing a stationery shop called Penz, Glenn's Frozen Yogurt, and a half-dozen other businesses. They all had OPEN signs up, and there were a few teens walking in and out, taking whatever they pleased. Again, no adults anywhere.

"This is so weird. It's like the Island of Lost Teenagers or something," said Natalie.

"Where could all of the adults have gone?"

"Maybe they didn't *go* anywhere. Maybe they were *taken*."

They stood in discomfort with this thought. Then Natalie looked down the street where a car was parked at an odd angle. The driver's door was ajar, the window smashed. The girls stared at each other.

"Maybe somebody's in there," said Natalie.

She took a step toward the car, but Emily stopped her.

"What if they're dead?"

"Then they won't mind if we look inside."

They walked to the car. There was no dead body inside, but Natalie did spot an iPod nano hanging by its earbud cord from the rearview mirror. It was creepy-looking: the cord was tied in a little hangman's knot. Natalie opened the door and took it, sliding it into her pocket. A couple of teens came out of the frozen yogurt shop carrying huge waffle cones and glanced over at them, so Natalie and Emily walked back toward the Volvo. The kids watched them for a few seconds, then got in their car and drove off.

"Why'd you take the iPod?" asked Emily once they were safely back in the car. "You wouldn't even let me take a scarf!"

"Did you see how it was hung? It looked like whoever put it there wanted it to be found."

Natalie pulled a charger from her purse and juiced up the iPod. She toggled through the menu items until she got to video. She opened the latest file and pressed PLAY.

Emily leaned close and they watched the video together. The images were shaky, as though whoever had shot the video was nervous. A woman's voice said, "Oh sweet lord . . . what is going *on*?!"

On the screen, four teen boys grabbed a man coming out of the stationery store. They pinned his arms behind his back, then slapped a piece of gaffer's tape over his mouth and threw him in the back of a delivery truck on top of three other squirming adults. Then the teenagers moved on to the copy shop and dragged the screaming owner, Albert Moore, out. He had a baseball bat and swung it. One of the boys got hit in the shoulder and was knocked to his knees. Albert was in a backswing to finish him off when a park bench slammed into him, hurling him to the pavement. Albert was unconscious. The demonteens threw him into the back of the truck.

On the video, the woman's voice said, "Oh my god . . . Denise!"

Several teen girls surrounded a pear-shaped woman as she emerged from a ThriftMart grocery store. It was Denise Gurney, a haggard redhead who ran the local bookstore. Trying to elude her attackers, she ran for her car but didn't make it, even after dropping her groceries to lighten her load. A brick lifted off the ground and flew, untouched, through the air.

Emily gasped. "How did they . . ."

The brick clipped Denise's ankle, and she went down hard. Then the demonteen girls were on her like jackals, wrapping her like a mummy with long scarves.

"Leave me alone!" she screamed. "What are you doing? Donna Marie, what's gotten into you?"

Denise was beet red, indignant with rage as she hissed at her tormentors, her turkey-wattle neck trembling. "You'll burn in Hell for this, you little bitches!"

The girls stared at her in concentration, and Denise lifted into the air and floated into the truck. Then the demonteen girls turned and looked right at whomever was recording the attack.

"Oh god . . . no!"

The girls started marching right toward the camera. A woman's face appeared on the screen: Elizabeth Morell, fifty-seven-years-old with bleached blonde hair.

"Please . . . help us!" she said into the camera. "They've gone crazy! They've all gone crazy! They're kidnapping all of us!"

The girls had reached Elizabeth's car and were pounding on the window.

"Open up, Elizabeth! Right now!"

The video image flipped upside down and swung all over the place.

"This must be where she hung it from the rearview mirror," said Natalie.

The video continued, showing the car window smashing, hands reaching in and grabbing Elizabeth, who screamed as she was dragged out. The girls put gaffer's tape over her mouth and she, too, was levitated into the truck. Then the truck roared away down Main Street.

"Rewind it," said Emily.

Natalie did.

"Stop it on the truck."

They could read the lettering on the back: CORWIN'S TOMATO FARM.

Natalie pulled the visitor's map out of her pocket and scanned it.

"Here it is."

Her finger was touching a "point of interest" on the map. It had a cute little smiling tomato above a logo for Corwin's Tomato Farm.

In Bingham High School, someone had set off the fire alarm. The hallways were filled with students running around, shouting angrily. They were looking for the intruders. In the book supply room, Will was losing patience with Frag.

"Open your mouth or drop trou. It's your choice," he said. He held the probing cockroach between his thumb and pointer finger. Frag was pale and looked dizzy.

"What happened on this island, Frag?"

Frag lowered his head and began to talk softly. "After the hot red rain, we all fell asleep. When we woke up, we could move stuff just by staring at it."

"The telekinesis," said Loreli.

"And then we heard the Voice."

Will and Loreli exchanged a look.

Will asked, "What did the voice say?"

"It told us to find the treasure. We could see it in our minds. Pieces . . . like diamonds. We had to find the treasure or . . ."

Frag stopped talking, not wanting to give away a secret.

"Or what?" asked Will.

"Our parents . . . ," whispered Frag.

"That's how he controls you? He took your parents?"

"Sort of . . . ," said Frag. He couldn't hide how guilty he felt.

"What happened to them?" Will demanded.

Frag shook his head. He was shaking, tears forming in his eyes.

"What did you do to your parents?"

Frag looked up, his eyes red. He was sobbing, but his lips were pressed together.

"I . . . I can't tell you," he said.

"We haven't seen anyone but teenagers. What about the little kids? And the old people? Where are they?"

Frag looked relieved to have an answer.

"Oh, they're okay. The little kids and babies and stuff are all at the old folks' home out on Hollister Road. The old folks are happy. They're all changing each other's diapers. It's a win-win sitch," he said, almost proudly.

"The treasure. Have you found it?"

Again Frag clammed up. Will moved the probing robot cockroach right next to Frag's nose, one of its little feelers actually touching it. Frag flinched backward.

"Oh god, please don't!" He looked like he was going to have a heart attack. "We found almost all of the treasure. But there's supposedly a few pieces left."

"Where are you searching? Can you show us on the map?"

"What map?" said Frag.

Will flipped up the face of his watch and spoke into it as he'd done the day they'd landed on the island.

"98450," he said.

The watch projected a map of White Island on the wall.

"Show me," said Will.

Someone banged on the door.

"You're running out of time, Fraggy, show me NOW!"

Will put the cockroach right on Frag's nose. That was it. He could hold out no longer. So he pointed to an area on the map, an area that caused Will to shudder with disgust. A deepening fear crept up his spine. Frag was pointing to the bay. The treasure was in the water.

"It's out in Puget Sound?" asked Rudy.

Will was already running the worst-case scenarios through his mind: hypothermia, black water, drowning, and very large sea creatures. "Damn," he said. "Why am I not surprised?"

He dropped the cockroach on the ground. When he stepped on it, it made a sickeningly familiar crunch. He moved his shoe and Frag squinted down at the crushed exoskeleton and the liquid guts splashed out in several directions.

"Hey," said Frag. "That was just a dumb old ordinary bug!"

Rudy chuckled. Even Loreli smiled.

"Not that dumb," said Rudy. "It fooled you." His chuckle was starting to turn into a gut-busting laugh, but he choked on it when something huge slammed into the door, bashing it half open. A dozen livid demonteens had used their power to smash the door with a seven-hundred-pound vending machine. Rudy was standing closest to the broken door and the demonteens reached in and grabbed him. He yelled as they pulled at him, trying to drag him through the splintered opening. Will whipped on the Paralyzer Glove and quickly zapped Rudy's attackers, who howled in pain.

"Hit the deck!" screamed Loreli.

They did, and a second later the massive vending machine blasted against the door again, knocking it wide open. Then suddenly every object in the room was flying around as if they were in the middle of a tornado. Will stood and picked up a two-drawer metal file cabinet and heaved it through the window. Loreli tossed a dense black smoke bomb through a shattered door into the hallway. The demonteens coughed their lungs out and were momentarily disoriented as Will, Loreli, and Rudy climbed out the window and sprinted to the Wagoneer.

Chapter Twenty:
The Black Depths

Will drove down to the Marina and parked. The front door to Dave's Dive Shop was open, so they went in. Loreli started assembling the gear they would need.

"You're a diver?" asked Will.

"Expert," she said nonchalantly.

Will was surprised, but he knew he shouldn't have been. His half-sister kept finding new ways to amaze him. He just wasn't sure what to do with her. Once out in the water she could either be an incredible asset, as she had been so far on the island, or—if she realized exactly how bad his fear was—she could be his worst nightmare.

Schlepping the scuba gear, they found a boat in one of the slips that was to Loreli's liking, a twenty-four-foot Cobalt Bowrider. She seemed to know all about boats, too, and quickly bypassed the ignition and hot-wired it.

Watching Will on Cappy's boat on the way over, Loreli had deduced that he wasn't exactly an expert seaman, so she took the wheel, throttling the boat out through the swells. Will was already feeling ill. They churned and slapped through the deep green water until they saw a group of boats anchored about a half-mile north.

Dive floats dotted the water, their red and white flags bobbing. A large cabin cruiser, the *Reel Love*, was anchored here. This must have been where Jasper and Boone and the other guys had been when Will and his crew had arrived in Bingham. He'd seen the boats speeding back into the harbor; he'd just had no idea what it meant at the time. Now he knew. They'd been looking for something sunken in the bay.

A slice of sun cut through the clouds. That was good, it would increase their visibility. Will struggled to put his gear on. Loreli could tell he was freaking but said nothing. Better not to acknowledge his fear with words. She just gave him reassuring looks and helped him when he had trouble with his weight belt. Rudy's wetsuit was so tight he couldn't get it on. But it didn't matter because he wasn't going down.

"Rudy, stay up here with the boat," said Will. "If someone surfaces, just put on a mask and look busy."

Will and Loreli put on their masks. Will looked at Loreli, who couldn't help smiling. Even though the situation they were in was deadly serious, she still got a little kick out of seeing her half-brother's nervousness. He held his nose and blew gently to equalize pressure in his ears.

"Don't worry, I've got your back," said Loreli.

"Why does that not exactly comfort me?" said Will.

His heart was pounding and he was perspiring heavily. He would rather be jumping out of an airplane without a parachute than jumping into this water. But he knew there could be no cowardly retreat. It wasn't in his DNA. Will silently asked the universe for some help, and sucked it up. Then he and Loreli put in their air regulator mouthpieces and fell backwards off the boat into the water to begin the dark descent into the cold waters of Puget Sound.

The world beneath the surface was shadowy and mysterious. Will immediately felt light-headed. All the old panic came rushing back. He struggled to keep breathing through the regulator—it was imperative *not* to hold your breath while diving—and he forced himself to focus on not passing out.

They had lights, but for now didn't need them. They paddled downward, controlling their descent with their buoyancy compensators. They both had spearguns with blaster tips, and Will had his cache of waterproofed gadgets strapped to his chest. He saw a large fish flash by, and it spooked him, so he swam faster.

They swam through a school of yellowtail rockfish and were inspected by some curious black-eyed gobies. More rockfish flashed by and Will shuddered, convinced that some underwater snakes had breached his wetsuit and were spiraling around inside. But he knew it was just the fear.

When they reached a rocky outcropping, they saw some bright red-plumed sea anemone, a few menacing-looking lingcod, and a spectacularly striped painted greenling. The creatures were beautiful, but Will couldn't have cared less; all he wanted was to find what they'd come for and get the hell out of there.

They kept swimming. A small wolf eel poked its head out of a cubby in a sudden, threatening motion. Will was duly warned and changed course accordingly. Loreli, spotting the little eel, hoped they wouldn't have to tussle with any of the larger ones. Wolf eels could grow to be six or even seven feet long, and though they didn't normally attack humans, considering the way the rest of the animals on the island had been acting, it seemed smart to steer clear. She sure didn't want to find out what a fish with that many teeth could do when possessed.

Up ahead, they spotted a few divers with scoop nets carefully searching rock piles. When the demonteens came to larger underwater rocks, they simply used their levitation power to slowly lift them. *That explains why the Dark Lord gave them that power*, thought Will.

Loreli motioned for Will to follow her, and they swam toward the group. Since the diving masks obscured their faces, they'd be difficult to recognize. Luckily, they'd brought small scoop nets themselves. They took them out and began sifting through some bottom sand in order to blend in.

Since they weren't exactly sure what they were looking for, they hung back and pretended to be searching like the other divers as a school of vermillion rockfish darted back and forth above them. Three divers were grouped over near the opening to some kind of cave. One had strands of long blonde hair whipping around in the water currents. It had to be Jasper. The huge diver next to him was undoubtedly Boone. They were gesticulating to the third diver, a stocky kid, who was shaking his head vigorously. But somehow Jasper and Boone's peer pressure worked, and the third diver reluctantly paddled through the opening and into the cave.

Will and Loreli swam closer. Ten seconds passed as Jasper and Boone looked on, shining their lights inside the cave to see what was happening. Then they jerked backward suddenly, as a blast of debris-ridden water came shooting out of the cave. It took Will and Loreli a few seconds to recognize that the debris was bits of wetsuit—mixed with flesh and blood from the unfortunate diver whom Jasper and Boone had ordered inside.

Will and Loreli exchanged a look as it occurred to them that what they had come to White Island to find was most likely inside that deadly cave. Otherwise, chances were it would already have been found.

Boone pulled out the body of the stocky kid—or what was left of it—and he and Jasper gesticulated to one another angrily. Then, together, they began to swim to the surface, towing the bleeding corpse behind them.

When they were out of sight, Will and Loreli swam toward the abandoned cave. They unhooked their AquaSun lights, turned them on, and shined them inside. Six pairs of reddish-yellow eyes looked back at them. Loreli shook her head. Bad luck. Wolf eels, the biggest she'd ever seen. All three of them had to be at least ten feet long.

They had huge muscular jaws that bulged with power, and their teeth looked like death itself.

Then Will saw what Jasper and the others had been attempting to retrieve. It was a fragment of crystal, sitting atop a jagged rock next to a sea anemone. The crystal seemed to be glowing faintly. Will knew that it must be part of the blade for the Sword of Armageddon, which meant that he was going to have to go into the dark eel-infested cave and retrieve it.

It wasn't going to be easy. Not only was he in the one place he hated the most, he had to somehow deal with not just one, but *three* huge deadly beasts—without the ability to time bend. *Oh well*, he thought—doing his best to fend off the impending panic attack. *Just another day at the office for Will Hunter*.

The eels swam languidly around inside the cave, and in any other circumstance Will would have marveled at how magnificent the creatures were. But this wasn't the Discovery Channel, and he wasn't there to admire the raw power of nature. He was there to kick its ass.

He loaded his spear gun and motioned for Loreli to do the same. He propped his light on a nearby rock so the beam shone into the cave. The wolf eels became agitated and darted back and forth, making for difficult targets. It looked like they were getting ready to attack, and Jasper and Boone could return at any time. Plus, Will and Loreli were starting to draw attention to themselves: some of the other divers kept looking over at them.

Will fired first and got lucky. His spear pierced one of the huge eels, the tip exploding on impact. The creature writhed in agony as its body was torn in two. Loreli fired and was not so fortunate. Her spear zinged past the second eel, which whirled and lunged at her. She was able to duck just enough that the eel's jaw glanced off her air tank instead of clamping onto her shoulder. She kicked her fins and swam backward as the angry eel pursued her. Confident Loreli could take care of herself, Will shined his light around, looking for the third eel, but he couldn't find it. The monster had slunk back into the black depths of the cave. It was his best chance to make a move. Will grabbed his light and swam in. In the commotion of the brief skirmish, the water in the cave had swirled about and become even murkier. Making matters worse, Will's mask was staring to fog up.

He looked frantically around for the crystal. It wasn't sitting on the rock anymore. As he searched, the currents in the cave became violent, tossing him and back and forth as underwater waves crashed around him. He blinked and felt his chest constrict with terror. All at once it hit him. *I'm underwater, getting air through a small tube. I could run out at any moment.* Suddenly he couldn't breathe. *I am going to drown. I don't want to die! Not here, not now, not like this!*

The fear was winning. He knew he had to do something or he'd pass out and drown for sure. So he let the fear in, all the way, just ushered it right on into his body, like a welcome guest. *You want me, then take me, I'm yours. Use me, become me, kill me if you have to. But I am not going to run from you anymore.*

That which you resist, persists. He'd learned that a thousand times, and yet it was a lesson he had to teach himself over and over again. *Let go*, he told himself. *Just let go.* He closed his eyes and thought of his mother and how badly she needed him. He breathed slowly and evenly. His mask began to clear and his heart rate slowed. By totally and utterly relinquishing control, he had regained it.

Just then, Loreli appeared at the mouth of the cave and shined her light inside on the sea anemone, which bloomed open. There it was, the crystal, nestled in the translucent tentacles. Will swam over and reached for it.

And then the third wolf eel, which had been lurking behind him in the darkness, lunged out with lightning speed. It clamped its mighty jaws on Will's hand, the razor-sharp teeth piercing his diving glove and sinking into the flesh of his palm. A jolt of pain shot up his arm, like he'd jammed his finger in a light socket.

Teeth still lodged in Will's hand, the wolf eel wrapped itself around Will's body and squeezed. Will's other hand was pinned to his chest, but he had enough wiggle room to reach into his vest and pull out a compact but deadly Heatblade, which he activated. With a quick thrust, he jabbed the Heatblade into the eel's flesh. The creature went berserk, coiling and recoiling, releasing its hold on Will's hand as it now, in ancient rage, prepared to strike directly at Will's face.

Loreli's second spear lanced the beast's head, the explosive tip detonating and blowing its brains to bits. The creature's body slackened, enabling Will to extricate himself.

Loreli reached down, grabbed the shard of crystal, and stuffed it in her catch net, then swam out of the cave. Will swam after her. As he emerged from the cave, he felt something behind him. A hand holding a diving knife came out of nowhere and slashed his oxygen line, and suddenly the water around him exploded with air bubbles. Will held his breath and, through the bubbles, got a good look at his attacker.

It was Loreli.

Fragments of Will's life flashed before his eyes as he held his breath. He was trying to keep from mentally punishing himself. How could he have been so stupid as to trust his devious half-sister after all she'd done to him? She'd already proven herself to be a Judas, time and again. Why on earth had he allowed himself to even begin to believe that she had somehow changed? Why did he continue to have faith that people's essential human nature was good?

Maybe it was hope. Maybe it was because deep down he figured that if people weren't basically, at their core, decent and kind and instinctively loving, then what was the point? He'd always believed that, given the chance, the average person would rather lend a hand than step on someone's throat, that love was stronger than hate. But if he was wrong in his belief, then why even bother trying to save humanity from the Dark Lord? Why not just let the whole stupid planet full of jackasses go right to Hell?

Will reached for Loreli even as she used her knife to slice off his scuba tank and rip it from him, completely depriving him of any chance of survival. There was no way he could make it to the surface before he suffocated.

A massive shadow blew by above him—*the shadow of Death*, he thought. He'd cheated its hideous specter so many times, and now it had come for him exactly where he'd feared it the most: underwater.

He felt a massive rush of water as something huge brushed past him and circled above. He looked up. It was indeed Death coming to collect his soul—in the form of a thirty-two-foot-long, nine-ton Orca. The massive killer whale was diving down at him, its huge mouth agape, ready to take him from this world. Beside him, Loreli appeared, and with timing bordering on the miraculous, she shoved Will's scuba tank forward, then shot her last spear into it to drive it down the Orca's throat. Will watched incredulously as the gigantic beast suddenly stopped like it had been rammed in the gut by a freight train. One second, two seconds, and then the creature's huge, round, black-and-white body twisted and convulsed before the exploding scuba tank blew a chunk out of the whale's side the size of an oil barrel. They were awash in blood and blubber and sinewy flesh.

Will was close to passing out when Loreli shoved her mouthpiece into his mouth. Together they began the slow ascent to the surface, trading precious breaths of air through the shared apparatus. When they broke the surface, Will gasped and gulped, dizzy from the oxygen loss and from the emotional roller coaster he'd just ridden.

He shook his head and focused on the quest. Always the quest.

"Where's the crystal?"

Loreli pulled the breathing apparatus from her mouth and spoke in between ragged breaths.

"Jasper took it from me. He and Boone were right there when I came out of the cave. They caught me by surprise. They looked so happy to see the crystal that they didn't even notice it was me," she said. "I was going to try and get it back when I saw the Orca. It was either you or the crystal."

Will kept sucking in air, trying to calm his heart. She'd cut his oxygen line because she'd had to get his tank off quickly enough to use it against the Orca. It turned out that she'd saved his life once again.

Loreli pointed behind him. Will spotted the Bowrider they'd taken from the Marina. On the deck, Rudy was waving at them.

"Over here!" he called.

"We've got to get you in the boat. Your hand is bleeding," said Loreli.

They swam over and hauled themselves back onboard. Once in the boat, Will dug out a healing patch and applied it to his hand. Then they were zooming along, Rudy at the wheel, piloting the boat back to the marina at full throttle. The island teens had a head start, but Will, Loreli, and Rudy were close on their heels.

Chapter Twenty-One:
Corwin's Beauties

Using the cutesy Bingham tourist map as a guide, Natalie and Emily drove up a winding road in search of Corwin's Tomato Farm. A light rain continued to fall, and the Volvo's wipers left streaks on the windshield. They passed another "point of interest," Dora's Quilt Shoppe. Dora must have been taken, too, because the shop was closed.

They turned left and kept on the road that snaked up the hillside until they found the farm. The large sign at the gate had a picture of Ed and Edna Corwin, presumably—from the looks of the big smiles plastered across their mugs—the founders of the sprawling enterprise. Ed and Edna looked like brother and sister, though they could have been husband and wife; often when people were married long enough they began to look alike. They were holding up big clumps of "vine-ripened beauties" and beaming with pride. A few of their "beauties" had faces painted on them, and they were smiling, too. Emily wondered why the tomatoes would be smiling, they were just going to be eaten.

Instead of entering the farm, Natalie kept driving because they spotted trouble. Dora Gurney, a heavyset girl in gray sweats, Doc Marten boots, and a black hoodie was smoking outside one of the large greenhouses. She had a sweet face and didn't look particularly threatening—except for the pump shotgun nestled in the crook of her arm. The twins didn't want to get introduced to the wrong end of that puppy, so they drove around the bend and continued up the hill until they were out of sight. Then Natalie pulled over.

"Who the heck would guard a tomato farm with a shotgun?" said Emily.

"Somebody's who got something to hide. Let's go."

They got out, slipped through a barbed wire fence, and made their way across a field of thick-headed sedge dotted with white yarrow plants. The rain began to come down harder. They slogged through the wet grass until they reached a canopy of big leaf maples. They were on Halstrom's Crest now, not far from the old barn. They gazed down at the tomato farm, which consisted of a dozen long, tent-like greenhouses—each one ninety feet long by thirty feet wide—domed with thick plastic sheeting the color of smoke. In one of the buildings they saw the same girls they'd seen at Price-Land coming in, wheeling a cart full of soup cans. And then they heard music. It was coming from inside one of the greenhouses. B. J. Thomas was singing "Raindrops Keep Falling on My Head."

"I've got a creepy feeling about this," said Emily.

"That makes two of us."

They waited and listened to the song for a few moments before succumbing to the inevitable.

"We gotta go down there," Natalie said.

"I know," said Emily.

"It's now or never."

"Can I vote never?"

"Let's go."

Natalie started walking down the hillside. Emily followed, but stopped her after a few paces.

"Wait."

"What?"

"In case something happens, you know, something bad . . ."

"Nothing's gonna happen. We're just gonna go and look. We'll be fine."

"Right. But what you said about Will really threw me off. If it's true, then that means I can't trust what I'm feeling. I can't trust *us*, you know? So tell me. Was it true? What you said to Will? Do you really not love him anymore?"

Natalie closed her eyes. She looked like she was debating whether or not to spill her guts, or maybe she was counting to ten. Emily couldn't tell.

"Just drop it," she said finally. "I am not having this conversation now."

They started walking again. Emily was starting to believe that their special twin bond, their unspoken communication, really had been damaged.

When they reached the farm, they moved toward the greenhouse where the oldies were playing. The plastic was too thick and opaque to see through. Then they caught sight of Dora tromping past. She didn't see them, but she spooked them, and they took cover behind a storage shed. They slipped the Vibroslammers on over their knuckles.

"I wonder how far these things shoot," said Emily.

"I don't know. But I wouldn't risk trying anything unless it's up close."

"We've got to take shotgun girl out."

"I know. I'll go this way, you go around there," said Natalie, pointing.

Emily went right and Natalie went left. They circled around the greenhouse. Emily ducked down when she saw the girls wheeling the now-empty cart out of the big side doors. She took furtive, quiet steps forward and had just made it to the door when she heard a distinctive sound that made the small hairs on the back of her neck rise. It was the metallic *click* of a shell being jacked into the barrel of a shotgun.

"Don't move."

It was Dora. She'd probably seen them after all and doubled back to sneak up on Emily. Two critical seconds passed—seconds when Emily might have spun around and fired her Vibroslammer. But instead she hesitated, then felt the cold steel of the shotgun pressing against her temple.

"Who are you and what the *hell* are you doing here?"

Emily hesitated a moment, then came up with the most effective lie she could think of.

"I just got lost, that's all . . ."

Dora thought about it, then pushed the barrel harder into Emily's temple.

"Get on your knees," she said.

Emily remained standing. "Please . . . could we talk? Listen to me. One minute, just listen to me," said Emily, doing her damndest to stall.

Dora didn't like it. She clenched her jaw. Her eyes narrowed as she stared at a bag of fertilizer. Using her telekinetic power, she lifted the bag up. It whipped through the air and slammed into Emily, knocking her down. *Now* she was on her knees.

"Where are all the adults?"

"Put your hands behind your head."

Emily complied. Shotgun girl's eyes widened as she stared at the Vibroslammer.

"That thing on your hand! It's a weapon!"

Emily was shaking, afraid to fire because if she missed her target, Dora might get spooked enough to blow her head off. Emily didn't want her brains dribbling into the dirt.

"I'm not going to hurt you," she said.

"You're damn right you're not going to hurt me."

Dora was getting more nervous by the second, her finger tightening on the trigger. She had the barrel of the gun shoved against Emily's head again. Emily closed her eyes, close to giving up. Natalie had tried to convince her that they didn't have their bond anymore, but Emily prayed she was wrong. This was her only chance. She clenched her jaw and spoke silently to Natalie. *Please hear me, please hear me now. I need you. I don't want to die. I don't want to leave you. Please help me. Please? Now . . . ?*

"Who *are* you? I asked you a damn question. Now talk!" said Dora.

Emily *was* talking, with her mind, reaching out to her twin. *I need you. I need you now, sister.*

"Okay, you don't want to talk to me? Then you better talk to God. You better say your prayers," said Dora, who had concluded that the only reasonable solution was to murder the girl lying face-down in the dirt. Then she heard a voice.

"Please don't shoot me . . ."

Dora turned. Her brain slowed down as she tried to understand what she was seeing. The girl in the dirt was now standing by the corner of the greenhouse, twenty feet away. How had she gotten up? And how could she be standing there begging for her life when she was clearly still on the ground ? Dora's brain was whirling. Maybe what had happened was she'd already pulled the trigger, and what she was seeing was a ghost! Her mind reeling, shotgun girl turned, momentarily lifting the gun away from Emily's head. Emily rolled over, clicked on her Vibroslammer, and blasted Dora directly in the ass. The vibration wave was so powerful, it blew her twenty feet in the air. She screamed and dropped the shotgun, waving her arms like she was trying to grab hold of something. The shotgun hit the ground and went off, blowing a hole in the side of the greenhouse plastic. Dora hit the ground at an awkward angle, her legs buckling beneath her. Natalie winced when she heard the unmistakable snap of a breaking bone.

The three girls who'd been wheeling the cart came running out, and Natalie calmly shot all of them with her Vibroslammer, blowing them backward into the side of the building they'd just emerged from. Two of them were out cold, and the other lay moaning.

Emily got up and smiled at her twin sister.

"You *heard* me."

"Of course I heard you."

"But then why did you—?"

Emily was interrupted when they heard someone calling from inside the greenhouse.

"Help! Help us!"

Natalie and Emily rushed to the greenhouse door, too preoccupied to see the girl on the ground pick up her cell phone. They opened the door to the greenhouse.

What they saw would haunt them as a dark dream for the rest of their lives. Among the rows of tomato plants were rows of another kind: rows of human heads. Each and every captured adult had been buried up to their neck so that only their heads were protruding from the soil.

The woman who was crying out, Denise, was the one they'd seen abducted on the iPod video. She had a baby bottle lying next to her. As Emily and Natalie looked around in horror, they saw that dozens of other heads were sucking on bottles. It was like some kind of perverted middle-aged nursery. Seeing the twins, some of the adults spat their bottles out and cried out feebly. One of them was the bleached blonde, Elizabeth Morrell, who'd taken the video.

"Please, help me!" said Denise.

"Oh god . . . ," said Emily.

Natalie moved over to Denise and picked up the bottle.

"Soup?"

"Yes," said Denise.

"They put drugs in it," said Elizabeth. "Some kind of tranquilizer, I think."

A man who had spit out his bottle was screaming, "Water! WATER!"

But he wasn't crying *for* water, he was freaking out because he *saw* water—coming right at him. The shotgun blast had not only blown a hole in the side of the greenhouse, but it had ripped through an irrigation pipe, which was now gushing water, flooding the floor of the greenhouse. For someone buried up to their neck, a couple of inches of water was a horrifying thing.

"We've got to get them out of here!" shouted Emily.

She dropped down and started scooping up the dirt surrounding Denise. But with only her hands, the process was too slow. Natalie looked around, scanning, and then her eyes lit up.

"Shovels!"

The shovels the demonteens had used to bury their parents were still piled up in the corner. Natalie ran and grabbed a couple of them, and the sisters started digging.

"Hurry!" cried Denise.

The other adults, seeing the approaching water, spit out their bottles and began screaming. One of them was Janie Walker, the owner of the bed and breakfast. She was trembling with fear. It was bad enough being nearly buried alive, but to drown on top of that would be unimaginable.

When Natalie and Emily had dug deep enough to free Denise's arms, the woman was able to wriggle out of her hole. Though her body was weak and limp from being in an inert state for so long, adrenaline kicked in. She fought through the pain and picked up a shovel, immediately starting to dig to free the man buried next to her, Doctor Swaggert, who had delivered Denise's own sons. Once he was freed, the two of them got to work to free Janie Walker.

The water kept gushing in, rising higher and higher. It was a sloppy, slippery, muddy battlefield. Once freed, people wasted no time rushing to grab a shovel and start digging up their neighbors. Natalie and Emily dug as fast as they could, working until their arms were on fire, aching with pain. They were fueled by a fierce determination. The memory of losing their own parents—even though they'd fought all the time and had been more or less awful to the girls—was still painful, and they were damned if they were going to let any of these moms and dads die.

The number of liberated souls grew exponentially, freedom begetting freedom as they worked feverishly to dig out their terrified comrades. The earthen floor of the greenhouse had turned into a muddy lake, and the last few people who were dug up had been forced to hold their breath until being rescued. They were gasping and coughing and sputtering, crawling out of the mud and shaking themselves like oil-coated birds. But the threat was over.

Suddenly Natalie and Emily found themselves in a situation they never could have imagined: standing in the middle of an enormous group hug. Dozens of half-naked, muddy adults with tears of gratitude streaming down their faces reached out to touch and hug the girls. The adults were a sight to behold. Most of them were chubby, and their dirty flesh sagged on their bodies. The women wore nothing but bras and granny panties, the men Jockeys or boxers. It was totally gross and downright embarrassing—and possibly the most beautiful thing Natalie and Emily had ever witnessed. The girls led the grateful throng out of their greenhouse prison and into the misty rain. Many of the adults raised their heads and arms to the sky as though they had just been blessed with a new life, which indeed they had. But how long would it last?

Chapter Twenty-Two: The Blade

Rudy throttled back the Bowrider and cruised into the marina. The slips were full of boats, but the marina was deserted. Rudy docked the boat, hopped out, and tied it up while Will and Loreli peeled off their wetsuits and changed back into street clothes. Then they put the weapons backpacks on and walked along the dock toward the parking lot. Rudy kept looking in the windows of the shops, complaining that he was hungry.

As they passed a large cabin cruiser, Will felt a presence. When he turned around, he heard something whistling through the air. *THWACK!* A spear sank into Rudy's crotch. Luckily, he wore his jeans so low that the spear had hit nothing but denim. He looked down and saw he was pinned to the wooden clapboard wall of the ice cream shop.

"Holy crap!" he yelped.

Wendy Childress was standing on her parents' boat, the *Reel Love*. She was wearing a wetsuit and looked like a villainess out of a James Bond movie.

"Don't move!"

Will underestimated her speed as he grabbed for a Flare-blade, and Wendy, using her telekinetic powers, sent a dive knife right at Loreli. Loreli ducked, but the knife sliced her cheek as it zinged past.

"Ahhh!"

"I *told* you not to move," said Wendy.

Will gripped the Flareblade and looked ready to backhand it at her. Wendy eyed it warily. She didn't like the way it was beginning to pulsate and turn red-hot. She mentally lifted four more spears into the air, where they hovered, waiting for her to send them hurtling into her victims.

"Very good," said Will, eyeing the spears. "If I throw this," he said, indicating the Flareblade, "your forehead's not going to like it."

"No doubt," said Wendy. "But then your friends will be dead."

It was a standoff. Loreli was holding her bleeding cheek. If looks could kill, Wendy would have already been dead. Will was looking at Loreli's choker.

"Tell you what," he said to Wendy. "Her necklace, it's worth thousands of dollars. You take it, and you let my friend go."

Loreli caught on immediately. "No way, Will! You gave this to *me*!"

"Sorry, babe," Will told her.

Wendy stared at Loreli. The striking necklace piqued her interest, and the fact that Loreli was so possessive of it made her want it even more. The ability to move things with her mind had made Wendy cocky and overconfident. She lifted a hand to her empty neck. Jasper was going to buy her a new necklace to replace the one he'd broken, but for now . . .

"Let me see it," said Wendy.

Will nodded to Loreli, who slowly unclasped the choker as Will touched the release button on his ring. Loreli walked over to the boat and handed the choker to Wendy.

She put the necklace on. Will smiled.

"What the hell are you smiling at?" she asked.

"Game over," said Will.

He pressed a button on the choker control ring.

"What are *talking* abo—?" said Wendy.

Panic rose in her throat—she knew something was wrong, she just didn't know what. Then she felt the choker constricting around her neck. She'd been tricked.

"I'll kill you!" she managed to gasp.

Wendy's mind played some nasty tricks on her. First she felt a boa constrictor wrapped around her neck. Then the sudden jerking of a hangman's noose. Her eyes were bulging out. The spears she'd been holding up telekinetically clattered harmlessly to the dock. She desperately tried to raise a knife up with her mind, but she hadn't had time to take a breath, and her brain was rapidly becoming oxygen-deprived.

"Where's Jasper?" asked Will.

He took two steps toward Wendy. She shook her head no. She wasn't going to tell him anything.

"I'm asking you nicely," said Will, even as he used the ring to tighten the choker even more.

Wendy managed to croak out a bleat of pain.

Will manipulated the ring, lessening the pressure so that she could breathe.

"You see how this works?" said Will.

Wendy nodded. Her goose was cooked and she knew it. Suddenly she wasn't a powerful demonteen, she was just a terrified sixteen-year-old girl.

"Now tell me, where's Jasper? Where'd he take the crystal?"

Wendy was shaking her head again.

"Our quest . . . We can't fail . . ." She started sobbing.

"Where is he?" asked Will.

Before Wendy could begin to muster further resistance, Will manipulated the choker. With a sudden surge of power, it began to strangle Wendy.

"One last time. Where. Is. *Jasper?*"

Wendy's eyes told the whole story. She was beaten.

"The old cannery," she gasped.

"We passed it on the way down here," said Loreli.

Will nodded.

"I've failed. You made me fail," whispered Wendy, raspy, dejected, beaten.

She'd almost never failed at anything—in school, in sports, in her personal life. She thought she'd been perfect. She was head cheerleader. She'd planned on being class valedictorian and marrying Jasper. These interlopers had ruined everything! She trembled with rage as an impulsive fury ripped through her body like hot lava. She let loose with what could only be described as a battle scream, using every last bit of her brain's power to raise the spears up and fling them at Rudy. He'd been trying to dislodge the one that had nailed his jeans to the wall, but he hadn't been able to make it budge. Now Death was coming right at him, and Rudy's life flashed before his eyes. He closed them and waited for the inevitable end. Will pressed a button on the ring, hard, and the choker did its final job, decapitating Wendy. Her head fell onto the dock with a *thunk* and rolled into the water and sank. The spears dropped in their trajectory and landed at Rudy's feet.

"Did I mention how much I hate this island?" he said, opening his eyes again.

Will tossed a healing patch to Loreli. While she was cleaning the wound on her cheek and applying the patch, Will freed Rudy.

"Thanks, dude. I owe you."

"Let's go," said Will.

They got in the Wagoneer and drove along Ocean Street, the asphalt giving way to dirt and gravel. Then the cannery came into view. It was an aged two-story red brick building with old-fashioned grille windows, at least thirty of the eight-inch panes cracked or broken. A wooden sign, bleached dim by the sun, identified the building as the Whiting Cannery. A dozen pickups were parked near the loading bays, so Will, Rudy, and Loreli knew the place was teeming with demonteens.

"Looks like we've found the party," said Will.

"Are you going to let me dance without my choker?" asked Loreli.

Her saving his life underwater could have still been part of a larger con. But at this point, he didn't have much choice but to trust her. He gave her a short nod, and Loreli smiled. Will stared at the building and formulated a rough plan of action, then consolidated the weapons he figured he would need into one backpack, which he then slung over his shoulder.

Rudy still had the Blaster Magnum. "Um, I think this is out of ammo."

Will checked it, saw that Rudy was right, and then chucked it into the pack like a piece of useless junk—which, without its powerful loads, it was.

"What do I get now?" asked Rudy.

Will pulled out one of the devices he'd given to Natalie and Emily. Rudy took it from him and looked like Will had just handed him a pair of panties.

"A Vibroslammer? This is a chick gun!"

"Suffer," said Will. "Let's go."

They got out of the Wagoneer, walked across the parking lot, and climbed up onto one of the loading docks. They kept moving until Will found some crates that he could stand on to look through the windows. It took a few seconds for his eyes to adjust to the darkness, but then he could see what was going on. Twenty White Island demonteens were standing in a circle holding hands. They were making horrible noises. The human larynx is capable of an almost infinite variety of sounds, none more hair-raising than the unholy cacophony heard by Will, Rudy, and Loreli now. Though the teens didn't know it, they were speaking in Satan's tongue. It was, Will thought, a sound he never wanted to hear again in his lifetime. The demonteens made sounds more akin to animals than human beings. And yet when combined, the voices created an odd, almost songlike dirge. They were calling out to the Voice, and the sounds they were creating, conjured from the darkest parts of their souls, made Will, Loreli, and Rudy's skin pebble with goose bumps.

"Catchy tune," said Loreli.

"Oh, man," said Rudy. "It's like the soundtrack to a nightmare."

Will pulled out a monocular and gazed through it, searching the room until he found what he was looking for. Cradled in black velvet in a large stainless steel tray atop a table in the center of the circle was the "treasure" the White Island teens had been driven to find. Will quickly processed what he was seeing. A look of recognition spread across his face. The fragments of crystals were power crystals, just like the one in his Power Rod.

Jasper was carefully arranging the crystals in two rows, piecing them together. Frag had been wrong. They hadn't had just a few pieces left to find, they'd only had one. The one in the underwater cave. And Will had helped them get it. As Jasper continued assembling the pieces like a puzzle, some of them began to fuse on their own.

Will finally made the connection. The two shafts that Jasper was forming were the very same Power Rods that had been part of the Triad of Power that was blown out of the volcano at Mount St. Emory. *This* was what the Dark Lord was after. He was going to use the two rods to fashion the blade for the Sword of Armageddon.

Will knew he couldn't leave without stealing them. He watched, his pulse racing, his blood pressure rising, as Jasper moved the last piece of the jagged puzzle into place. The Power Rods began to shine as they rapidly fused into solid shafts. There was not a moment to waste. Will's whole body was tingling, his brain jacked up to high alert as it often did just before a seminal battle. Loreli saw the look in his eyes.

"It's in there, isn't it . . . the blade?"

Will ignored the question. "Can you create a diversion?" he asked her.

"Are you kidding me? I could start World War Three."

"Do it. Then mess up their rides. Give me exactly sixty seconds. I'm going low, you go high," said Will. He pointed to a stairwell that led to a basement, then he pointed to the roof.

Loreli nodded. "Got it." She reached for the fire escape, but Will stopped her and handed her a power zip-line kit from his backpack.

"This will get you up there quicker. Take Rudy with you. Okay—go!"

She did: 60 . . . 59 . . . 58 . . . , the seconds ticked down. Loreli shot the zip line up onto the roof. The hook caught on some pipes and she pulled it taut. Then she grabbed the motorized handle with one hand and Rudy with the other. She pressed a button and up they went, Rudy stifling the urge to yelp: 49 . . . 48 . . . 47 seconds and counting.

Will used a Flareblade to cut open the basement door and went inside, then carefully walked off forty-three paces, the distance he'd calculated between the door and the center of the room above. Moving fast, he sprayed a six-foot-diameter circle of blaze foam on the ceiling and waited: 25 . . . 24 . . . 23 seconds.

Loreli climbed onto the roof, helped Rudy up, and looked around, quickly locating two vent pipes and a skylight. She reached into her duster and pulled out two small red orbs that she handed to Rudy.

"Drop those in the vent pipes when I tell you to," she said. Rudy nodded and walked to the first vent. He stood waiting while Loreli moved to the skylight and peered down. She lifted a blue cylinder from her duster and then looked at her watch: 5 . . . 4 . . . 3 . . . 2 . . . 1.

"Now!" she said.

Rudy dropped one red orb down the first vent pipe, then ran and dropped the other one down the second. At the same time,

Loreli broke the skylight window and dropped the blue cylinder. *Boom! Boom! KA-BOOM!* Spectacular diversion completed and their job done, Loreli and Rudy zip-lined back down to the ground and set upon their next task.

In the basement, Will heard all hell breaking loose above him, the demonteens shouting and running around. He zapped the foam circle with the Flareblade and the foam caught fire. It sizzled for two seconds before exploding, and the section of floor above it collapsed into the basement. The table holding the Power Rods landed with a bang and a clatter. Will grabbed the rods and stuffed them into his backpack, then glanced up at the hole he'd left in the floor. Looking down at him was Jasper.

The two young men locked eyes, and Will was puzzled. He'd squared off with hundreds of demonteens, and their eyes had all been more or less the same, containing varying amounts of enmity, malice, rage, greed, and the like. But in Jasper's eyes he saw suffering. With his seventh sense, his ability to deftly and expertly pick up meta-communication, Will was getting some surprising vibes from Jasper. Usually a demon's anger and hatred was a flood, drenching everything in its path. But Jasper was sending out feelings of utter despair.

Will tossed aside his bravado and spoke. "Jasper, listen to me. He's using you. The Voice you've been hearing, it belongs to the Dark Lord, to Satan."

"I. Don't. Care," said Jasper. "Give them back."

"I can't do that, Jasper."

"Then you will have to die."

Jasper leapt down, his heavy boots smashing the table. He made a guttural roaring sound as his eyes shifted from wet black to fiercely glowing red.

"I should have killed you when I had the chance!"

"Sorry, no do overs," said Will.

Jasper glared at the stainless steel tray, and it became a deadly weapon as he used his powerful mind to whip it around the room, a spinning disc capable of taking Will's head off. Over and over the tray rocketed at Will, who had to bend time in order to duck and feint away from the flying guillotine. Coming in faster, it grazed his scalp, and blood dripped down into his eyes. Enough. He managed to grab a short-range Turboflayer from his backpack and fired off two rounds. They caught the steel tray in midair and tore it to shreds.

Jasper was not impressed. He started ripping pipes from the walls and flinging them at Will with shocking speed and intensity. Will used the Turboflayer to deflect the onslaught of projectiles, but he took a shot to his chest from a brick that had penetrated his defenses. He felt like he'd been punched in the heart by a pile driver and went down hard. He had to get out of the basement—if he didn't, it was going to become his grave.

He dug into his backpack and retrieved a Series 9 Sonic Flash Bomb, wasting no time pulling the pin and flinging it at Jasper. The Series 9 went off and the room erupted in a flash of white light and a high-pitched wailing sound that caused Jasper to reflexively try to cover his eyes and ears at the same time. Will seized the opportunity to bend time and run for the door.

Outside, Loreli was behind the wheel of the Wagoneer with the engine running, Rudy in the passenger seat with the window rolled down. Demonteens spilled out of the cannery, their eyes blazing with manic anger as they roared and spat and hissed. Will blasted out of the basement door and screamed at Loreli.

"Drive! *NOW!*"

Loreli floored it in Will's direction as Rudy started firing away with the Vibroslammer through the open window, knocking three demonteens off their feet with invisible blasts.

"Cool!" said Rudy.

The Wagoneer's rear wheels burned rubber on the pavement and then kicked up rooster tails of rocks when they hit the gravel. Rudy leaned back and flung open the back door. Will bent time again and ran, diving in and slamming the door shut behind him, barely escaping the demonteens on his heels.

Jasper emerged from the basement and yelled demon curses to the others, and the pack ran for their pickup trucks. They exploded with rage and hurled expletives when they saw that all their tires were flat. When Jasper began running, the others followed.

Will, Loreli, and Rudy had a huge head start. But would it be enough?

Chapter Twenty-Three: Battle at the Farm

Natalie and Emily were leading the nearly naked throng of disoriented, malnourished, traumatized adults out through the front gates of the Corwin Tomato Farm, intending to more or less herd them safely back into town. But when they saw a fleet of vehicles speeding up the hill toward them, they realized that one of the demon sentries must have alerted their comrades. So, running back and forth and barking orders like a couple of sheepdogs, the twins guided the drove of adults back through the farm and up the grassy hillside toward the tree line.

Natalie looked back at the tomato farm as a half-dozen cars and trucks skidded to a halt. A mass of demonteens spilled out and, seeing them, began shouting angry curses. Then they stood as a group and began to use their telekinesis to raise gravel from the driveway. Concentrating, they sent a hail of rocks through the air.

Natalie shouted at the adults, "Hurry! To the trees!"

The adults understood and hastened their pace. Small stones hurled down from the sky and struck many of them. Those hit cried out in torment. Natalie risked another glance down at the teens. They were slowly bringing larger rocks up through the loamy earth to the surface. She screamed again at the slow-moving adults.

"Hurry! Faster!"

They redoubled their efforts, but they were still totally exposed. It was imperative that they get to the tree line.

"Natalie! Over here!"

Emily waved her sister over, and they watched as the first of several larger rocks—ten pounders and bigger—came arcing up from below. They slammed into the ground like cannonballs, and the adults screamed in terror. As Natalie raised her Vibroslammer, so did Emily, and together they aimed and fired, sending powerful pulses skyward, deflecting most of the deadly projectiles heading their way. However, one found its target, striking Denise in the shoulder and knocking her down. She brayed like an injured beast, and while Emily kept up the shield of defense, Natalie rushed over to help Denise back to her feet. The woman's eyes were feral with panic.

"Come on," said Natalie. "You've got to get to the trees!"

Denise appeared to vaguely fathom Natalie's entreaty, and up she went, waddling like a terrified duck, her formidable buttocks swaying ignobly. Natalie never saw the rock coming, but she sure as hell felt it as it slammed into her elbow, sending a lightning bolt of electric pain up her arm and into her neck and head.

"Ahhhh!" she screamed.

For a moment her mind was buzzing with nothing but pain, granting no room for rational thought. But she managed to fight through it. She moved the Vibroslammer to her left hand, then whirled and fired it, blowing rock after airborne rock asunder, firing with a vengeance until the weapon's power source was depleted. Emily blasted away with hers until it, too, was dead.

Most of the adults had reached the relative safety of the tree line by then, and they crouched behind the thick firs and pines. Now the flying rocks slammed into the tree trunks instead of striking fragile human bodies. Natalie ran as fast as she could, fighting to keep her balance. She attempted to reject the basic notion of pain, though it threatened to overtake her entirely. *Will does this all the time*, she thought, gritting her teeth. With her arm dangling uselessly, she reached the tree line.

"Are you all right?" asked Emily.

"I can't feel my arm."

The huddled adults looked over at the twins. Emily ministered to Natalie, rubbing her own elbow as well, because she could feel the pain, too. She began to manipulate Natalie's arm, causing them both to yelp in pain. Natalie clenched her teeth.

"I don't think it's broken," she said.

They looked down at the tomato farm and watched as the assembled demonteens huddled in evil consult, then spread out and began trotting up the hill. Natalie looked farther up the hill and saw their only hope: the old barn on Halstrom's Crest.

"The barn!" she shouted. "Let's go!"

They ran for their lives.

As Loreli sped through the streets of Bingham, Will wiped the sweat from his brow. They were safe. For now.

"Did you get it?" asked Loreli.

Will stayed silent. She'd been doing double duty as his guardian angel, saving his butt over and over, and a voice told him that maybe it was time to bury the hatchet. But another voice reminded him that he had vowed to never, ever forgive her. She could still be planning to sabotage him like she had before. He was waging an internal war that at this point he could ill afford. Yet he couldn't seem to resolve it.

Loreli checked her rearview mirror. Far in the distance, Jasper and the demonteens were in pursuit.

"I'll take that as a yes, which means we need to get our butts off this island."

"Right after we get the twins," said Will.

He pulled out his cell phone and dialed Natalie.

She picked up almost immediately, sounding out of breath. "Will?"

"Where are you?" he asked.

"By the tomato farm, just up the hill." Her voice was thin with fear.

"What happened? Did you find an adult?"

On the other end of the line, Natalie looked at the thundering herd of naked muddy prisoners whom she and Emily had liberated. They were rushing into the barn with Emily.

"We found them all. It's horrible what they did to them! Hurry, Will. We're in the barn on the hill, way at the top of the island. We need help!"

Will hung up, his mind racing. He looked at Loreli.

"When you came and seeded the clouds, you went to the highest point on the island, correct?"

"Yeah, some old farm. That's where I did the seeding."

"Okay, good. Get us there. Fast."

Loreli slammed her foot onto the gas and the Wagoneer shot forward, tires screaming as she whipped around a corner and headed up the winding road that led them up into the hills.

Will held on and set his jaw in grim determination. He wasn't about to let anyone or anything stand between him and saving the girl he loved, even if she no longer loved him back. He turned around to dig into his weapons backpack—and found himself looking into a double-barreled Burn Pistol. Behind the pistol, Frag was grinning from the very back of the Wagoneer, clearly enjoying having the upper hand this time around.

"Are you feeling lucky, punk?" Frag cackled and shot a mocking glance at Rudy, adding, "Sorry, I couldn't help myself!"

The Burn Pistol was a wicked compact weapon that shot white-hot bursts of pure flame up to fifty feet. It was like a small double-barreled flamethrower. Frag's eyes were bloodshot, his pupils enlarged. Will guessed that he was high on something. He looked just out of it enough, and dumb enough, to fire the Burn Pistol. If he did, the flame would ricochet off the interior roof and bloom in seconds, turning the whole interior into a blast furnace. They'd all wind up incinerated.

Frag was still grinning like he'd just won the lottery. "I was outside taking a leak when I saw you guys pull up. When they went up on the roof and you went into the basement, I knew you were up to something. Oh, man, this is so sick. I'm gonna be a hero! Jasper's gonna be majorly proud of me!"

Frag's finger was tightening on the trigger. Will knew he had to do something, and pronto. *Think. Think!*

"How about your parents?" he asked. "Are *they* going to be proud of you?"

Frag's eyes flickered with guilt. Will had touched a nerve. As the gears turned in Frag's head—as he thought back to how his mom and dad had been hunted down like animals and buried up to their necks—Will made his move. He bent time and twisted the gun in Frag's hand, cracking the proximal phalanx bone in his middle finger. Frag should have immediately dropped the gun, but his hands were small. His third finger, unbroken, was still on the trigger, squeezing. Will could feel it all happening, knew a blast was coming, so he shattered the side window with his boot and shoved the pistol away from his face. *Ka-boom!* The Burn Pistol's load fired, and twin jets of flame shot out of the Wagoneer's window, striking a parked VW bus, which caught fire instantly.

Will yanked gun out of Frag's hand. He decided Frag needed some motivation to cooperate, so he hit him with a right cross that twisted his head violently to the side. Frag slumped backward. Will caught him by his shirt. He was woozy but still conscious.

"Smooth move, hero" said Will. "Your little stunt could have killed us all."

Loreli kept driving. Behind them, the VW's gas tank blew and the bus exploded.

"You'd better come up here beside me," said Will.

He yanked Frag up into the backseat next to him. Frag was like a rag doll in Will's powerful grasp.

"Don't hurt me anymore, man," he pleaded.

"We should just waste him," said Rudy from the front seat.

"That's not necessary, is it Frag?"

"No. Definitely not. Definitely not necessary."

Frag gazed out the window. He wasn't thinking malicious thoughts. He was thinking about how it had all gotten away from them, from all of them.

"What did you do to your parents?" asked Will.

Frag shook his head from side to side, determined to stay clammed up, even though the truth—and the guilt that came with it—was like a parasite, eating him from the inside out, just like that cockroach was going to do. Will grabbed Frag by the scruff of his neck and positioned him next to the window. He shoved the Burn Pistol in his face.

"Talk or fry. Your choice."

Frag began shaking, then made his decision.

"The Voice told us what to do. It made us capture all the old people and bury them up at Corwin's. It was like we were in a daze, like zombies or something. The Voice, man, we can't disobey it or our parents will die. This one kid resisted, and then his dad . . . ," Frag swallowed hard. "The dive club recruited everyone, and they started searching for the treasure. And we got it. Maybe now the Voice will stop."

Will was starting to get the full picture. The Dark Lord had not only infected the island's teens, but had forced to them to hold their own parents in hideous confinement as collateral, to make sure the teens did his bidding. A little way of saying, "My way or the highway." If any of the newly minted demonteens dared rebel, the Dark Lord would command the others to kill his or her parents.

Will had always known that demonteens retained some of the same feelings they'd had before they were infected, but he hadn't realized just how much. Even though demonteens appeared heart-less, it seemed they remained connected, a thin filament of familial love running to their roots. Or at least *these* demonteens did. Will was beginning to look at them in a totally different way.

He cuffed Frag with a zip-tie and slapped a length of gaffer's tape over his eyes and mouth for good measure.

"Don't give us any trouble," said Will.

Frag shook his head slowly as Loreli saw the sign for Corwin's Tomato Farm and turned the wheel hard. They were less than a min-ute away. Will tucked the Burn Pistol in his jacket, then leaned back and checked the contents of his weapons backpacks. He was well stocked, and damn glad of it. He had a feeling they were in for a real donnybrook.

They sped past Corwin's Tomato Farm. When they reached Hal-strom's Crest, Will saw the demonteens grimly marching across the field toward the old barn.

"Here!" he said.

Loreli yanked the wheel and the Wagoneer bounced off the road, through the ditch, and began crossing the field. When the demon-teens saw the speeding vehicle approaching them, they used their powers to lift a fallen fir tree and send it hurling through the air right at the Wagoneer. Loreli braked just in time as the tree cartwheeled past them and slammed into a jutting boulder, splintering. Will looked toward the barn and its heavy old doors. They were open, and he could see Natalie and Emily watching from inside.

"Keep going! We've got to make the barn!" yelled Will.

"Take the wheel!" said Loreli, grabbing Rudy's hand and putting it on the wheel.

Keeping one foot on the gas while a wide-eyed Rudy steered, Loreli dug into her duster and grabbed a slingshot. The Wagoneer lurched and bounced across the ruts in the field. She loaded the slingshot with a ceramic ball and let it fly directly at the demon-teens. The ball exploded, creating a massive cloud of black smoke.

Meanwhile Will pulled out a Diversion Ball, activated it, and threw it as hard as he could. Seconds later the hillside was alive with a cacophony of human voices, disorienting the demonteens. Loreli took the wheel back, and they blasted across the meadow, through the open doors, and into the barn.

As the Wagoneer skidded to a halt, Will and Rudy jumped out and ran to close the heavy barn doors. Will looked out through an opening and saw that, though they'd regrouped, for the moment the demonteens in the meadow were holding back. Jasper and the others had arrived. Jasper had surveyed the situation and was formulating a battle plan.

Will turned around and took in the horde of half-naked muddy adults. They looked like Neanderthals. Will blinked in disbelief. Natalie and Emily approached him.

"You're here," said Natalie.

Will's soul lit up when their eyes met. Her radiant eyes were beaming. Before she'd been infected, they would have hugged each other tightly. Things had changed, but the look in her eyes made Will hope they could change back. He reached out his left hand toward her right—it was a cautious gesture, a gesture of reconciliation; he yearned to once again take refuge in her heart. But her arm remained at her side. *She won't even raise her hand to meet my touch.* He was crushed. What he didn't realize was that her arm remained at her side not because she chose not to touch him, but because it was still numb.

She opened her mouth to explain, reaching out with her other arm. "Will, my—"

The roof of the barn exploded. A two-hundred-pound boulder came crashing through and slammed into the dirt floor, raising a cloud of dust and debris. The adults screamed and wheezed and dove for cover. Will pulled out the Burn Pistol and handed it to Natalie.

"Take this!"

She took it with her left hand while Will grabbed a backpack
and quickly climbed to the hayloft, where he swung open one of the
upper doors. Emily yelled up to him.

"Will! We need one of your healing patches!"

He dug one out of his jacket sleeve and tossed it down to her.
Emily immediately applied the patch to Natalie's elbow as, above
them, Will stared out the hayloft door.

Jasper and the other demonteens were gathered in the meadow.
Boone was grimacing.

"What about our . . . my mom, she's in there," said Boone.

"So's my dad," said Jasper, "and my aunt Janie."

Jasper, too, was in turmoil. How could it have come to this? How
could it be that he had to make a choice between saving his father
or heeding the powerful Voice that resonated in his brain? No one
knew what would happen should they disobey the Voice. They only
knew that they could not. The present quandary was eating away at
what was left of their hearts and souls. Jasper searched inside himself, imagining how he would lead a revolt against the Voice, how
he could defy it. With this notion came a sudden assault of images,
thousands of hellish scenarios played in his brain at warp speed,
each and every one featuring either Jasper or someone he loved suffering through immense pain. Jasper shook his head. Better that his
father die quickly.

"We gotta do what we gotta do," he said.

"Come on, man," said Boone. The big bullet-head was on the
verge of tears.

Jasper just shook his head slowly, and made a deadly pronounce-
ment. "We must obey the Voice."

So Jasper and Boone and the other demonteens stood grimly in
the field, stock still, and began focusing their power. Another huge
boulder rose up—as though birthed from the earth—and became
airborne, hovering like an alien ship before blasting toward the barn.
Will saw it and screamed to the others.

"Incoming!"

After the catastrophic impact of the first boulder, everyone knew what *incoming* meant and they hit the dirt, bracing themselves. *Ka-bam!* The second boulder struck with the force of a howitzer, ripping a huge hole in the side of the barn as it passed right through. Everyone in the barn had the same thought: We're all going to die.

Will knew he had to get proactive, and fast.

Chapter Twenty-Four: Love Unbound

Unzipping a backpack, Will pulled out the long-range Broad-Beamed Shock Bombardier. Dialing it up to 9, he waited for it to power up, then aimed it at the demonteens and fired.

The shockwave hit the demonteens hard, knocking them backward, blowing them off their feet. As Jasper climbed back upright, bowed but unbroken, he had sudden irrefutable confirmation of what he'd suspected earlier at the cannery: he was dealing with an equal, an adversary who would be every bit his match. His eyes burned with fury and he opened his throat to unleash an unearthly howl.

Galvanized by their leader, Jasper's battered compatriots leapt to their feet and joined in, letting loose a jarring wail, their eyes glowing fiercely. Jasper roared, "Attack again!"

Like their leader, the demonteens were not about to be deterred. They strained their brains, causing more boulders to bloom from the earth. Another one soared across the meadow and hit the barn's front door. *Ka-boom!* Another crashed through the roof. Miraculously, Rudy dove and knocked Emily out of the path of the boulder just in time, and together they rolled into a stall. He landed on top of her, shielding her with his body, as the huge rock slammed into the floor right where she had been standing.

She looked up at him. He'd just saved her life. He looked back down at her.

"Are you . . . ?"

"I'm okay," she said.

Rudy could have stayed like that for hours. But there was too much going on. He knew he had to get up. He was thrilled, however, that she hadn't shoved him off. With a huge force of will, he climbed off her, stood up, and pulled her to her feet.

"Thanks," she said.

Her eyes were locked on his and he couldn't suppress a hard blush.

"Come on," said Loreli, interrupting them. She ignored a surge of envy at the way they were looking at each other. "Help me start moving these people further back."

Up in the hayloft, Will quickly unpacked and assembled the Death Twister, a singularly vicious weapon which, when first viewed, appeared to be a small rocket launcher like an RPG. But what it launched was far deadlier than a simple grenade.

Will shouldered the Death Twister. He was about to pull the trigger when he heard a voice from below saying, "Garfield!"

Mary Dressing, a slight woman with long stringy red hair, saw Frag in the Wagoneer and rushed to him. She pulled him out and yanked the tape from his eyes and mouth.

"Ow! Geez!"

"Frag! Can you see? Can you see Mommy?"

Will lowered the Death Twister and frowned. *Mommy?* He had let her be buried up to her neck, fed and watered like a plant, and she was still *Mommy*?

Frag blinked, pulled all the images into his brain, saw the naked grubby adults, including his own mother, whose sagging breasts he'd once suckled on.

"Garfield, are you alright?"

"My . . . hands . . ."

Mary tried to break the zip-tie but couldn't. She turned to Natalie.

"Cut him loose."

Natalie looked to Will in the hayloft, who shook his head no.

"I'm sorry," Natalie said.

"I SAID CUT HIM LOOSE!"

"I'm sorry," said Natalie again. "It's not safe."

When Natalie turned away again, Mary marched over to a wall, where she found a rusty old scythe blade, and promptly used it to start sawing through the plastic zip-tie.

The sound attracted Will's attention.

"Ma'am, please don't do that," he said, struggling to keep his voice calm. "He can't be trusted."

Mary kept sawing. Will couldn't believe it.

Loreli made a move to stop Mary, but two older women blocked her path. She looked at Will. Should she kick their asses? Will shook his head, deciding instead on appealing to their logic. They were adults and they weren't infected; hopefully he could reason with them and avoid using violence.

"Ma'am, he doesn't have control of himself right now. As soon as you cut through that, he's going to run and join the others."

"No, he won't!" cried Mary. She stopped sawing. Frag looked at her with pathetic puppy dog eyes.

"You won't, will you Garfield? You won't leave Mommy?"

"No," he said. "Just cut me loose, Mom . . ."

She sawed again. *Snap.* The plastic broke and Frag started rubbing his wrists.

"I'm sorry, Mom," he said. His voice was small and full of shame.

"It's okay, baby," she said. And then she hugged him and wept. "I forgive you."

Will shook his head. It was unreal. The little rat bastard had allowed her to be put in the ground, and she forgave him?

Then Frag pushed his mother away. "Thanks for letting me go . . . but . . ." He ran to a gaping hole in the wall. "I can't help it, Mom. I have to obey the Voice."

And he was gone. Mary rushed to the doors and opened one, watching in disbelief as Frag ran to his infected comrades. More adults went to the barn door and peered out at their mutated offspring.

The demonteens were busy. Boulders continued to slam into the barn, tearing through the roof. When one hit the foot of an older woman, she screamed and fell, clutching it.

Will re-shouldered the Death Twister and took aim. As he pulled the trigger, he felt hands clutching at him, pulling him backward. The shot went high and the load was fired into the trees. The Death Twister's load was a thing to behold: a thousand whirling micro-blades of doom. When they hit the treetops, they exploded in a cloud of mind-bending annihilation. The tops of the trees were obliterated in seconds.

Will looked back to see who had grabbed him. An older man, Bill Brownlie, stood watching the destruction, then he looked Will in the eye.

"Those are our children out there," he said.

"They're trying to kill you," said Will calmly.

A voice came from below. "Better I should die from my son's hand than he from mine!"

It was Hannah Winter, a tall brunette who'd had plenty of work done on her face, but had long ago let her body go entirely.

"And I tell you right now, Boone would not lay a finger on me!" she said.

Will knew she was in total denial—how could she think that, after everything that happened at the farm? But he wasn't prepared for what she did next. Hannah, still wearing only her bra and under-wear and caked with mud, drew herself up regally. "I'm going to prove it," she said. "Boone!" As she yelled his name, she bolted through the open door. The others watched in amazement as she ran out screaming.

"Boone! Boonie! *Boone!*"

As she ran, she lifted her arms in hope, reaching for her son, for love, for honor. Will hoped she was also saying a silent prayer, because he had an awful feeling about what was coming next.

Although the bonds of family run deep, the infected demonteens were driven to place the Dark Lord above all else. And so the boulders kept coming. Poor Mrs. Winter had no chance. A mighty hunk of granite the size of a dryer came hurling down out of the sky and crushed her.

The adults in the barn sucked in a collective gasp. Out in the meadow, the barrage abated as Boone Winter dropped to his knees and cried out, heart breaking.

Jasper approached Hannah Winter's body, which was now little more than a pulpy mass with a hand jutting out, still reaching for love. Jasper calmly reached down and slipped Hannah's wedding ring off her finger, then walked over and presented it to Boone.

The big kid took the ring and put it on his little finger, then stood up and roared, "I'm going to kill those sons of bitches!"

Boone ran forward, but Jasper stuck out a foot and tripped him. The big guy fell to the dirt.

"You'll get your revenge, Boone. But not yet. We still have a quest to finish!"

Boone got up, his body shaking with rage, but stood down.

Jasper stepped in front of him and yelled across the battlefield to Will Hunter, "Give us the treasure and no one else will be harmed!"

Inside the barn, the adults conferred in staccato whispers. "What treasure?" "Who has the treasure?" "Give it to them!" "Give them what they want!"

Out in the meadow, some of the demonteens whispered among themselves as well. Could they really keep up the barrage and kill their parents? What if they didn't? They knew they had to obey the Voice.

Will considered the situation. He knew he could not relinquish the Power Rods. Yet the adults seemed fully prepared to sacrifice themselves rather than watch their offspring perish in a battle, even though the kids were demonically possessed. He thought about the bond he had with his own mother, how he knew he would go to the ends of the Earth to save her, and knew she would do the same for him. So he knew their wounds, felt their pain, and when all was said and done, he would probably have done the same.

Through all of what had happened, Will had gained a clearer understanding of the teens on White Island. When he'd arrived, he'd expected everything to be business as usual—they were demons, and it was his job to wipe their kind off the face of the Earth. But this group was different than any other group of demonteens he'd encountered. They hadn't *chosen* to become infected. Infection had literally been dropped on their heads, in the form of a freak demonic rain. The Dark Lord was using them as pawns. They were only fighting to please the haunting Voice that had promised that if they did what was asked of them, their parents would be spared. In twisted way, they were only behaving this way out of love.

Will was caught between a rock and a hard place. He couldn't give up the rods, but he also couldn't bring himself to set about wiping out the sons and daughters of the adults whom Natalie and Emily had liberated. Not if there was another way.

Jasper decided he needed to send a message, so he shouted to his subordinates, "Hands together!"

They formed a semicircle and joined hands. They concentrated their power and unearthed a massive granite boulder ten feet in diameter. The immense rock vibrated in midair, then took flight, soared across the meadow, and crashed into the side of the barn. A section of the barn collapsed, and the adults inside screamed and shrieked in terror. Jasper was pleased.

"You have ten minutes! If we don't have what we want by then, you're all going to die. If you don't believe me, then watch this!"

His searching eyes found something. He spoke to his peers.

"Again! They need to know we're really serious."

They all did as Jasper did, focusing their energies upon the rusty old five-ton logging truck at the foot of the meadow. It was a behemoth, a monstrous wreck. As the demonteens' stares grew more intense, the truck creaked and groaned and rose up like some prehistoric beast. It hovered ten . . . fifteen . . . fifty feet off the ground, then flew across the meadow as though flung by Zeus himself, arced up, and smashed down through the roof of the barn.

Will was deep in thought, locked in his moral conundrum. He should have been prepared, but he wasn't. So when the massive truck breached the roof and plunged toward him, even though he bent time, he was still a half second too slow, and the truck's right rear axle clipped the side of his head. His head slammed down hard and he slipped into an inky black void.

Natalie's heart rose into her throat. She rushed to Will's fallen body and cradled his head in her hands. "Will!"

His breathing was ragged. The wound on the side of his head was brutal. She touched his cheek.

"Will?"

He was unconscious, for who knew how long. Natalie tore into his jacket pocket and pulled out a healing patch and applied it to his wound. His body jerked at her touch, which she knew was a good sign. Holding his head in her lap, she realized she hadn't been this close to him for a long time. Not since she'd lied to him, right to his face. She'd hurt him, put up barriers, obstacles meant to protect him. It had been only days, but it felt like a lifetime. She had been in agony every second she'd withheld the truth. She'd told him she didn't love him. The words were like a sickness in her soul, yet she'd felt she had to speak them. But now things were different. What if he never woke up? Natalie's heart pounded. She had to tell him the truth, even if he couldn't hear it.

"Will, I lied to you. I have never, ever, not for one second, stopped loving you. I just . . . I almost *killed* you! When you brought me back, all I could think of was how stupid I had been, how I'd almost destroyed the one thing in my life that matters to me the most."

Will's eyes remained closed, almost as though he were sleeping. Was he dreaming? Was he dreaming of her? She touched his cheek again, this time with her lips.

"Will, come back to me. Don't go. I only said what I said because I'd betrayed you and I couldn't forgive myself for what I'd done. I wanted you to go on with your life and leave me behind. I wanted you to find *true* love, someone better than me. That's why I lied. But I don't know how I'll go on if you die now, thinking I could ever stop loving you."

Emily heard Natalie's confession, and she flushed with relief. She *knew* Natalie had never stopped loving Will!

Loreli heard it too, and hung her head in shame, overcome with guilt over what she'd done.

Under Will's eyelids, his eyes were flicking back and forth. He could hear Natalie's voice, but he was in the grip of a nightmare. *He and Natalie were alone on the deck of a huge ghost ship at night in a churning sea. Massive waves crashed around them like giant greedy hands. A huge tentacle rose up out of the inky water and snaked across the deck toward them, wrapping around Will's leg, dragging him across the slippery deck as Natalie screamed and fought to hold on to him. The ship began to list to one side and spun slowly in the water. As he was being dragged over the side of the ship, Will saw that the vessel was being pulled into a deep swirling vortex. They were being sucked down to Hell.*

In the barn, George Sholes had had it. He couldn't wait anymore. While the others bickered and watched the drama unfolding in front of them—the handsome young man lying in his girlfriend's arms, his life bleeding away—George slipped unnoticed over to Will's back-packs and rifled through them. He was startled and amazed by the strange weapons he found. But it wasn't weapons he was looking for. His son, Jasper, had said they were to relinquish the treasure. George pulled out and unfurled a long piece of black velvet. Inside were two glowing crystals. George's heart beat with a sudden surging hope.

"I have the treasure!" he called out.

The other adults rushed over to surround George. They gazed in awe at the crystal rods.

"This is what they want!" said Janie Walker.

"So let's give it to them!" said Mary Dressing.

Loreli's head shot up. This was not how it was supposed to be! Her brother was lying on the barn floor, perhaps mortally wounded. These crazed adults had gained possession of the thing that they'd all risked their lives for. Everything had come undone. They were on the verge of defeat. If the adults gave the rods to their children, there would be no stopping the Dark Lord from assembling the Sword of Armageddon.

Clearly, reason and logic had failed. It was time for Loreli to take matters into her own hands. Slowly, she reached inside her duster.

Chapter Twenty-Five: Help from Above

The adults were ecstatic. Now that they had the "treasure," it was as if all the problems of the world had been solved. They would hand it over to their kids, and then all of this would be over.

Boom! The barn was rocked by an explosion and filled with a blinding white light that rose from the ground and bloomed into an intense and dazzling mushroom. The adults cried out. George Sholes felt the rods being wrenched from his grasp.

"No!"

The light abated as swiftly as it had intruded. Now the adults were greeted with another sight: Loreli stood holding the crystal rods, feeling their power in her hand. She stared at them, succumbing to their magic, magnetic pull.

The adults knew they had Loreli and the other teen warriors vastly outnumbered. They began picking up what crude weapons they could find: rocks, chunks of wood, old rusty farm tools.

Rudy stepped forward and aimed the Vibroslammer at them. "You'd better stand back," he said. "This thing hurts like—"

He choked on his words. Felton Possnack and Dan Winter had snuck up behind him and thrown a rope around his neck, and now they yanked him off his feet. Felton stepped on Rudy's hand and he yelped in pain as Dan confiscated the weapon. Emily screamed and raced forward.

"Leave him alone!"

She pounded her fists into Felton's chest. He relaxed his grip on Rudy, who fell to the floor. He was fuming, but now unarmed. Emily helped Rudy to his feet as Felton spoke.

"We're grateful that you saved us, and we're sorry to have to do this. But you have to understand. They're our *children*. No matter what, we still love them. We can't let you harm them."

Natalie had dropped the Burn Pistol when Will was hit. She was staring at it now. She made a move toward it, but Frag's mother, Mary, beat her to it. She held it at arm's length and pointed it at Rudy. It was occurring to Rudy and Emily that they might be living out their last moments on Earth in the bowels of this decrepit old barn. What a place to die. Rudy took Emily's hand. Loreli glared at the adults.

"You may think you're doing the right thing, but you're not," she said. "We're fighting the powers of darkness here! If you get your way, the whole world's going to be doomed!"

The adults all heard her words but apparently could not bring themselves to believe them. They were shaking their heads, muttering among themselves.

Loreli was still holding the crystal rods and was doing her best to appear menacing. "We can't allow you to hand these over," she said

The adults spread out and took small careful steps in the dirt, moving closer and closer.

Will was still clinging to the deck, with Natalie a few feet away as the ship was pulled down into the black whirlpool. Malicious creatures swirled around them. He reached for Natalie—but she was swept overboard. He screamed his throat raw, but he made no sound.

Suddenly he was in a clearing in the woods. The skies above him were choked with pewter clouds. They cracked and rumbled. He felt the first drops of rain, salty on his tongue.

I must still be in the ocean, he thought.

He opened his eyes.

Natalie's face was just inches from his. Her eyes were closed tight and she was weeping, her tears spilling down upon him. He saw the world with acute clarity. Not only were Natalie's tears hitting his face, but rain was now falling down through one of the huge holes in the roof of the barn. The skies were really opening up, the rain coming down harder by the second. Will drew in a sharp breath and Natalie's eyes opened wide. She gasped, too.

"Will . . ."

"Did you mean it? Do you—"

"I still love you, I love you, I love you!"

Her skin was flushing and prickled as he smiled and pulled her down, kissing her ear and whispering, "I never stopped believing that."

It was true. Deep in his heart, he had always known that she loved him. He told himself to listen more closely to his heart from now on.

Satisfied, he glanced around the barn and assessed the situation. The adults, murder in their eyes, were surrounding Loreli. The crystal rods were in her hand. Rudy and Emily were weaponless.

It was, of course, up to him. He had to rise to the challenge or they'd all die like dogs, the demonteens would get the Power Rods, and the Dark Lord would win.

He rose on unsteady feet, reached around and touched the retrieval patch on the back of his neck. Mary Dressing's hand shook as she aimed the Burn Pistol at him.

"Don't try to stop us!" she shouted.

"I'm not going to *try*," said Will.

Things happened very quickly. He tapped the Power Rod Retrieval Patch on the back of his neck, and *his* Power Rod came screaming down from the clouds, whooshed through the hole in the roof, and slapped into his waiting palm. He activated the dual laser blade function. He bent time and, moving as silently as a ghost, swept through the barn, disarming the muddy, befuddled, disoriented adults in seconds.

Mary Dressing stood blinking, staring at her hands where the Burn Pistol had been. Will stepped toward Loreli. She was still holding the crystal rods, their faint glimmering reflecting a golden light in her eyes. The adults' threat diffused, Loreli was gazing at the rods.

"They're so beautiful . . . ," she said.

"Give them to me," said Will.

He reached out a hand. Loreli hesitated. Will knew that she could, should she choose, use the crystals as a weapon against him. But she just took one last longing look at the crystals, then re-wrapped them in the black velvet and handed them to her brother. Powerless against Will and his Power Rod, the adults stood and watched in silence. Save for the sound of the falling rain, the barn was hushed. Jasper's voice rang out.

"Your time is up! Surrender or die! Ten seconds!"

They all counted the seconds down in their minds. Mary Dressing looked at Will with pleading eyes.

"Please . . . ," she whimpered.

Silence. Then the barrage hit. Two boulders hit the barn broadside, knocking the door down, splintering it into a thousand pieces. More boulders rained down from above, smashing through the roof and thudding into the ground. A massive uprooted fir tree soared across the sky and rammed the corner of the barn, causing the entire structure to creak and groan as it began to list. Will and the others gazed up at the rafters. The barn could come down on them at any second.

Rudy shouted at Will, "Dude, you've got to stop them! You've got to kick their asses!"

"No!" said George.

"You gotta smoke 'em! It's the only way!" said Rudy.

Will had envisioned a battle that would end in a river of blood. But maybe it didn't have to go down that way. He remembered his mother's words: *When you let anger in, it crowds out everything else. It crowds out empathy, compassion, love.* Usually when he fought he was so angry, so full of hate, that violence seemed like the only solution. He'd started out hating Jasper and the other demonteens, but he no longer did. Now he understood them. If there was a way to end this standoff without any more bloodshed, he had to try.

The raindrops had given him an idea, but he had to act fast.

More boulders and trees hit the barn. A huge boulder smashed into the barn's floor, crashing through an old horizontal door that led to a root cellar. A rafter beam cracked in half and the huge slab of wood crashed to the floor, nearly killing Mary Dressing, who screamed. Will saw the entrance to the root cellar and shouted to Natalie and Emily, "Over there! Look! Get everyone into the cellar!"

With Rudy's help, the twins set about herding the middle-agers into the root cellar as instructed. Since the roof was starting to cave in, the adults saw little choice but to cooperate. Will rolled sideways out of the way of a falling beam and grabbed Loreli's arm.

"The cloud seeder. Is it still there?"

"Yes. I saw it on our way up the hill."

"Will it still work?"

"It should."

Will ran to one of his backpacks and pulled out the two vials he'd tucked there in case Natalie relapsed. He gave them to Loreli.

"The cure. Seed the clouds with it!"

Loreli understood immediately. Taking the vials, she zigzagged through the falling debris and out the back door. She dashed out of the barn and through the rain to the rise where Karl Mulligan's silver Iodide generator still stood. She fired the old machine up and added the amber liquid from the vials. The machine started chugging, belching smoke that rose swiftly into the dappled gray clouds.

Will was at the front door of the barn. The demonteens had spread out and were sending projectiles at them from various vantage points. He dodged an incoming boulder, then used the Broad-Beamed Shock Bombardier to fire off several blasts into the sky, which temporarily acted as a force field, knocking the various flying objects off course. Tree stumps and boulders and assorted bricks and scrap iron from the Halstrom farm came flying through the air. Will fired again and again, blasting them in the sky, blowing them asunder. But the Shock Bombardier finally ran out of loads, and the sky became Hell itself as the demonteens heightened their efforts. Will ducked back into the barn a millisecond before an old-growth fir tree came crashing down, crushing everything in its path.

Will was knocked off his feet. Loreli came running back in just as he was standing up, and together they dove through the root cellar door, Will dragging a backpack behind him. A few seconds later, half of the barn collapsed with a thunderous roar.

Outside, Jasper and the demonteens began a slow, steady march toward the ruins of the barn, their battering assault continuing. Will, Natalie, Emily, Loreli, Rudy, and the adults huddled in the root cellar, doors pulled tight, and awaited their fate. Will pulled a flashlight from his backpack and turned it on. He was met with a sea of faces, rife with raw fear.

Emily was huddled with Rudy. She was shaking. She pulled him close and whispered to him, "We're gonna die down here . . ."

Rudy swallowed hard. Even though he'd just been thinking the same thing—his heart was beating so hard he thought he was going to pass out—he knew he needed to put on a brave face for Emily.

"We'll be okay. It's gonna be all right," he said.

Somehow he'd gotten the valiant words out, and for that he was grateful. He held Emily tight, thinking, *This might be a good time to kiss her.* He'd read about how in England, during the blitzkrieg, people had huddled in the tunnels for hours during Hitler's reign of horror, and, fearing death was imminent, total strangers embraced one another and shared passionate kisses.

Approaching what was left of the barn, Jasper raised a hand, signaling for the onslaught to cease. A few more timbers collapsed, creating a cacophonous noise as they hit the ground. The demonteens stood and stared at the wreckage. Nothing moved.

"Come out now and give us what we want!" shouted Jasper.

Still no movement came from the barn. Jasper reached out with his hands as though performing a magic trick. His body trembled as his eyes bored into the battered barn door, which was lying on its side. Then suddenly the door sailed up into the air and whirled away, flipped telepathically by Jasper. The other demonteens took their cue and began lifting and hurling the debris away until there was nothing left of the barn but its foundation. They saw no bodies, and the crystal rods weren't there, either. Jasper took a careful step forward and stared hard at the cellar door. In a few seconds, it banged open upward, ripped off its hinges, and it, too, was pitched away, flying through the air like a Frisbee.

"Come on out now," said Jasper.

The demonteens once again held hands, this time focusing their powers upon the opening to the root cellar. And then Will Hunter began to rise up, trapped in the invisible web of their power. He had his backpack on, the greatly sought-after crystal rods wrapped back up and tucked inside it.

"You have no idea what you're doing!" he shouted.

"I know *exactly* what I'm doing," said Jasper.

Will was still holding his Power Rod, and he activated the fireball function. He managed to fire off two blasts at the demonteens, who ducked and dove and scattered as the fireballs struck the ground near them, exploding. But they quickly regrouped and redoubled their efforts. With tremendous force, they concentrated on the Power Rod. Will could feel that it was going to be wrenched from his grasp, and he knew he couldn't risk his prized weapon falling into the hands of the demonteens. So he flung the Power Rod upward with all his might. It flew into the sky, rising higher and higher until it disappeared into the clouds.

The Power Rod was safe, but Will was in big trouble. He locked eyes with Jasper. The next thing he knew, he was flying across the meadow. He slammed into the trunk of a towering fir and then slid to the ground, his neck and shoulder raking against the rough bark. He felt like his back had cracked in half. He couldn't feel his arms or legs.

A shadow fell across him. He looked up. A massive boulder was hovering above him. The thing was absolutely huge, as big—and no doubt twice as heavy—as a garbage truck. When it landed on him, it would crush him to death for sure. Will's brain was buzzing from having slammed into the tree. His thoughts were jumbled. What move did he have? He couldn't think of a single one.

Just then, the falling rain suddenly became a hammering downpour. The demonteens shielded their eyes, gazing skyward at the roiling clouds.

One second . . . two seconds . . . three seconds. Then it happened. Absorbing the cure through their skin, Jasper and the other demonteens collapsed like slack-stringed marionettes. With all the strength he had left, Will rolled to his left, barely avoiding being crushed by the falling boulder. He looked over at the demonteens. Their bodies were jerking spasmodically as they writhed in agony, just as Rudy and Natalie had when they'd been injected with the cure.

Will stared up into the sky. Even though it was bubbling with thick black clouds, he was so glad to be alive he felt like the sun was shining. He gradually regained the feeling in his arms and legs and struggled to stand, holding his back. He gazed across the meadow. The demonteens's spasms had subsided and they were now stone still. For a moment Will thought the cure might have killed them, but then he saw their chests begin rising and falling rhythmically. They were breathing now and asleep.

Will reached into the backpack, took out the velvet, and unwrapped it enough to see that he still had possession of the two crystal rods. He put them back in the pack and walked across the field until he was standing directly above Jasper.

He pulled a Flareblade from his combat vest, knelt down, and held it to Jasper's throat. When Jasper's eyes blinked open, with no trace of demon black, Will knew that the cloud-seeding gambit had worked. But he had to be sure, so he pressed his fingers into Jasper's temples to read his eyes. They remained clear.

"What happened?" said Jasper.

"I just saved your sorry ass, that's what happened," said Will.

Natalie, Emily, Loreli, and Rudy climb up out of the root cellar. George Sholes, Mary Dressing, and the other White Island adults came spilling up after them. They wasted no time rushing to their offspring. It was a baptism, a rebirth of sorts, as every one of the demonteens had been cured by the healing rain. Many tears were shed as parents and children embraced.

Watching the touching scene, Will decided it was time to get the hell out of there. The teens were confused and awash in a river of guilt over what they'd done. But Will had no time for explanations or recriminations, or to accept heartfelt thanks. It was time to go.

The five of them climbed back into the Wagoneer and took off without so much as an adios. After all, what was there to say? They'd gotten what they came for, and saved the possessed teens besides. It was time to move on to the next phase of their adventure, time to go back to the mainland, back to the mansion.

It was time to vanquish the Dark Lord and save the world.

Chapter Twenty-Six: Love and Theft

As they sped down the hill through Bingham, the rain let up, and as the setting sun cut through the clouds, the trauma receded behind them. They were tired and dirty, but, for the moment at least, they were out of danger.

Will had called Cappy as soon as they got back in the Wagoneer, and when they got to the harbor, the *Oleana* was just chugging into the marina. It was a sight for sore eyes indeed.

"Ahoy!" Cappy shouted, a broad smile on his face. He waved at them like they owed him money, which Will figured they technically would after the return trip. The *Oleana* slid up to dock. Cappy threw a line to Rudy, who tied it off on a cleat on the piling.

"Did you find what you was lookin' for?" asked Cappy.

"We sure did," said Will. "Can you take us to the mainland, right now?"

"Soon as you get on me boat and stop yappin', I can," said Cappy.

Will helped Natalie aboard. When their hands touched, the old electricity sparked through them. Their eyes met and they smiled. There was so much to be said, but it could wait. For now they were content to just look at each other.

Cappy cast off, then swung the *Oleana* around and throttled the old boat to the hilt. The appearance of the sun had been, as usual in the Northwest, a mere flirtation. The skies darkened once again, and the wind blew hard and cold. Cappy had Cokes and chips, which he gave to Rudy, Emily, and Loreli. Up on the bow, Will held Natalie close.

"Will, I'm so sorry . . ."

"I know," he said.

Natalie wanted to let all her feelings pour out. She wanted to tell Will that lying to him—even if it had been for his own good—had been the hardest thing she'd ever done. She wanted to tell him that she would never lie to him again. She had a thousand questions she wanted to ask him, the first being, of course, *Do you still love me?* She felt like he did, but she wouldn't have blamed him if he didn't, after her betrayal and dishonesty, not to mention the fact that she'd almost snuffed him from the face of the Earth. He'd been pretty clear about how he felt, but she still worried that things might have changed after all they'd been through. She shuddered just thinking about it. Will set the backpack holding the two crystal rods down and wrapped a blanket around Natalie. He held her tighter.

"There's so much I have to say . . . ," she said. Her eyes found his again, but this time they weren't as welcoming, because Will was distracted. Of course he wanted to give Natalie his full and absolute attention, but his seventh sense was kicking in.

"Hold on," he said to her.

They were moving into a patch of dark, ugly fog, and Will sensed that something was very wrong. He saw a rat on the deck, watched it sniff the air, then leap overboard and swim for its life. Not a good sign.

Will thought about the crystal rods. As soon as he'd seen their fragments fusing together in the old cannery, he'd known the time would come when he would combine the two rods with his own Power Rod to form the Triad of Power. It was the most powerful weapon the world had ever known, and he knew he could try to use it to destroy the Dark Lord once and for all.

It occurred to him that the time to do all that was *now*.

He reached back to tap in the code on the Power Rod Retrieval Patch, then felt a sudden burning pain bursting in his right shoulder. He cried out in agony.

"I'm sorry, sonny boy," said Cappy.

With one hand, the old guy was holding the handle of a harpoon, the lancing end of which was sticking out of Will's shoulder. With his other hand, Cappy was holding the backpack that held the two crystal rods. Natalie saw the blood pouring out of Will's arm and screamed.

Will looked over Cappy's shoulder and saw Rudy, Emily, and Loreli entwined, trapped like flies in a bloody web of fleshy red filaments. All three were screaming, but their mouths were covered.

The water around the *Oleana* was going crazy, whitecaps churning, water swirling as a huge whirlpool began to spin the boat clockwise. One of Cappy's eyes shifted from bloodshot to the stomach-turning liquid black of a demon. His head jerked left and right. He gurgled, then shouted.

"I tried to stop him!" yelled the old man.

Even through his pain, Will realized Cappy was at war with himself. Cappy's left hand still held the backpack. With his right, he let go of the harpoon and dug into the *Oleana*'s utility box. He came up with a flare gun, which he put to his head. He was drenched in sweat and convulsing. Cappy's body had been invaded by evil, but his good side was putting up a fight.

"He got me when I weren't paying no attention!"

Cappy's body twisted around grotesquely. There was the sound of bones cracking.

Natalie managed to yank the harpoon out of Will's shoulder. Will wanted to reach up again to call down his Power Rod, but he was losing blood so quickly. He collapsed, watching the world spin around him. Cappy began laughing, but not with his own voice. It was the spine-chilling voice of the Dark Lord emanating from the old man's mouth.

"Blind fool!" he said.

Natalie fumbled in one of Will's jacket pockets, trying to find a healing patch. But she was yanked away by centrifugal force and slid across the deck as wave after huge wave pounded the *Oleana*. Gritting her teeth, she clawed her way back to Will and managed to rip a healing patch from his pocket. She opened it and pressed it to his wound.

"Stay with me, Will!"

Will nodded, wanting to. He tried to grab a weapon, but the pain shot through him like a bolt of lightning. He wasn't going anywhere, not just yet. He knew he had to wait a few precious seconds as the patch did its job.

Cappy's good half was still fighting. He pressed the flare gun harder to his head and cocked it. He looked at Will. For a moment his eyes were not the eyes of a demon, but those of a sad old man who knew his life was coming to an ugly end.

"Lord, forgive me," he said.

He pulled the trigger. The flare gun detonated against his jaw, the potassium perchlorate and magnesium exploding, and his head became a fiery globe. Cappy's last sound was a horrifying scream. The poor old man was trying to kill the devil inside him, but he had only succeeded in stripping the flesh from his body, allowing the Beast within to emerge. It was a grotesque sight, the Dark Lord expanding out through Cappy's worn old body, the aged flesh falling away like a cheap Halloween costume. Will knew the Dark Lord had the ability to take over a human body like this, but he'd never witnessed it before. He wished he wasn't seeing it now.

Like a hideous mutation of the legendary phoenix, the Dark Lord was rising from the flames, growing larger and more menacing every second. With his clawed hands, he tore open Will's backpack and clasped the two crystal rods, his saffron eyes widening with delight as he eyed them lustily.

"Good work, my son! Excellent work!" He laughed. "You have an uncanny ability to locate what is missing." Then his eyes narrowed. "The time is nigh. There are profound decisions to be—"

In a flash, Will pulled the Megashocker from its holster, leapt up, and thrust with it. The Dark Lord dodged, but the blow landed above his thigh. He bellowed in pain. Will threw a Flareblade that caught the Beast in the neck. The Dark Lord froze and locked eyes with his progeny.

"You never cease to amaze me, young Will Hunter."

Moving insanely fast, he grabbed the harpoon, skewered Natalie, and flung her starboard into the Sound.

Will screamed, "No!"

Then the Dark Lord, crystal rods in hand, leapt off the port side of the boat.

"Make your choice, boy. Me or the girl!"

Will jumped in after Natalie. The Dark Lord laughed, then dove deep into the brackish water and disappeared.

Will's shoulder was still bleeding, not yet fully healed, but nothing on Earth was going to keep him from saving the girl he loved; not the stormy sea, not the searing pain, not the Devil himself. Swimming with just one functioning arm, he found Natalie in the dark depths. She clung to him as he kicked them both to the surface, where they floated, gasping for air. Natalie was losing consciousness. Will kicked hard to the boat and fought through the debilitating pain to hoist her onto the deck.

He climbed up and immediately applied a healing patch to her wound, which wasn't mortal, but the water was cold and she was trembling violently. Will covered her with a blanket, then cut Rudy, Loreli, and Emily free from their heinous bonds. Emily rushed to Natalie and lay down beside her to share her body heat. Will started to do the same, but Loreli stopped him. She was on the verge of tears.

"I'm sorry, Will, it all happened so fast! I'm so sorry, I—"

Rudy chimed in, "We would have stopped him if we could, Will—"

Exhausted, freezing, and in terrible pain, Will sagged against a railing. "Cut yourself some slack, you guys," he said. "It was the *Devil*. And we're all okay."

Loreli was shaking her head. "Yeah, but I should have—"

Will held a finger to his lips. "Shhhhh . . ."

They listened. And heard, in the distance, the sound of beastly, demonic laughter.

Loreli took the wheel of the *Oleana* and navigated the old boat out of the storm. Once in calmer waters, they made for the mainland.

When they docked at Beech Bay, Will carried Natalie straight to the Hummer and wrapped her in the blanket he kept in the back. He told Rudy to drive, and Rudy gladly obliged. When everyone was loaded in, he fired up the Hummer and sped off. He never bothered looking in the rearview mirror. If he had, he might have noticed the skinny blind girl they'd seen in the bait shop the day before climbing onto a motorcycle and following them.

By the time they reached the mansion, Natalie's wound had healed, but she was still shivering from her plunge into the Puget Sound. Rudy pulled the Hummer into the garage and closed the door behind them.

The girl on the motorcycle pulled up, stared for a beat with her black, not-so-blind eyes, and then rocketed toward Pioneer Square.

In the mansion, Will activated the security system and told everyone to get some sleep. They would undoubtedly need it. The Dark Lord had the crystal rods now and was planning on striking a fatal blow to mankind.

Most likely the Dark Lord had retreated back to the Under City. Will knew he had to somehow prevent him from using the Sword of Armageddon, but trying to attack the Beast now, especially when they were all exhausted, would be suicide. They would have to rest, and then come up with a plan of action.

Loreli retreated to the guest room, where she showered, trying to wash away the trauma from White Island. It didn't work, but she felt a little better anyway. Totally spent, she flopped on the bed and closed her eyes. She remembered how, on the *Oleana*, while still in Cappy's body, the Dark Lord had looked at her with surprise and maybe even a little pride in his eyes. "You survived! Amazing. Just amazing," he'd said. Then he had bound her with the flesh web instead of killing her. Had some part of him actually wanted her to survive and somehow return to him? She tossed the thoughts around in her head until she was too tired to think any longer and then fell asleep.

Rudy and Emily were both weary as well, but they didn't want to be apart in their respective bedrooms, so they kicked back on the couch in the media room. It wasn't long before they were asleep, too, their hands touching.

Will took Natalie into his room and laid her down. Then he went down the hall into the lab and checked the security cameras. All was quiet. He checked on his mother. All was quiet there, too. He sent her a quick *I love you* and a prayer. Then he went back to his room and laid down next to Natalie. She opened her eyes and smiled at him as he pulled her close.

"I love you . . . ," she whispered.

"I know," he said.

"I love you more than anything . . . more than the next beat of my heart . . ."

Their eyes met in a brief dance, passing adoration back and forth. Natalie opened her mouth to speak again. She wanted to share her remorse, her fears, everything. But Will put a finger to her lips. Her eyes had told him everything he needed to know. He just wanted to hold her until she stopped shaking.

She felt so warm and calm and safe in his arms that she drifted off to sleep, the dreams pulling her away, like a warm river. As she slept,

Will stared out the window, watching as the night winds outside whipped the leaves of an oak tree against the glass and thinking about the task ahead of him, and the low likelihood he would survive it.

In the huge cavern deep beneath Pioneer Square, the Dark Lord entered his lair, unwrapped the two crystal rods, and gazed at them. Their beauty brought a smile to his scaly face. He placed the crystals on a slab of marble, the two ends touching. Then he closed his eyes and conjured up his favorite images—war and pestilence, famine, and death. Thinking of such things gave him power. Sufficiently fueled, he spit a stream of fire at the joint where the two shafts were touching. In moments they were fused together, forming one long shaft of crystal power. It was now a massive rod, the magnificent, splendid, deadly blade for the sword he so craved. The fused rods glowed brightly, then dimmed somewhat. The Dark Lord's eyes narrowed with concern. But then the rods glowed brightly again. It was time to assemble the sword.

The handle, forged from evil by Jared Wasserman, was embedded with blood-red rubies and polished to a brilliant silvery luster. The Dark Lord had shocked the humble craftsman by not killing him, but rather releasing him. He had intended to simply let Jared go—he had done an exemplary job, and that warranted rewarding— but he was, after all, the Prince of Pain. So he could not help but plant within Jared the twin destructive seeds of jealousy and paternal rage. Jared's life would unravel in a storm of violence, and this pleased the Dark Lord.

Smiling wickedly, he slid the crystal blade into the handle up to the hilt, spitting a constant flame like a blowtorch, and fused the blade to the metal.

Thus was born the Sword of Armageddon.

Out in the main cavern, the sound of thousands of drums was deafening. The demons were attempting to please their leader by hammering out rhythms in his honor. As he entered the cavern, the drumming reached a crescendo. The demons were mad with glee. The slight girl who had followed Will to his mansion bowed, then approached the Dark Lord and told him what she'd learned. He smiled and nodded. Very good. He now knew where the boy lived. Everything was falling into place. The Dark Lord lifted his fist into the air.

"Silence!"

The cavern fell into a hush, save for the sound of one drum, pounded by a whacked-out demonteen with glazed eyes who hadn't heard his master. The Prince of Darkness shot out a tendril of flame that swiftly engulfed the hapless demonteen, who screamed as he burned to a crisp and then disintegrated.

Now the cavern was stone quiet. Everyone was holding his or her breath. The Dark Lord smiled. Fear was such a wonderful thing. He spoke in a booming voice that echoed off the walls.

"With this sword, victory will be ours! With this sword, the human race will be vanquished! With this sword, all the rivers of Earth will run with blood!'

The demons screeched and shrieked until their throats bled. The Dark Lord smiled and shouted: "Behold! The Sword of Armageddon!"

With his right hand, the Dark Lord held up the mighty sword with the evil handle and the crystal rod blade.

"Now, *bring me Will Hunter!*"

The underground cavern was bedlam. The demons were working themselves into a murderous frenzy, picking up weapons and fighting amongst themselves.

The Dark Lord watched, his saffron eyes gleaming. The sword's blade was glowing brightly, but then it flickered and grew dimmer. The Dark Lord growled so loudly as to give the mob pause. The assembled demons, observing the inconsistency of the mighty sword's blade, sought to will the thing to brightness by pounding their drums and screeching their throats even more raw, raising a hellish ruckus in the great hall. But the blade grew only dimmer. This was a public humiliation, an embarrassment of epic proportions. The Dark Lord blushed a hue even more vivid than his usual scarlet, then screamed in rage as the demons reacted by fiercely wailing and pounding on their drums.

"I gave you an order! Go now! Go and get Will Hunter!"

Hungry for the opportunity to prove themselves, the demons amassed into a tide of death, surging up and out of the cavern, a swarm of evil creatures all of a single mind, all with a common goal: to hunt down and capture the Devil's son, the great demon foe, Will Hunter. They blasted up through Smiling Bob's Underground Tours, roaring past an elderly woman from Kentucky, her weak heart failing as they nearly trampled her. They poured up onto the streets of Pioneer Square in a terrifying horde. Nothing could stand in their way. They clambered up First Avenue, smashing cars and kicking the ass of anyone in their path. They were on a mission of destruction. Led by the little "blind" motorcycle girl from Beech Bay, they were headed for the London mansion on Queen Anne Hill.

The Dark Lord retired to his lair and sat upon his throne. As he held the sword, its blade was only flickering now, he furiously wondered what to do. How was he to dominate his greatest adversary with an impotent sword? He closed his eyes and called forth the winds of anger. The vault became a maelstrom as debris and books and papers lifted up off the ground and swirled around. An airborne magazine slapped the Dark Lord in the face and he opened his eyes in rage. It was a copy of *Seattle* magazine, and on the cover was a photograph of the Space Needle in a lightning storm. The Dark Lord's eyes narrowed into knowing slits, and once again he smiled.

The first wave of demons swarmed over the tall wrought iron fence surrounding the mansion without making a sound. They moved across the grounds like ghosts, passing the marble statues and topiary animals. They all knew that the one to capture Will Hunter would be immortalized. An alarm was tripped. The mansion and surrounding grounds lit up like a football stadium. The demons froze for a moment, then many of them surged forward. That was a mistake. Will had armed this fortress well, and the infrared detectors sensed the elevated body temperatures of the demons. The lawn spikes were activated, and the first demons to cross the line were noisily and messily impaled from below, their screeches of agony rousing every dog on Queen Anne Hill, their howls filling the night sky.

Will leapt out of bed and ran to his lab, Natalie's bewildered voice following him down the hall. The monitors were lit up with images of the attacking demons, as alarms throughout the mansion began to sound.

Chapter Twenty-Seven: Under Siege

Will hit the panic switch for the security shutters a moment too late. The mansion was breached. Four demons came crashing through the first floor windows. Will ran out of the lab, jacked two Flareblades into his palms, and threw them. The first demon took a blade to the neck and spurted blood, managing only a single step before falling over dead. The second lived a moment longer and was leaping at Natalie, who was coming down the hallway out of the guest room, when Will hit him in the back of the head, blowing his brains out. The other two intruders flew up, sprang off the ceiling, and dove down in attack mode. Will was waiting for them with his Megashocker. With four deft strokes—two for each demon— he ended their miserable lives. As their bodies disintegrated, the onslaught continued. Other demons, attempting to enter through the windows, found themselves sliced in half by the tremendous force of the slamming steel shutters. Those outside set about pounding on the shutters with all their might. Rudy, Emily, and Loreli, hearing the alarm, had come running. Will turned to them.

"We don't have much time."

"What's happening, Will?" said Rudy.

"What's happening is that they're trying to break in here and kill us all," said Loreli.

Will rushed over and yanked open a case, pulled out two hand-fuls of healing patches, and tossed them to the others.

"You might need these."

Everyone pocketed their healing patches, and Will then went to a tall weapons case. He pulled out two Thunder Lances and handed them to Emily and Natalie.

"And these, too."

The Thunder Lances were long tubes the same size as the sticks the girls had practiced with under Will's tutelage when they'd first moved into the house. The weapons looked like fluorescent light bulbs until Will turned them on and they fired up, burning a deep blue. Natalie and Emily stared at the dangerous-looking weapons. They'd spent a lot of hours with the practice sticks, and they were psyched to finally use the real deal.

"How do they work?" asked Natalie.

Will grabbed hers, and with one swipe he cut a chair in half. He handed it back.

"I think I got it," she said.

"When they come, don't hesitate, don't think about it, just kill."

The girls nodded and twirled the lances.

"What about me? I want one," said Rudy.

Will moved across the room. Rudy was on his tail.

"Come on, man, I want a weapon!"

"Cool down, I'll get to you."

Will motioned to Loreli, and she followed him to a cabinet. He pulled out three firearms: a Turboflayer, a Death Ripper, and a Force-Field Chopper. He grabbed a stack of Dart Blades, Cutchucks, and some Chemo-Chiller Pellets, too. He handed the chopper and pellets to Loreli, then showed her how to use them.

"Cock it like this, and then fire away."

She cocked and shot off a round that sent a wave across the room, blowing a hole in the wall.

"This will do," she said.

Will looked at Loreli. "There's just one little thing."

"Okay . . ."

Will grabbed another Blaster Magnum from the cabinet and held it threateningly. "Can I trust you?"

"Yes, Will, yes!" Not even a second of hesitation, and her eyes looked solid. For the first time, he believed her completely.

"Then let's get this done."

Will ran out of the lab, with Rudy hot on his heels. In fifteen seconds they were on the roof. Rudy was frantic.

"First I get the chick weapon, which, hey, okay, it kind of rocked, but now I get nothing? Come *on*, man! Please don't lay some little tiny gun on me. I want something to kick demon ass with, dude!"

Rudy was eyeing the Blaster Magnum. But Will tucked it in his belt, then used a code to open a sliding panel. Up rose a bulletproof glass bubble cockpit, the rotating firing station for the pulse-blast laser cannons mounted on the mansion's five turrets. There was also a laser cannon mounted on the front of the half-bubble firing cockpit itself, so the thing resembled the swiveling underbelly gun turret on a World War II B-52 bomber.

Will powered everything up and then jumped into the cockpit, which rotated a full 360 degrees. He quickly got a demon in his sights—a huge one climbing over the fence—and fired away. *Kablam!* The laser pulse slammed into the demon and blew him in half. His head continued to scream as he fell back off the fence.

"Whoa! This is *exactly* like the pulse-blaster cannon in *Demon Hunter*!" Rudy's eyes were about to fall out of his head.

"You said you were good with the *Demon Hunter* weapons," said Will. He jumped out of the seat and motioned for Rudy to climb in. "Kill as many as you can. Try to keep them away from the perimeter."

Rudy was so happy he was frozen to the spot. "What . . . are you . . . are you serious? I can . . . I can . . ."

"Just get in there and start firing!"

"You got it, man!"

Rudy leapt into the cockpit. With a gleeful glint in his eye, he started firing the pulse-blasters. *Ka-blam!* He took out four demons who'd just pulled up in an old Sebring. *Ka-blam!* He took out two more who were tearing down a tree to make a battering ram. Rudy was literally having a blast. He paused and turned to shout to Will:

"Hey, do these kills count on my *Demon Hunter* score?"

Will heard a loud crack and started running back downstairs. A security shutter had buckled, then split as a lamppost came ramming through. The crack wasn't wide, but it was enough to let two demons squirm through. It didn't take them long to wish they hadn't, as Natalie and Emily launched their first attack with the Thunder Lances, swinging swiftly and efficiently, cutting the intruders to ribbons.

Emily wrinkled her nose as the demons' toxic blood spewed out. Their bodies sparked and dissolved.

"Is it just me, or is this really gross?"

"It's totally gross," said Natalie. "But don't stop."

"I wouldn't dream of it," said Emily. "But I kind of miss the Vibroslammers."

Another demon breached the torn shutter and landed behind Natalie. He hissed out a yellow cloaking cloud, buying himself time to morph into a larger beast with a tail and jagged claws. Coughing, Natalie swung her Thunder Lance, but the creature dodged the blow. Then it whipped its tail around and swept Natalie's feet out from under her. She went down hard, her head slamming into the tile floor. The creature leapt at her, primed to kill. Loreli whirled and fired the Force-Field Chopper, blowing off the beast's legs. It howled and died.

Natalie looked up at Loreli with gratitude. "Thanks."

Loreli smiled. "Don't mention it." After all she'd done to Natalie, a small measure of payback felt good.

Arriving back on the first floor, Will ran to the breached shutter and, powering up his Megashocker to full load, used the heat to fuse the shutter back together. For the moment they were safe.

Will went to check all the monitors, including the one that sent the signal from April's still-quiet hospital room. Will checked the area surrounding the mansion, front, sides, and back. Out front, the gathering horde was growing larger.

Emily spoke first. "What do they want?"

"I'm guessing it's not what, but *who*. Me." Will turned to Natalie. "I want you and Emily to take Rudy and get out of here. Plan B. You remember what that means?"

They did. Will had briefed them on it before, and it was intended to be implemented if he went out on a mission and never returned. Plan B meant that they evacuated the mansion and fled, taking enough cash to last them for years.

The twins exchanged a look.

Natalie shook her head, and then stared at Will. "We're not going. I'd rather die by your side than live without you."

He knew what she was talking about because he felt exactly the same way.

Up on the roof, Rudy was rotating in the firing cockpit, blasting demons as they continued their frontal assault. He was in hog heaven, wasting them by the dozen.

"Hey, you like that?" *Ka-blam!* "How about some of this!" *Ka-blam!* "Oh yeah! Come on, who's your daddy!" *Ka-blam!*

Rudy was decimating them. The only problem was, like ants pouring out of an anthill, they just kept coming. For every demon he toasted, two more took its place.

A group of demons had commandeered a big lumbering "duck," an amphibious landing craft from World War II that had been re-appropriated by a sightseeing company. The duck churned through Lake Union, past the houseboats, then sped on its wheels up through the streets of Queen Anne Hill. When it got close enough, Rudy got it in his sights and fired away. *Ka-blam!* Goodbye duck!

Rudy was feeling on top of the world. But then a group of demon-teens, some of whom he recognized from the week they'd spent at LBJ High School, arrived on motorcycles, blasting up the hill in a V-formation. In unison they leapt off their bikes and into the air, where they sprouted hideous flesh wings and took flight. The bikes crashed to the ground, twisting and sparking against the pavement. The flying demonteens were carrying chains.

Now Rudy was under siege from above. The lasers were useless because he couldn't fire straight up, which was where the demon-teens were coming from. The first one swooped down and swung his chain, and Rudy let out a yelp as it smacked against the glass of the cockpit dome. They took turns dive-bombing him. He tried rotating way back and firing all five lasers as far skyward as they would go, but he couldn't reach his attackers. Meanwhile, down below, doz-ens of demonteens had breached the perimeter. A Hummer smashed through the front gate.

Will was watching the whole thing on the surveillance monitors. He cursed under his breath and grabbed the Turboflayer, yelling to the girls.

"Keep your backs to the wall and don't stop killing!"

He tossed Loreli the Blaster Magnum, which she caught with the hand not holding the Chopper. Then Will was up the stairs. Loreli tucked the Blaster Magnum in her belt.

The girls backed themselves against the wall and waited. One. Two. Three. Four. Silence.

Then the front door blasted apart as it was hit full on by the Hummer. Wood splinters flew everywhere. Plaster rained down. Amid a horrible keening sound, the gaping wound that had been the front entrance was filled with a swarm of flying demons. Loreli cocked and fired the Force-Field Chopper repeatedly, wave after wave of death, knocking the demons backward and blowing them to smithereens. Natalie and Emily swung their Thunder Lances like whirling dervishes, slicing and dicing the creatures as fingers, arms, legs, and even heads went flying. All their hours of stick-fighting practice and their real-life combat on the island was paying off. Using the Force-Field Chopper and the Blaster Magnum, Loreli was blowing away her fair share of demons too.

On the roof, Will sprang into action, defending Rudy, who was still under aerial assault from the flying, chain-wielding demonteens. Will had the Turboflayer in one hand and the Death Ripper in a shoulder holster. He ducked an oncoming demon, then aimed and fired the Turboflayer as two more flying demonteens dove down to bash Rudy with their chains. The Turboflayer was the size of a shotgun and it fired unique rounds. *Blam!* Out came a white-hot load, which dispersed into hundreds of whirling metal microfilaments capable of cutting through hardwood. When the metal hit and engulfed the diving demonteens, it was like they'd flown straight into a blender. The sky filled with their blood. Three more dove down with their teeth bared. *Blam-blam!* Will fired again, and the Turboflayer's double loads minced the demons in midair. Blood rained down, body parts falling in chunks onto the roof.

Rudy wiped the sweat from his brow and gave Will a thumbs-up. Will hit a button, and the bubble cockpit hissed open. He snagged a pair of night-vision binoculars and scanned the streets leading up the hillside.

"Let me have a shot, Rudy."

Rudy slid out, and Will handed him the Turboflayer.

"You see anything flying down at us, shoot it."

Rudy glanced skyward, but for now the aerial attacks had ceased. Will powered up the five pulse-blast laser cannons and started finding and eliminating targets. The city streets were swarming with demons. Will went into rapid-fire mode, firing at five different targets simultaneously. Motorcycles exploded. Cars and trucks burst into flames. Then Will saw a fleet of city busses that the demons had commandeered and reinforced with thick slabs of iron. He fired at them repeatedly, and the lasers did some damage, but not enough to slow the advancing fleet. Will kept firing, but he couldn't stop them. The big armored busses rumbled closer.

"What are we going to do?" asked Rudy. He had panic in his eyes.

"I'm thinking," said Will.

He fired off another volley of shots at the busses, but they were too well-fortified. Will looked from one turret-mounted laser to another, taking in the position of all five.

"Okay, I've got an idea," said Will.

Opening the control panel, he recalibrated the laser cannons, then sent out their thin red tracer beams. The five beams found one another and joined together into one large beam. Now all five pulse cannons could fire together with one massively powerful stream of destruction. Or so Will hoped—the system wasn't designed for this, and of course he'd never tested it out.

The armored busses continued to rumble up the street toward the mansion. Will took careful aim, then pulled the trigger. The ensuing blast was a thing of beauty, a shimmering shaft of white-hot power that carried massive laser pulses along its length until they exploded on impact. The armored busses were lifted up off the asphalt and tossed into the air like toys, the demons inside trying to fend off death with their screams.

A lone demonteen came swooping down from above, surprising Rudy, who dropped the Turboflayer. The weapon went skidding across the roof tiles. Swinging a chain, the demonteen struck Rudy in the leg, and he cried out in pain. Will dove and tucked, snagging the Turboflayer as he rolled. He came up firing. *Blam!* The load unfurled all around the demonteen, enmeshing him in a metal web of instant death. Will rushed to Rudy.

"You okay?"

"I think so, man, but my leg's bleeding."

Will whipped a healing patch out of Rudy's pocket, then tore open Rudy's jeans and slapped the patch on the wound. Then he jumped back into the bubble cockpit and began sweeping the entire hillside with the mega-powerful laser cannon beam, decapitating dozens of demons in mere seconds. It was a slaughter. Eventually the stragglers shrank back into the darkness, retreating.

A preternatural calm settled over the city. It was a deathly hush. Will climbed out of the firing cockpit, stood on the roof, and gazed out at the city lights. He watched, his eyes narrowing, as the dark sky thickened with roiling clouds.

Nineteen-year-old Janet Masurer was wrapping up her shift as the elevator attendant at the Space Needle when she sensed that something was wrong. She'd taken a group of tourists up and was on her way down when she thought she heard noises. As the doors opened, she saw the frightened tourists who'd been waiting in line scrambling for the exits, their eyes wild with fear. She heard shouts, the sound of fists striking flesh, and glass breaking. Then she smelled something horrible, like the wind of Death itself. This was what preceded her meeting the Dark Lord, who, throwing aside a security guard and impaling him on a cap rack, stepped into the elevator, surrounded by his elite shedemons.

Janet's throat constricted with fear and she blurted, "I'm sorry . . . this elevator only goes up."

She wasn't sure why she said it, but at the moment it was the only thing that made sense to her. Clearly the creature that had just accosted her was the Prince of Darkness. She'd had nightmares about the Devil ever since she was a little girl, but the beast that stood in front of her was worse than anything her sleeping mind had ever conjured up. His hideous yellow eyes narrowed into slits, and he threw his head back and laughed a horrible laugh that echoed throughout the entire first floor. Janet wanted to say something, anything to buy her more time on this Earth, but her lips were locked, her tongue swollen with terror.

"Don't worry, I'm not going to throw you out of the elevator," the Prince of Darkness rumbled. "Let's go up, shall we?"

Janet touched the controls and the elevator began to rise, her tour spiel spilling nervously out of her mouth.

"The Space Needle was built for the 1962 Seattle World's Fair at a cost of two million dollars . . ."

The Dark Lord held a finger to his lips. "Shhhh . . ."

Janet's blood went cold. She saw herself dying even before it happened. As the elevator rose higher, the Dark Lord moved closer to her. When it was nearly to the top, he spoke again.

"I changed my mind. You'll be getting off here."

With a mighty fist he smashed the elevator's thick glass window. Then he threw Janet out. Her body was perfectly still in mid-flight, and for a few magnificent seconds she experienced true bliss and time froze as she streaked toward the plaza below. She was thinking about Francis—a boy she'd known in school—when she hit the pavement going fifty miles an hour.

The demon attacks on the mansion were now only sporadic. Rudy was back up in his new favorite spot on Earth, the bubble cockpit. He was firing the laser-pulse cannons, gleefully blasting almost all the demons who were stupid enough to continue to charge. He delighted in blowing their heads off and watching them disintegrate. Loreli, with help from Natalie and Emily, took care of the few that made it past Rudy.

Will was using a telescope to observe the unnatural color of the clouds forming around the Space Needle. He had seen these violent purple clouds only once before: when the Beast had invaded his boyhood house and kidnapped his father.

Something fell from high up on the Needle, and his heart jumped as he realized it was a body. He knew that the Dark Lord was up there. The entire Seattle sky was coming alive, choking with thick purple clouds, which crowded together tightly, unleashing torrents of rain. Within seconds the sky was torn apart by massive bolts of lightning, slender claws reaching down from the heavens at 130,000 miles an hour to snatch the Earth's soul.

The Dark Lord stormed through the restaurant and up onto the observation deck, scattering terrified patrons with each step. Two security guards made fatally foolish mistakes: one stepped forward to block the Dark Prince and paid for it by having his heart ripped out and eaten; the other drew his weapon, a measly .03 amp taser, and moments later found himself lying in a pool of his own blood, his body convulsing as he blinked his last bits of consciousness away staring at his severed limbs.

Moving onto the roof of the Space Needle, the Dark Lord lifted his arms into the storm, and the violet clouds reacted according to his desires, churning and bashing into each other as more lighting shot out. The Space Needle's roof was equipped with twenty-four lightning rods, including one on the very tip. The shedemons ripped out twenty-three of them and threw them off the roof, overlooking the one on top. When they were done, the Dark Lord pulled the Sword of Armageddon from its scabbard on his back. The blade was flickering only faintly.

The Dark Lord held it aloft. In seconds, the lightning that he'd been calling forth came to greet him, cracking down out of the sky and striking the crystal blade. This was just the beginning, as more and more bolts slashed down, slamming into the sword. The bolts reached temperatures of 64,000 degrees, striking the sword, electrifying it, energizing it. The sword shimmered with immense power. The Dark Lord's laughter rang into the night. *It was working!* The Dark Lord roared, imploring the purple sky to give him more, and it did, unleashing a veritable onslaught of thunder and lightning. People with hillside views of the Space Needle could not believe what they were seeing.

• • •

Will stared at the Space Needle through the telescope, watching as the Dark Lord continued to steal the lightning from the sky. First he built a satanic cathedral in the bowels of a volcano, and now he was commandeering the Space Needle to steal lightning from the sky; Will had to admit, his adversary definitely had a flair for the epic.

The Dark Lord had succeeded in capturing an electrical maelstrom with the sword and was controlling it, flicking it here and there like a bullwhip. Will wondered what would come next. What was he up to? What was his next move? Will was running the various scenarios through his head when he saw a blast as the Dark Lord sent fifty separate tendrils shooting out from the sword. They arced across the sky and connected with their targets: the crosses and spires of churches and synagogues and mosques throughout the city. The buildings erupted in flames. People screamed in terror. All they could think was, *This is it, this is the end.*

And they were right.

Then the Dark Lord turned right toward Will, swung the sword once more, and sent a mega lightning bolt, a massive stream of electrical energy, right at the mansion. The bolt hit an outbuilding, a gardening shed, blowing it to smithereens. The main power generators were housed there. The mansion's lights flickered and then went out.

Simultaneous to his storming of the Space Needle, the Dark Lord had orchestrated another takeover, this one at the Swedish Hospital. A crew of demonteens burst through the front doors and felled the security guard with a piano wire. Then they ascended the stairs. Using broad axes, they chopped their way into the wing that housed April, and then they obliterated the alarm system. Triggered by the intrusion, the automated wide-beam lasers Will had set up sensed the presence of inhuman creatures and fired, frying half of the crew to a crisp. But there were too many of them, and the backups were able to march over the charred bodies of their comrades and smash the lasers, too. Moments later, April's body, clinging by the thinnest of strands to life, was wheeled into a waiting ambulance outside. The Dark Lord knew he could not depend on his followers to be able to capture Will Hunter and bring the boy to him. So he would lure the boy with April, the perfect bait.

Atop the Space Needle, the Dark Lord laughed into the storm, enjoying this immensely. He called out to Will though the night sky: "Come to me, my son! We have unfinished business to attend to!"

Though the Dark Lord's voice could not carry across such a great distance, Will could still hear it—in his head. As always, the Prince of Darkness tormented him. Now he was taunting him, challenging him to come and fight. Will knew it would be utterly foolish for him to attempt to battle the Dark Lord on his own terms. In the bowels of Mount Saint Emory, Will's defiance had caught the Beast by surprise, and that was the only reason Will had prevailed. But this time the odds were stacked completely against him. He had planned on sneaking into the Under City and somehow stealing the Sword of Armageddon. But it was too late for that. *Somehow* he had to battle the Dark Lord and prevent him from using it to strike a fatal blow to mankind. But how?

The backup generators came on. Will heard an alarm. He rushed to his bank of surveillance monitors. What he saw chilled his heart. His mother's hospital room was *empty*. They'd taken her, respirator and all.

Again the Dark Lord called out to his son.

"My son, I'm waiting! It's time to face your destiny! Come, boy, come to your father!"

Will ran back to his telescope. He saw the ambulance arriving, saw the gurney pulled out and wheeled into the Needle. His blood ran cold. He knew that he had no choice but to accept the Beast's challenge now. By taking April's body, the Dark Lord had guaranteed

Will's cooperation. If the Dark Lord destroyed April's body then, well, there was just simply no bringing her back from that. There would be no recovery, no do-over. He would have to face the Beast on his terms.

Will answered the Dark Lord's challenge. He didn't need to move his lips to communicate. He knew that Dark Lord would hear his thoughts.

Here I come, he thought, loud and clear.

Chapter Twenty-Eight: Stairway to Hell

There are 848 stairs in the Space Needle from top to bottom, and Will was climbing them fast. They spiraled up the centermost spine of the Needle, exposed to the elements and enclosed by chain-link fencing. He'd tried the elevator but had only risen one hundred feet when the demons above cut the cable and he'd plunged to the ground, barely diving out of the car before it crashed into the cement. He decided the stairs were a better option. He had his Megashocker strapped to his leg, the Death Ripper holstered on his hip, and a supply of Flareblades in his pockets. So far he hadn't encountered any demons, but he knew it was only a matter of time

He'd left Natalie, Emily, Rudy, and Loreli with strict instructions to lock down, defend, and stay put until he'd either returned victorious, or gone down in defeat. They had all protested, demanding to go with him, but Will was adamant, explaining that he had a specific plan that relied on stealth, and that they needed to guard the mansion, especially his lab. If his secrets fell into the wrong hands, it could be disastrous. Loreli protested the loudest, saying she desperately wanted to be part of the attack to take down the Dark Lord, but Will stood his ground, and finally she acquiesced.

In the event that Will didn't come back, they were to activate the escape plan, which meant abandoning the mansion for good. Will made sure that they would do as he instructed by arming the doomsday bomb in his laboratory that only he could disarm. It was sunk deep in the foundation so it could not be removed. He'd set the timer for ninety-nine minutes. Plenty of time. With Will's time-bending speed the Space Needle was only a couple of minutes away. In ninety-nine minutes it would all be over, one way or another. Either he'd succeed quickly, or not at all. He showed them the bomb, and the timer, and explained why it had to be this way. If he lost, he could not afford to have his enemies plunder his laboratory and steal his secrets. If he won, he would be back in time to deactivate the bomb. He'd hit the switch. For a few seconds, he and Natalie, and Emily, Loreli, and Rudy had watched the bomb ticking down: 99:00 . . . 98:59 . . . 98:58 . . . 98:57.

He whispered to Natalie, "No matter what happens, we'll always be together."

She pulled him to her. Their lips met. It was a kiss so extraordinary that they forgot for a moment that they were on the precipice of Hell. When Will finally pulled back, Natalie's eyes spilled tears.

"Do you promise to come back to me?"

"I promise."

Will took her hand and placed it on his chest. "Feel my heart. Every beat is for you."

He kissed her again. And then set out to conquer.

After he'd gone, the demon attacks died down. Rudy, Natalie, and Emily took turns packing up in case they had to evacuate. Loreli couldn't stand the waiting. She paced; she sweated. She was crawling out of her skin. She'd agreed to stay behind, and even felt like it was her duty to protect Natalie and the others, but as the seconds ticked away she realized she just couldn't keep away from the final battle. She had incurred debts—debts that needed to be repaid. Holding her stomach and feigning cramps, she excused herself to go to the bathroom. Then she grabbed the Force-Field Chopper and slipped out a side door.

Will was halfway up the stairs when all hell broke loose. A strong wind picked up. Rain began to pound. The wind kicked into gale force and Will had to brace himself against the onslaught as he pulled himself up against the column and stared up. He heard a massive clattering and then felt as though an army was firing at him with pellet guns. It was hail: big stones, coming down fast and hard. Then the hail stopped abruptly. The air went calm and dank. And then something else began to fall from the sky.

Toads. Will had expected the Dark Lord to be a little more original, but he was old school all the way. Down came the toads, hundreds of them, fat and green and ugly, smacking off the crossbeams and slapping as they hit the asphalt way below, splitting open, their guts squishing out in all directions. The few that had landed near Will and still had heartbeats immediately morphed into beasts as big as bulldogs, their jaws powerful, teeth spiky, eyes glazed, and mad with primitive aggression.

They attacked. He swung his Megashocker in wide arcs, mowing them down. Will looked at his watch. The ascent up the Needle was taking longer than he'd thought. He had to get up there quicker.

A news chopper from KIRO TV began to circle above the Needle, the pilot and cameraman overwhelmed by what they were seeing. The cameraman trained his HD video lens on the creature on top of the Needle. He knew that he was witnessing pure evil. He prayed. He knew they should turn their eyes away and get out of there fast, but he was willing to risk his life for the footage. The people of Seattle deserved to know what was going on, and the glory that would surely accompany the story didn't hurt either. He yelled at the pilot to maneuver the craft closer. His instincts told him to leave that instant, but his ego shouted for him to go for it.

In the pit of his stomach, he felt as though these might be his last moments. He was correct. The Lord of Darkness swung the sword and cracked his lightning whip into the chopper's blades, blasting it out of the sky. Trailing black smoke, it tumbled down and crashed into the monorail, the gas tank detonating and exploding in a roiling fireball. The Dark Lord smiled. He would never tire of murdering humans.

Will kept climbing. He looked at his watch. More time than he'd thought had passed. He had to hurry. But then he realized he could sense the shedemons coming. He had first encountered them at the Gas Works Park. Moving viciously fast, they had surrounded him and would have put him six feet under had Loreli not come to his rescue. He'd had several battles with them since, and each time he survived he was left with the uneasy feeling that one of their battles was going to be his last.

He hunkered down on a landing near one of the massive steel crossbeams so his back was covered. The shedemons' inhuman voices filled the sky. They sounded more like a pack of coyotes than a group of humanoid creatures, their yips and yelps and howls growing louder the closer they got. They were crawling down the columns toward Will and looked like geckos from space, their hands and feet somehow binding to the metal as they slithered down, their cold-blooded eyes peering at him.

The first one leapt out to draw Will's attention, releasing her grip on the Needle and hanging in midair as she sprouted flesh wings. Will flung a Flareblade at her, but she dodged it, diving right. He'd anticipated the move, and he immediately threw another. This one struck her shoulder and she shrieked, clutching it as she fell. She was cursing and yanking at the burning blade as she hit the cement and splattered.

The next two shedemons swooped down at him from the left and the right, crossing in front of him, slashing with their razor-sharp nails. Then they merged in midair and came again, this time carrying something between them. Will didn't see what it was until it was almost too late: piano wire, strong and thin and sharp. They planned to decapitate him. He barely managed to lift his Megashocker up in the nick of time, blocking their attempt. But the Megashocker, while burning the wire, fused to it. They yanked the weapon from his hands. All he could do was watch helplessly as it tumbled to the ground below.

The shedemons took out daggers and attacked again. Will kicked into time-bending speed and parkoured up another hundred feet until he was looking down on them, then he whipped the Death Ripper out of its holster. It fired saw loads: bullets that flared out into whirling ripsaws. He fired two shots down just as the shedemons were back-flipping in midair and throwing their daggers up at him.

The actions happened simultaneously. The first dagger came dangerously close, slicing Will's left earlobe. The second he deflected in a shower of sparks with his titanium wrist plate. Then his shots hit. The first Death Ripper shot hit a shedemon in her thigh, burrowing in and sawing. She screamed in agony as the ripper pinballed around, sawing back and forth through her flesh and then sinking into her femur. She fell backward out of the sky and plummeted, trying to flap her wings but tumbling badly out of control until she crashed to the ground. Will's second Death Ripper shot was even more deadly, blasting into the other shedemon's brain via her right eye. Her head shook and she opened her mouth to scream but could only spit out clots of blood. She, too, fell from the sky and kissed death face-first on the pavement below.

The Dark Lord, mind-watching, found this all very engaging and was quite proud of his estranged son's courage and battle prowess. He knew the boy would make his way up to him soon. And then the real battle would begin.

In the meantime there was malice to be wrought. After all, this was the beginning of the End of Ends! The Dark Lord swung the Sword of Armageddon and sent more tendrils of evil out across the

Emerald City, this time connecting with cemeteries. Within seconds of being struck, the graveyards erupted. Corpses came alive and clawed their way out of their graves. Once upright, they began a deathly march into the dark night, hungry for human flesh.

Will caught his breath. He looked up and thought about his mother. He knew her only chance at survival—and, for that matter, the survival of the entire human race—depended on him making a rapid ascent and crushing the Dark Lord. Will forged ahead until he came to the underbelly of the dome that capped the support columns. He was directly beneath the housing for the massive turntable that caused the famous sky-high restaurant to rotate.

He climbed higher and found himself staring in through the tinted glass of the restaurant. People were cowering on the floor. Some were praying. Others were tucked into fetal positions. They saw Will Hunter scaling the windows. They saw the fearless look in his eyes, and their hope for survival rose with him.

He climbed up past the sun louvers, and from there onto the observation deck. He saw the bodies of the guards—poor souls—and moved past them. He heard a noise, a kind of huffing sound. He rounded a corner and there was April, lying on a gurney, hooked to a respirator. She was alive, but she looked bad, her face a mask of pain.

"Mom?"

He went to her side and touched her hand. It wasn't yet deathly cold, but it was cool to the touch. He felt like crying. He knew she wouldn't be able to talk.

"I'm going get you out," he told her.

He heard laughter. The Dark Lord appeared.

"So brave. So loyal! But you don't seem to understand," he said. "It's over."

With one swipe of his claw, the Dark Lord cut through April's respirator tube and then blew a door off its hinges and flew up the stairwell. Will knew that if he didn't defeat the Dark Lord soon, his mother would die.

He was after the Beast in a flash. Every second counted. He entered the staircase and heard a hellacious screeching sound. Two shedemons launched themselves down out of the darkness, knocking him backward against the wall and then tossing him over the railing. He tumbled down a flight of stairs.

He looked up at them. "You're really starting to piss me off."

He pulled out two small Blast Missiles—each about the size of an ordinary ballpoint pen—activated them, and fired them at the shedemons. The shedemons tried to fly away, but the little heat-seekers quickly tracked them down, pierced their bodies, and obliterated them with two eardrum-busting explosions. Will covered his head as shedemon blood rained down on him. His anger was wearing on him, pulling him down. He was tired of being furious. To defeat the Dark Lord, he would need to find a different path. But what was it?

He thought about Natalie, and the thought made him stronger. He ran up the stairs and kicked open the roof access door. Blue Streak was waiting for him, and she slashed at him with a tri-blade saber. He ducked and rolled. She leapt after him. He came up with a right cross that caught her under the chin. She dropped the tri-blade. Will dove and got his hand on it, but her boot stomped down on his wrist. She was standing above him and had a dagger ready to plunge in his eye. He pressed down with his right toe, and a blade shot out of the tip of his boot and into her thigh. She screamed.

Will flipped up onto his feet and jammed the tri-blade into her side. Her eyes flared with hatred as she tumbled backward off the edge of the Needle and plummeted down. Twice wounded, she appeared destined to smash headfirst into the concrete. But Blue Streak had great reserves of malevolence, and she drew upon them now to give her strength. Sprouting fleshy wings in the nick of time, she managed to pluck herself from death. And then she flew away into the night.

Finally, on the roof of the Needle Will faced off with the Lord of Darkness. The Sword of Armageddon glowed in his father's hand.

"You're a death machine. I'm so proud of you, my son."

"You may have fathered me," said Will, "but I'm not your son—and I never will be."

The wind howled. The skies continued to unleash a torrential downpour of rain and hail. The maelstrom of lightning continued to smash down out of the sky and into the Sword of Armageddon that the Dark Lord held in his hands. It pulsed with pure energy. He sent tendrils from the sword downward into the streets, the evil penetrating the souls below, conscripting them into his cursed army, turning people against each other. Violence broke out in waves. Knives were plunged, shots were fired, screams rent the night.

"Tonight is the night!" crowed the Dark Lord. "Angels will fall from the sky! You cannot stop what has begun!"

"Maybe not. But I can sure as hell try!"

Will reached back and tapped a code into the retrieval patch on the back of his neck. It was time for his Excalibur, his Power Rod. He held out his palm and the Power Rod soared down out of the clouds. The dual blades crackled to life.

The Dark Lord was the greatest foe any hero had ever faced. Will knew he had very little chance of surviving. Nonetheless . . . he would give it everything he had.

The Dark Lord swung first, the mighty Sword of Armageddon making the sound of thunder as it cut through the air. Will ducked as the massive sword passed over him, its intense heat singeing his hair and clothing. As the Dark Lord advanced, swinging the sword, Will leapt and ducked out of the way of its scathing blade. When the Dark Lord swung it a second time, Will blocked it with his Power Rod. The sound of the mighty weapons clashing was a clap of thunder that rattled every window in Seattle and set off car alarms all the way to Everett. Will had reflexively closed his eyes, expecting his rod to shatter under the Sword of Armageddon's force, but now he opened them. The Power Rod had held!

The Dark Lord was surprised as well, but seemed to relish the challenge.

"That's my boy! You don't give up, do you?"

Will didn't want to waste any energy on useless banter. Instead he cartwheeled right and swung his Power Rod as he deflected two blows by the Dark Lord. Each time the weapons met, thunder filled the air and the sky lit up in a shower of sparks and cinders. The Dark Lord spewed some venom Will's way.

"How did it feel when I killed your pathetic stepfather, boy?"

The ploy worked. Anger flared up within Will. His blood boiled.

I hate him!

He's baiting you.

I will kill him for Edward!

Keep your wits; don't falter!

I want him dead, dead, dead!

Calm down, think, concentrate.

The Dark Lord laughed and struck again, the Sword of Armageddon growing more puissant with each passing moment, throbbing with energy. Each time Will struck at it, it fed on the angry lust for vengeance in his soul. The Dark Lord taunted him again.

"Edward suffered greatly! Was it not like a dagger in your heart, Will?"

Will could not help but replay that dreadful moment when the Dark Lord had murdered Edward. With those thoughts polluting his mind, the red curtain of rage came down. Will found himself fighting not only the Dark Lord, but himself as well. He knew he mustn't let this rage prevail!

The Dark Lord knew Will's anger was a liability, knew it weakened him, so he exploited the weakness, striking again and again. He would bring the boy to his knees and make him see: the dark side was his only path!

Will was using every bit of his time-bending powers to dodge and deflect the deadly blows. The huge sword was spitting bolts of lightning like a giant sparkler. The monster was reveling in his power.

And then the Dark Lord's eyes softened, and he spoke calmly. "I knew you could not be killed by anyone but me. I foresaw that you would make it up here, to be in this fateful moment. Don't you see, Will Hunter, you have been your father's pawn all along. You found my head. You found the blade. Though you've fought it mightily, you *are* part of the great prophecy!"

A wave of guilt surged through Will as he faced the idea that, in trying to do good, he had actually aided and abetted the Dark Lord at every turn.

The beast held out a claw-hand in a gesture of reconciliation. "I offer you this one last chance, my son. Renounce all attachments to your human half and embrace the darkness. Do not force me to kill you. Choose to live. Come with me and rule by my side!"

Will did not have to waste a second pondering the offer. His response to the Dark Lord's offer was embedded in his brain, woven into his soul, and repeated with every beat of his heart.

"I would rather die!"

Will swung his Power Rod. The mighty weapons clashed once again. The Dark Lord, his momentary sadness at Will's rebuke transforming rapidly into rage, began to growl.

"Then you have sealed your own fate! The time has come for your life to end, bastard son!"

The Dark Lord morphed into an even larger and more grotesque embodiment of himself, his face flattening out, his scaly skin becoming more muscular and glistening with excretions. The spiked horns on his head enlarged. His eyes burned a fearsome fiery yellow. He struck repeatedly at Will, who could do little but backpedal, until he suffered a glancing blow to his shoulder that knocked him to his knees. The Dark Lord moved swiftly, and slowly brought the Sword of Armageddon to his son's neck.

"Put the Power Rod down."

Will's hand trembled.

"Do it now! And listen to what I have to say!"

It was game, set, and match. Having no other choice, Will set his Power Rod down on the roof. But he kept his hand only inches from it.

"You cannot win, Will Hunter. On this Earth, it is not goodness and light that prevail, but darkness and death. Humans are innately evil. They follow my teachings! Look what has become of the Earth! Greed, mass destruction, pollution never before seen on such a massive scale! I have *won*. Humanity has proven me the victor. Now, with the Sword of Armageddon, I will usher in the End of Ends. Demons will rule the Earth. Take this lesson with you to your grave. And now . . . it seems," bellowed the Dark Lord, "that you are about to lose your head!"

The Beast drew back his sword and was preparing to deliver the deathblow when a voice rang out.

"*Not yet!*"

It was Loreli. The Dark Lord, upon hearing the haunting voice of his other progeny, turned to gaze at her. She was gorgeous and formidable. Her magnificent strawberry-blonde hair billowed in the whipping winds. Her emerald eyes were filled with righteous fury. She'd just climbed the Needle, toasting several surviving demons on her way up, and her blood was pumping, her cheeks flushed.

"My beloved Loreli . . . you made it. I suspected you would."

Loreli hesitated. "Did you?"

"Of course. You're my daughter."

The Dark Lord smiled. Even though he'd sent Loreli to her death, here she was, crawling back for one last chance at redemption. Perhaps she thought she was here to save the boy, but he knew that his power was overwhelming. He saw it in her eyes.

"Come to me. I want you at my side when I dispatch this traitorous worm."

Loreli did not move.

"Lower your weapon and come beside me," the Dark Lord said. "I am amending my earlier decree. You have proven yourself worthy. So bask in your glory! Come and rule by my side, beloved daughter."

These were the words the Dark Lord knew Loreli wanted to hear; words she'd been yearning for so passionately for so long. Something flickered in her emerald eyes. Then she smiled wistfully. She slowly moved toward her father, lowering the Chopper.

"That's good, that's a good girl."

Will eyed his Power Rod. Should he make a move for it while the Dark Lord was distracted? Loreli moved closer to the Beast. Will couldn't believe his eyes. What was she *doing?*

"Yes, daughter, that's it . . ."

She was right beside him now, the Chopper by her side but still clenched in her hand. Trembling, she held it out to the Dark Lord, who snatched it and crushed it in his claw.

Will's heart seized in his chest. *I am a fool! Why did I let her live? How could I have ever let myself trust her again? The Dark Lord was right, evil does trump goodness.*

The Dark Lord smiled at Loreli again. "That's my girl. Now watch your brother die!"

The Dark Lord drew back the Sword of Armageddon.

This was the moment Loreli had been waiting for. Her bluff had worked! She unsheathed a hidden dagger and plunged it deep into her father's neck and twisted, hard.

The Dark Lord roared in pain. The path of the mighty sword changed, and Will was able to duck out of the way and snatch up his Power Rod.

The dagger imbedded in his neck, the wound spurting blood, the Dark Lord exploded with rage, glaring at Loreli with disbelief.

"You . . ." His eyes actually showed pain. "How *could* you? How could you turn on me, betray me?"

"I'm my father's daughter," said Loreli. "It's my nature."

The gash in his neck spewing blood, the Dark Lord pursued Loreli. She was fast, but even gravely injured, he was still faster, and the mighty sword sizzled with power. Loreli dodged and feinted and flipped away from him, but she couldn't keep it up forever.

Will switched his Power Rod to freeze and sent a volley of arctic blasts at the Dark Lord. It was enough to buy Loreli a few precious seconds, but there was nowhere for her to go. She was on the edge of the roof. Her eyes found Will's.

"I'm sorry for everything I've put you through, brother. I hope someday you'll find a way to forgive me."

The Dark Lord swung his sword.

"Loreli!" screamed Will. "Loreli, I forgive you!"

And with a powerful, burning slash, the Beast cut Loreli, his only daughter, in half.

Will screamed so loud his throat burned. *"No!!"*

But it was too late. Her body toppled backward off the edge and pinwheeled in two pieces to the ground below.

The Dark Lord turned and faced Will, blood still pouring from the wound Loreli had left in his neck. "Now it's your turn, my son."

Again the Sword of Armageddon and Will's Power Rod clashed, sending fireworks into the sky. The Dark Lord was bigger and stronger, but Will had speed and cunning. He had expected the curtain of rage to hamper his efforts, but this time it did not appear. He had done the right thing in forgiving his sister, and this knowledge gave him strength. The hot red anger was gone; in its place he experienced something entirely different, a strange new kind of calm, a serenity that gave him strength and clarity. But could he make it last?

Will dodged strike after strike and landed retaliatory blows of his own, blows that caused the Dark Lord to yell in agony. But Will was half human, after all; he only had so much strength. And that strength was waning.

The Dark Lord struck and missed, but then turned and kicked Will and sent him sprawling across the roof so fast that he skidded to the edge and rolled over, just managing to grab on to the edge cap. He was dangling six hundred feet in the air, hanging on with one hand, the Power Rod still clutched tight in the other. He was running out of time, running out of options. Somehow, he had to dispatch the Dark Lord, save April, and make it back to the mansion before it exploded.

The Dark Lord approached the edge and swung his sword. Will knew this was it. He had one more chance. He swung his Power Rod upward with all his might. As the magical, mythical weapon once again crashed against the Dark Lord's Sword of Armageddon with a deafening rumble, it did something it had never done before.

It flickered, and then it went out. It lost its power. It died.

"And so it shall be . . . ," the Dark Lord said. "I think that should be a sign to you that it's time to give up."

With that, the Dark Lord reached down with blinding speed and yanked the now-dormant Power Rod out of Will's hand and flung it backward over his head. It landed on the roof. Lightning continued to slash down out of the sky, slamming into the single lightning rod that remained on the very tip top of the Needle.

He knew he was nearly beaten, but Will was not about to give up. Not when he still had any fight left in him. He swung himself back up as the Dark Lord swiped at him with the sword, catching his leg. Will screamed in agony.

The Dark Lord swung again. The sword missed, but he caught Will with his other hand and his huge claws raked across Will's chest, drawing blood.

Will saw his Power Rod lying on the roof. He saw the thunderbolts slashing down and hammering into the lightning rod. He had one more move left, and he knew it would either kill him or save him. It was a million-to-one shot, but it was the only one he had. He ran and dove for his Power Rod, scooped it up, and as the Dark Lord gave chase, he climbed the tower.

The Dark Lord paused and watched curiously.

"What will you do, Will Hunter? Climb all the way to Heaven?"

The Dark Lord laughed an ugly laugh, his voice raspy with hubris. Will had climbed all the way up to the very top, to the flashing aircraft-warning beacon. He held his impotent Power Rod straight up into the sky and then sent a prayer into the clouds.

Thunder rumbled. The Dark Lord's eyes widened. A massive bolt of lightning sliced down—and connected with the Power Rod.

Miraculously, Will was still alive. The Power Rod had absorbed the entire strike. It flickered—and then blasted back to life, brighter and stronger than ever.

Holding it tightly, Will dropped down onto the roof and squared off with the Dark Lord once more.

"One of us is about to die," said Will, "and it's not gonna be me."

Again they dueled.

Back at the mansion, Natalie, Emily, and Rudy had dispatched the last of the attacking demons. From his perch on the roof, Rudy switched on the infrared scope and did a wide sweep. The entire hillside was clean. He could see the Space Needle. Something big was happening on top. He prayed that Will was up there kicking ass and would be back soon. He'd better be, because time was running out.

Rudy hurried downstairs and joined Natalie and Emily. The mansion was a battlefield, littered with broken furniture and the remnants of demon ashes. A stubborn demonteen body, the legs having been blown off, shuddered in the corner. The legs were miraculously still kicking. Rudy picked up the Blaster Magnum Loreli had left behind, cocked it, and fired a shot that put the creature out of its misery. The body took the shot, then disintegrated in tiny flashes. Rudy set the Blaster Magnum down and wiped the sweat from his brow.

"Well, that's the last of them. It looks like the demons have given up. Where's Loreli?"

"I don't know. But we don't have long before this thing goes off," said Emily.

She was staring at the doomsday bomb. An hour and twenty-seven minutes had passed since Will left. The timer had ticked down to eleven minutes and counting. Although they all hoped, only Natalie was utterly convinced that Will would return in time. They waited in silence. When the timer hit seven minutes, Emily took Natalie gently by the arm.

"Okay, it's time to go."

But Natalie wouldn't budge. "I'm not leaving without Will," she said. "But you guys should. Go on!"

Time was flying by. Emily and Rudy were dumbstruck.

"Nat . . . I'm your twin sister, I can't make it without you! Come on, please?"

Emily tightened her grip, but Natalie wasn't going anywhere. It was simple. She would rather die than live without Will. She spoke in a soft, calm voice.

"He's going to make it back. He *is*."

She wanted to sound convincing because she held on to hope so strongly. But she saw the doubt in Emily's eyes.

"And if he doesn't . . . then what's the point?" said Natalie. "Will's the only hope we have. If he doesn't make it, if he doesn't defeat the Dark Lord, then the world that will be left is a world I don't want to live in."

Emily understood, but she still wasn't keen on sticking around and being blown up. Yet she couldn't leave without her twin.

"Rudy, a little help?"

Rudy came over. "What do you want me to do?"

"Grab her other arm. We'll drag her out of here if we have to. Natalie, please, I'm begging you!"

The sisters were staring at each other fiercely, and Rudy was watching them both, when a voice startled them all.

"Save your breath. Nobody's going anywhere."

It was Blue Streak. She had the Blaster Magnum aimed at them.

. . .

Will was locked in battle. The Dark Lord continued to taunt him.

"Your adoptive father is dead, your sister, too. Your mother will go soon! And all at my hand."

Crash! The Dark Lord swung the Sword of Armageddon again and again, and Will met each mighty blow with a defensive blow of his own. His Power Rod was pulsing with energy and was serving him well. But the Master of All Demons was crafty and knew Will's weak spot.

"Come on, boy! Speak up! Have you no choice words for me? You hate me, don't you?"

Yes I hate you! I hate you and want to kill you! You are evil and cold-blooded and heartless! You are a malignant tumor on this Earth! You deserve nothing but the painful death I am going to bring upon you!

Will lunged, swinging his Power Rod. But the Dark Lord had anticipated the overly aggressive move and he sidestepped the blow. As Will lurched past him, the Beast swung the Sword of Armageddon and clipped Will in the shoulder. The wound was bad, and Will was running out of time. He knew his mother was just below him, her body succumbing to death's grasp. The tide had turned. Will was battered, bleeding from numerous wounds, his energy waning even as his anger grew. Maybe the Dark Lord was right. Maybe mankind's nature *was* evil. If that was the case, then Will wanted no part of living and was ready to surrender. Let the dark side take over. Mankind deserved it.

Will lowered the Power Rod in defeat.

Then something amazing happened. A crack appeared in the sky, a gap, a calming in the midst of the furious clouds. And through that gap Will was able to gaze, ever so briefly, at a star. It was the brightest star he'd ever seen in his life.

Hairs rose on his neck. His skin tingled. He thought about how he'd forgiven Loreli, and how right it had felt. He remembered how Natalie's refusal to forgive herself had nearly ruined their love. He remembered how once he'd forgiven the White Island teens and chosen to save them rather than destroy them, things had worked out.

With a deep breath, Will was calm again. And in that moment of clarity, he knew that he had to complete the most difficult task yet set before him. It was likely impossible, and yet it beckoned.

The Dark Lord thrived on hatred and malice and all that was evil and wrong in the world. He lived for the death of others, seeking disease and destruction with every breath. He was evil incarnate. But Will believed that, blood or no blood, the sins of the father need not be visited upon the son. Just because his father was the Devil didn't mean *he* had to have a dark heart.

Will realized that right now the most potent weapon he had was not hate, but . . . love. But could he possibly do the one thing that was most difficult in the world for him to do? Could he *forgive* the monster who had slaughtered his father Edward, killed his sister, and most likely destroyed his mother? Could he find the place in his heart—*could such a place possibly exist?*—that would enable him to reach out and actually *love* his mortal enemy, the Prince of Darkness?

The Dark Lord could hear Will's thoughts, and he began to twitch and shudder. Will knew that he had to act quickly before the Beast could say anything or send any more evil his way, and so he began to speak. The words that came were the most difficult he had ever spoken.

"Father"—*I called him father*, he thought, *I can't believe it*—"I no longer hold you in contempt."

The Dark Lord roared. He struck repeatedly with the Sword of Armageddon.

"I don't believe you! You hate me with every fiber of your being!"

Will fended off the blows and leapt away from still more.

"No, father. I have no more malice toward you."

"You're *lying*!"

Now it was the Beast who was in the blind throes of anger, and Will who was calm and collected. There was no damage left to be done by the Dark Lord. He lashed out. Will deflected the blows.

The Dark Lord screamed; grating, jagged words came up from the depths of his guts, words that caused him great pain.

"I am unforgivable! *He* could not forgive me for my insurrection! And *you* cannot forgive me for killing those you loved!"

"I ask you this, Father. Whose image are you made in?"

The Dark Lord's head shook. The words assaulted him.

"I was made in the image of the Mighty One! You know this. Ask me no more foolish questions, boy! It is time for you to die!"

But Will was not ready to die. New hope had sprung up within him. He fought hard now, and his Power Rod was equal to the task.

"And am I not made in *your* image, Father?" he said.

The Dark Lord was again flummoxed by Will's words. The truth had to be spoken here now, and the Beast loathed the path they were taking.

"Yes! And what of it? So *what*?"

"So . . . ," said Will, "therefore I am *also* made in the image of the Mighty One. And should I choose to forgive you, then He Himself would be forgiving you, through me."

The Dark Lord responded as though he'd been struck with a thousand lances. "No! This is not the prophecy!"

Now the Beast was not only lashing at Will, but beating himself as well, scratching and clawing at his own body, trying to tear out the torment that was eating him from within.

Will saw something he never thought he would see in the Dark Lord's eyes: fear. He knew he had to strike hard. Not with the Power Rod, but with the mightiest of words.

"Father . . . I pardon you."

"No! You cannot!"

"But I do. I absolve you."

"DO NOT! DO. NOT. SPEAK. THOSE. WORDS!"

Will was smiling and had tears spilling from his eyes as he not only spoke the words, but actually *felt* them. He had no other recourse. No other feelings would fulfill his destiny.

"Father, *I forgive you.*"

The Dark Lord wailed as though his body were on fire. He raised the Sword of Armageddon straight into the air and bellowed a roar so loud it rivaled the thunderclaps that had torn the sky asunder. He stared at Will, frozen, powerless. With words alone his son had delivered the most powerful blow imaginable and the Beast was staggered.

And then Will did what he'd wanted to do for so very, very long. He thrust the scalding tip of his mighty Power Rod into the Dark Lord's beating heart.

The look on the Dark Lord's face was not one so much of shock, but rather of resignation, perhaps even something approaching relief. It was over. His own End of Ends had come. The Sword of Armageddon faded, dimmed, stopped thrumming, and lost its power. He dropped it and the crystals shattered into a million pieces. The Dark Lord clutched at his chest. He staggered backward. Blinking back what appeared to be tears—how human-like he was in this fleeting desperate moment!—the Prince of Darkness, the Dark Lord himself, pitched backward off the edge of the Space Needle. As he fell, his body morphed—for a fraction of a second—into that of a falling angel. And then he disintegrated in a whirling, swirling explosion of sparks and cinders.

Will watched in awe. All that was left of the evilest villain the world had ever known was a wisp of smoke. Now that smoke drifted up, higher and higher. It lingered, as though in momentary limbo, and then the last bit of the Prince of Darkness, the tiny, powerless wisp of vapor, was sucked up into the clouds—back, it seemed, to Heaven.

Will was stunned. The Dark Lord was really gone. Which meant . . . he had to get to April.

Will rushed off the roof and down the stairs. So much time had passed while he was battling the Dark Lord that he was terrified she had died. He prayed that he was wrong.

As he saw when he rushed to her side, he was.

The sky had cleared rapidly, and the light of a brilliant full moon illuminated April's face. Her expression was calm, her breathing strong. Will touched her hand. It was warm.

"Mother?"

She opened her eyes and spoke. Her voice, though raspy, was pure bliss.

"We made it."

"Yeah, Mom. We did."

He leaned down and kissed her. She was going to be all right. Will had saved her, and she would know that with every breath she took for the rest of her life. Ever since his quest had begun, he'd doubted his abilities and blamed himself for his mistakes and defeats. It occurred to him that now that he had vanquished the Dark Lord with forgiveness, he could finally forgive the one person he'd never been able to: himself.

He looked at his watch, then whipped out his phone and dialed.

The bomb timer ticked down. They had less than two minutes to get out of the mansion before it exploded. Rudy pointed at the bomb, never taking his eyes off Blue Streak.

"Just so you know, that bomb's about to go off and blow us all to smithereens."

Blue Streak nodded. "Unless Will Hunter arrives in time to diffuse it," she said. "And then I will kill him."

Natalie wasn't about to let that happen. Even if it meant throwing herself at the shedemon, sacrificing herself to give Rudy and Emily a chance at somehow taking the creature out. Natalie's muscles tensed. The timer on the doomsday bomb kept ticking down: 59 seconds . . . 58 . . . 57 . . .

Natalie felt a vibration. Then she heard a noise. It was her phone ringing on the counter.

Startled, Blue Streak swung the Blaster Magnum and fired, blowing the phone to bits. Rudy dove and killed the lights. Natalie and Emily dropped behind the counter as Blue Streak fired off four quick rounds and blew the top of the counter off its base. Debris rained down, but Natalie, Emily, and Rudy were still alive.

Rudy looked at Emily. If he was going to die, then there was something that he wanted to do first, and as he watched the timer tick down, he became emboldened. It was now or never.

Before Blue Streak could figure out where they'd gone, he grabbed a canister that had been blown off the counter and flung it across the room. Blue Streak fired at the sound: 40 seconds . . . 39 . . . 38 . . . 37 . . .

Will was moving at time-bending speed. Horns honked. People yelled. But the sounds and voices fell away in a muted hush, drowned out by the sound of Will's blood rushing through his veins. He'd miscalculated; he should have set the timer for longer! But there was still time. He dared not even glance at his watch as he ran up the street and leapt over fences: 25 seconds . . . 24 . . . 23 . . . He hoped that Natalie, Emily, and Rudy had abandoned the mansion as he'd instructed, but he couldn't be sure. He'd done the emotional math, and the calculation included factoring in what he himself would have done. He knew that, given the choice, he would never have chosen to live without Natalie. And she'd said it herself before he left: she didn't want to live in a world without him. He could hear Natalie's heart beating along with his own. He was determined that they would not perish together.

• • •

Blue Streak kept firing until the Blaster Magnum was empty. Then she threw it aside and took out two daggers. Rudy's heart was galloping. Emily was staring at him. Her eyes were full of need. They moved closer together: 19 seconds . . . 18 . . . 17 . . .

Out front, Will ran through the wrecked gate: 15 seconds . . . 14 . . . 13 . . .

He blasted through the front door. Blue Streak turned and ran toward him.

"Will, lookout!"

He heard Natalie's scream and dropped into a forward slide as a dagger whizzed overhead and thunked into the wall. Blue Streak burst out of the lab screeching, aiming the remaining dagger. She swiped at him, hissing, spitting: 12 seconds . . . 11 . . .

"This ends here!" yelled Will.

He flicked on his Power Rod. She struck and sliced at his shoulder, but the pain was nothing compared to the thought of losing Natalie. He leapt up, and with a huge force of will, he decapitated her with the Power Rod.

Then he threw himself forward into the lab: 5 seconds . . . 4 . . . 3 . . . 2 . . . 1 . . .

Click. Will flicked a hidden switch and disarmed the bomb.

He turned on the lights. Rudy and Emily were locked in an embrace, kissing like there was no tomorrow. Will smiled and cleared his throat. They paid him no mind.

Will's eyes found Natalie. She was staring at him, a smile slowly spreading across her face as she realized he was really here.

Rudy and Emily finally broke apart. They were blushing. Rudy blinked like a baby bird seeing the sun for the first time.

"Did we die and go to Heaven?"

Emily laughed and pulled him into another hug.

"I'm kind of crazy about you, you know?" she said.

Natalie could not take her eyes off of Will Hunter, and she didn't want to try, not for all the money in the world. He was here. Her hero. Her love. The person who made her life worth living.

Her body was suddenly wracked with shuddering sobs of joy. Will ran to her, took her in his arms, and kissed her long and deep, and when they broke apart, she smiled and spoke the words she'd believed in her heart all along.

"I knew you'd make it."

Will tried to think of something to say, but there were no more words. Not now. He decided to kiss her again. And he did.

THE END